The Cipher's Heart

A Tale of Love, Codes, and Hidden Messages

Morgan Logstone

First Edition: May 2024

Table of Contents

Chapter 1
Cryptic Beginnings

In the shadowy, cramped quarters of the German intelligence headquarters in Berlin, Anna Richter sat before an array of flickering screens, her eyes scanning rapidly as her fingers danced over the keyboard. Her workstation, a fortress of solitude amidst the buzz of military activity, was littered with scribbled notes and intercepted messages. Anna, a cryptographer of unmatched skill, decrypted an intricate Allied code that had stumped many before her. Her concentration was palpable, each keystroke a step closer to revealing secrets meant only for the highest echelons of enemy command. She prided herself on her ability to unravel the webs of deceit woven by the war, yet each success deepened the creases of concern on her brow. Her disillusionment with the purpose behind her assignments grew, a silent question mark looming over her head: "To what end?"

As the decrypted message revealed its contents—a planned Allied maneuver that would endanger countless lives—Anna's heart sank. The thrill of solving the puzzle was overshadowed by the grim reality of her contributions to the war. She leaned back in her chair, the glow from the screen casting ghostly shadows on her face. "Is this the cost of loyalty?" she whispered to the empty room, her voice a mixture of defiance and despair.

Moments later, another message intercepted from the Allies piqued her interest. This one was different; it was personally addressed to her codename. The sender, known only by his own cryptic signature, challenged her with a puzzle more complex and playful than any military command. Intrigued and slightly amused, she set her professional duties aside and engaged with the mysterious correspondent, her mind alight with curiosity.

The exchange with her unknown adversary brought a rare smile to Anna's lips. As she decoded the playful messages, her usual environment of war and strategy transformed into a private battlefield of wits. The flirtatious undertone of the messages was undeniable, and for a fleeting moment,

Anna allowed herself to indulge in the fantasy that there was more to life than war. "Who are you, my enigmatic friend?" she mused, her spirits lifted by the intellectual camaraderie forming through lines of coded text.

This opening beat sets the stage for Anna's complex journey, illustrating her exceptional abilities, her moral conflicts, and the beginning of a cryptic relationship that promises to transcend the boundaries of war. The chapter establishes her character, her environment, and her initial connection with James, leading into a story of intrigue and clandestine romance.

Across the Channel, in a dimly lit, cluttered room of the Allied codebreaking facility in England, James Bennett sat hunched over his desk, littered with papers and old coffee cups. The constant hum of activity buzzed around him, but he was engrossed in a particularly challenging code—a direct message from an Axis cryptographer which was unusual in its complexity and directness.

James, with a reputation as a sharp and somewhat unconventional codebreaker, was both intrigued and excited by the challenge. The message wasn't just any scrambled set of orders; it was personal, crafted with a cunning that matched his own. He rubbed his chin, a grin spreading across his face as he murmured, "Looks like I've caught someone's eye." His colleagues were too absorbed in their own tasks to notice his amusement.

He poured over the message, his eyes scanning back and forth between his notes and the encrypted text. The room's only light flickered as he tapped a pencil against his lips, deep in thought. Slowly, the pieces began to fall into place, revealing not just a coded communication but a playful challenge from the Axis cryptographer. "Clever girl," he chuckled, appreciating the intellectual flirtation hidden within the wartime correspondence.

Excited by the challenge, James decided to respond in kind. He crafted his reply with care, embedding his own clever twists and turns in the code. This was no ordinary exchange of intelligence; it was a duel of wits that sparked a light in his eyes that had been dulled by the relentless war. He encrypted his message with a personal touch, hoping to stir curiosity and perhaps a bit of admiration from his mysterious counterpart.

As he transmitted his response, James leaned back in his chair, a rare moment of satisfaction washing over him. The exchange, though risky, brought a human connection to the impersonal shadows of war. "What are you like, my distant adversary?" he wondered aloud, allowing himself a brief escape from the drudgery and moral ambiguity of his daily life. The thrill of the intellectual chase momentarily overshadowed the grim realities of his surroundings.

In this chapter, James's character is fleshed out through his reactions to the coded message, highlighting his intelligence, his playful side, and his longing for connection amid the war's isolation. The beats underscore the beginning of his intriguing interaction with Anna, setting the stage for a deepening intrigue and complexity in their exchanges.

The exchange of coded messages between Anna and James grew more complex and personal. Through veiled language, they debated the philosophy of war and the dreams that sustained them beyond the battlefields. Each message deepened their connection, serving as a lifeline in the lonely expanse of war.

As winter deepened over Europe, the clandestine exchanges between Anna and James grew in complexity and frequency. Back in Berlin, in her now familiar sanctuary among machines and codes, Anna sat with bated breath each time she received a new message from her elusive counterpart. The war outside felt distant as she delved into this secret world that was theirs alone.

Anna's fingers hovered over the keyboard as she decrypted the latest message from James. Each decoded line brought a mix of thrill and intellectual satisfaction. The codes were no longer just sequences of letters and numbers; they were intimate conversations disguised in cryptic language. She couldn't help but smile as she pieced together his witty retorts and clever challenges, a spark of joy igniting in her usually somber existence.

The messages began to include subtle personal revelations hidden deep within layers of encryption. James shared glimpses of his life before the war, encoded as if they were mere data. Anna responded in kind, her messages sprinkled with veiled details of her own past, wrapped in the safety of codes. These snippets painted pictures of who they were beyond their roles as cryptographers, bridging the vast distance between them.

One evening, as the snow fell softly outside her window, Anna crafted a message that ventured beyond personal anecdotes to philosophical questions about the war, morality, and fate. It was a risky shift, but her curiosity about James's thoughts on matters beyond tactics and strategies was too strong to resist. She encoded her thoughts carefully, sending them off like a message in a bottle thrown into the digital sea.

After sending her message, Anna leaned back in her chair, her eyes lost in the rhythmic patter of the snow against the glass. She wondered about the man on the other side of her screen—his reactions, his beliefs, his feelings. The waiting for his response was filled with anticipation and a bit of apprehension. She realized how much this secret connection had come to mean to her, how it had become a beacon in her shadowed world.

In the bustling English facility, James Bennett leaned back in his chair, a smirk playing on his lips as he cracked the code sent by the mysterious Axis cryptographer. He quickly tapped out a playful response, challenging her skill. "Let's see if you can solve this," he mused, intrigued by the intellectual connection he felt with his unknown adversary.

Across the channel, in a dimly lit, cluttered room of the Allied codebreaking facility in England, James sat hunched over his desk, littered with papers and old coffee cups. The constant hum of activity buzzed around him, but he was engrossed in a particularly challenging code—a direct message from an Axis cryptographer which was unusual in its complexity and directness.

James, with a reputation as a sharp and somewhat unconventional codebreaker, was both intrigued and excited by the challenge. The message wasn't just any scrambled set of orders; it was personal, crafted with a cunning that matched his own. He rubbed his chin, a grin spreading across his face as he murmured, "Looks like I've caught someone's eye."

His colleagues were too absorbed in their own tasks to notice his amusement.

He poured over the message, his eyes scanning back and forth between his notes and the encrypted text. The room's only light flickered as he tapped a pencil against his lips, deep in thought. Slowly, the pieces began to fall into place, revealing not just a coded communication but a playful challenge from the Axis cryptographer. "Clever girl," he chuckled, appreciating the intellectual flirtation hidden within the wartime correspondence.

Excited by the challenge, James decided to respond in kind. He crafted his reply with care, embedding his own clever twists and turns in the code. This was no ordinary exchange of intelligence; it was a duel of wits that sparked a light in his eyes that had been dulled by the relentless war. He encrypted his message with a personal touch, hoping to stir curiosity and perhaps a bit of admiration from his mysterious counterpart.

As he transmitted his response, James leaned back in his chair, a rare moment of satisfaction washing over him. The exchange, though risky, brought a human connection to the impersonal shadows of war. "What are you like, my distant adversary?" he wondered aloud, allowing himself a brief escape from the drudgery and moral ambiguity of his daily life. The thrill of the intellectual chase momentarily overshadowed the grim realities of his surroundings.

In this chapter, James's character is fleshed out through his reactions to the coded message, highlighting his intelligence, his playful side, and his longing for connection amid the war's isolation. The beats underscore the beginning of his intriguing interaction with Anna, setting the stage for a deepening intrigue and complexity in their exchanges.

Chapter 2
Codebreaker's Response

In a quiet corner of Berlin, under the low hum of the ever-present war, Anna Richter continued her clandestine exchanges with the mysterious Allied codebreaker. Their messages had woven a tapestry of intellectual challenge and subtle flirtation, which had grown into a thrilling yet dangerous rapport. Each coded letter was a delicate dance around their true intentions, wrapped in layers of secrecy, as much for protection as for the allure of the unknown.

It was early evening when Anna received the latest message. The soft glow of her desk lamp cast long shadows across her notes, the coded words flickering on the page like the distant echoes of an unfamiliar melody. As she deciphered the message, her mind raced, not just with the technical challenge, but with the emotional stakes now intertwined with each transmission. The person on the other end of these messages was no longer just an adversary or a faceless entity in the vast machinery of war. He had become a beacon of humanity in the midst of chaos, a source of solace that was as disconcerting as it was comforting.

The message this evening was different. It was bolder, threading through philosophical musings and veiled personal inquiries that ventured beyond the usual boundaries of their previous exchanges. James had asked about her dreams, those woven not from the fabric of war but from the threads of a life she might wish to lead in a world at peace. The inquiry was tentative yet revealing, and it prompted Anna to pause, her fingers hovering over the keyboard, her heart caught in the quiet tension between duty and the stirrings of a distant hope.

In crafting her response, Anna found herself reflecting deeper than before. She shared thoughts of her love for the stars, not just as celestial bodies but as symbols of guidance and mystery. Her words, though cloaked in the language of astronomy, hinted at a yearning for navigation through life's uncertainties, a map to follow toward something more than the war that had defined so much of her existence.

As she encrypted her response, embedding her personal revelations within the complexities of code, Anna felt a strange sense of vulnerability. It was a departure from the strict boundaries of her professional identity, a step into a more personal domain that the war had compelled her to wall off. Yet, there was also an undeniable thrill in the act, a feeling of crossing into unknown territory that was both exhilarating and terrifying.

The click of the machine as it transmitted her message marked the end of her momentary introspection. The room returned to silence, filled only with the soft ticking of the clock and the distant rumble of the city under curfew. Outside, the stars were obscured by the smoke of factories, leaving only the dim glow of a city at war. But inside, in the quiet of her room, Anna allowed herself a brief moment to dream of open skies and uncharted journeys, guided by the stars she had always loved.

As the coded conversation continued to unfold, the atmosphere in James Bennett's cramped office in England became one of suspended anticipation. Each new message from Anna, though shrouded in the necessary veils of cryptography, brought a nuanced layer of her personality into sharper focus. She wrote of the stars not just as celestial objects but as symbols of hope and guidance, resonating with James's own undisclosed fascination with the night sky.

With a careful blend of the professional and the personal seeping into their exchanges, the intellectual game they played had subtly shifted. It was no longer just a battle of wits; it had evolved into something more profound—a shared exploration of not only each other's minds but of possible futures beyond the confines of war.

James sat back in his chair after decrypting Anna's latest message, the glow of the computer screen casting blue shadows across his thoughtful expression. He pondered her metaphor about the stars, realizing that it mirrored his own hidden desires for peace and exploration.

"This is getting complex, isn't it?" he mumbled to himself, tapping a pen against the desk. "She's more than just codes and war games."

Choosing his words with care, James crafted a response. He incorporated a coded analogy about navigators and explorers, subtly weaving in his admiration for her intellectual prowess and his curiosity about her personal worldviews.

"Anna, this discourse on celestial navigation you've started is intriguing," he typed, encrypting the message with a new layer of complexity as if challenging her to delve deeper into the metaphor. "Do you think we, too, might be explorers in a way, charting unknown territories in this war-torn world?"

Upon receiving the message, Anna was taken aback by the depth of James's response. Her fingers hesitated over the keys as she processed his words. There was a shift in the air, a subtle realignment of their connection. She typed back, her response careful yet candid.

"James, perhaps we are," she encrypted. "In our quest for understanding, maybe we are mapping out more than just strategies and codes. Perhaps we're discovering paths to places we've only dared to dream about."

As she sent her reply, Anna felt a mixture of exhilaration and trepidation. This exchange was unlike any she had engaged in; it was personal, reaching into the depths of her aspirations and fears. The war continued to rage outside, but in the quiet of her office, a different kind of battle was being fought—a battle for understanding and connection.

In his office, James read her message and allowed himself a rare smile. Their dialogue had opened a window to a new kind of intimacy, one that transcended the physical and delved into the emotional and intellectual. He was no longer just an Allied codebreaker to her, nor she merely an Axis cryptographer to him. They were individuals caught in the throes of a global turmoil, finding solace in shared dreams of a different reality.

He looked out the window at the darkening sky, where the first stars of the evening were beginning to twinkle. James felt a kinship with those distant lights, wondering if Anna was looking up at the same stars, pondering the same questions about fate and the future. As he turned back to his desk to draft another message, the lines between friend and foe, between duty and desire, continued to blur, charting an uncertain course through the night.

In the dim glow of her office, surrounded by the soft hum of the intelligence machinery, Anna found herself increasingly drawn into the night's task. She sat poised, ready to decode another message from James, her heart oddly syncopated with the rhythmic tapping of her fingers on the keys. Tonight's message was delayed, and the tension of waiting added a weight to the air, thick as the encroaching darkness outside her window.

Finally, the machine sprang to life, churning out the coded message that she had been anxiously awaiting. As she translated the symbols into words, James's voice seemed to echo through them, almost palpable in its presence.

"Anna, our conversations have taken on a life of their own, haven't they?" began the message. "It's as if we're no longer just soldiers in opposite trenches but rather two minds converging on a battlefield of ideas."

"Yes, James," she typed back, her response quick and unguarded. "It feels as though we're crafting a bridge over a chasm wrought by war. Do you ever wonder what it would be like to speak without these encoded veils?"

"I do," his reply came swiftly. "To converse openly, without layers of ciphers between us, would be a strange freedom. Do you think we could maintain this... connection, unguarded and honest?"

"There's a part of me that longs to try," she confessed, her fingers hesitating momentarily. "But there's also fear, James. Fear that reality won't live up to this mysterious rapport we've built."

"Understandable," he typed, the delay in his message suggesting he was pondering his words carefully. "There's a purity in our exchanges, isn't there? Shrouded in anonymity, we're perhaps more honest than we might be in person."

"That's just it," Anna replied. "Here, in the realm of codes and metaphors, we can be our ideal selves. Outside this... Are we not just cogs in the war machine, defined by our duties and the expectations of our sides?"

"Perhaps," James acknowledged. "But I like to think that this connection has revealed truths about us that transcend the war. We are not only what we are made to be, Anna. We choose who we become, through every word we exchange, every idea we dare to share."

"Your optimism is infectious," she smiled to herself as she typed. "Maybe, just maybe, this is the start of understanding that can bridge more than just the physical distance between us."

"Let's hold onto that thought," he suggested. "And maybe, when the war is over, we can test that theory, meet in a world without encrypted messages and hidden identities."

"An intriguing proposal, James. A meeting in a neutral place, where the war is just a backdrop to a conversation between two friends?"

"It's a promise then," his message concluded. "A conversation in peace, in a place where we are just Anna and James, not cryptographers, not soldiers, but simply two people who were once connected by the stars."

As Anna ended the transmission, she leaned back in her chair, the buzz of the machines around her fading into a distant murmur. The war raged on, but in her office, a tiny sanctuary of peace had formed around her, a space filled with hope and the promise of a different kind of connection. As she looked out into the night, the stars seemed a little brighter, a little closer, as if reflecting the newfound closeness she felt to a once distant ally.

The winds of war carried a chill through the streets of Berlin, rustling the papers on Anna's desk as she sat contemplating her next move in the ongoing game of coded exchanges with James. The stakes of their communication had risen; each message now bore not just the weight of intellectual challenge but also the subtle warmth of budding friendship, or perhaps something more.

Tonight, she worked meticulously, decoding another message from James, her hands steady despite the internal turmoil the words provoked. Each sentence seemed to draw them closer, a dance of intimacy choreographed within the confines of war.

"Anna," the message began, "I find myself looking forward to our exchanges more than I should. In these words, I see a respite from the shadows of conflict."

"James," she responded, her fingers hesitating just a moment before continuing, "it's the same for me. Your messages are like a light in the darkness that surrounds us both."

The room around Anna felt suddenly too vast, too empty. She was acutely aware of the silence that enveloped her between the bursts of static from the radio equipment.

"Tell me," James wrote, breaking into her thoughts, "what is it about the night sky that fascinates you so?"

"It's the vastness," she typed back, her gaze drifting to the small window and the sliver of dark sky it framed. "The stars remind me that there is so much more beyond this war. They are constant, yet untouchable—much like our correspondence."

"Do you ever wish," his reply came quickly, as if he were right there with her, "that we could step out from behind these coded veils? To meet, not as soldiers on opposite sides, but as two souls beneath those very stars?"

Anna paused, considering his words. "Sometimes, I do. But wishes are dangerous things in times like these."

"Yes, they are," James agreed. "But sometimes, they're all we have. And sometimes," he added, "they lead us to moments of truth we never expected to find."

Their dialogue continued, the room around Anna filled with the soft clicking of the typewriter keys, each word a step deeper into shared confidences. She felt a connection to James that transcended the physical barriers of war, reaching into a realm where fears and dreams could be shared without reprisal.

As the night wore on, the coded messages grew more personal, weaving between the lines of duty and the threads of a connection that was as fragile as it was unexpected. The world outside her office continued its relentless march, but within those walls, a sanctuary of shared secrets and whispered dreams had formed, protected by the very codes that bound them.

The promise of a meeting under neutral skies, once merely a fanciful thought, began to take root in their hearts, a possible endpoint to their journey of words. As Anna sent her final message of the night, a simple sign-off that belied the depth of her newfound feelings, she allowed herself a rare moment of hope.

Outside, the stars twinkled in the cold night sky, witnesses to the silent unfolding of an unlikely bond forged in the shadow of war. Anna leaned back in her chair, her eyes fixed on the heavens, pondering the paradox of finding human connection in the midst of humanity's greatest discord.

Chapter 3
Intricate Dialogues

In the soft shadows of dawn, as the city of Berlin began to stir under a cloak of cautious optimism, Anna sat at her workstation, her fingers poised over the keys. The previous nights had seen a growing bond between her and James, one nurtured not just by shared secrets but by the burgeoning need to understand each other beyond their roles as soldiers. Today, she awaited what she hoped would be another message from him, the continuation of a conversation that had surprisingly become the highlight of her days.

The buzz of the incoming transmission broke the early morning silence, and Anna quickly set to work decoding the message. Her heart raced with a mixture of anticipation and anxiety—each message now carried a weight that was hard to ignore.

"Good morning, Anna," the message flickered onto the screen once decoded, "I found myself watching the sunrise today, and it made me think of our conversations. How are you this morning?"

"Good morning, James," Anna replied, her response tinged with the warmth that had started to characterize their interactions. "I'm well, thank you. The sunrise here was obscured by clouds, but I can imagine its beauty through your words. It seems our roles as morning observers have added a new layer to our exchanges."

"Indeed, it has," James typed back, his words flowing quickly now. "It's strange, isn't it? How two people, so far apart, not just in distance but in circumstances, can find solace in the simple beauty of a sunrise?"

"It is," Anna agreed, her fingers moving deftly over the keys. "It makes me wonder about the simple pleasures of life that we often overlook. Tell me, James, what other simple pleasures do you find yourself missing these days?"

"There are many," he confessed. "The smell of fresh coffee in the morning, the sound of laughter in a crowded room, the feel of a book in my hands. What about you, Anna? What simple things do you long for?"

Anna paused, her mind wandering to the days before the war when life was a tapestry of simple joys. "I miss the sound of the piano," she admitted. "I used to play, you know. Now, the music halls are silent, and the pianos are left unplayed."

"That's a beautiful, yet sad image," James replied. "I hope one day you'll return to the piano, Anna. Maybe you could play for me, in a world where music is not a memory but a celebration."

"I'd like that," Anna smiled slightly as she typed. "And I'd like to hear your laughter in that crowded room, perhaps even share a coffee with you, as we discuss the books we've read."

"Let's promise then," James suggested, "that when this is all over, we will meet not just to talk under the stars, as we once dreamed, but to share those simple pleasures—to laugh, to drink coffee, and to listen to your piano playing."

"It's a promise, James," Anna responded, a sense of commitment resonating through her words. "A promise for a future where we can be just two people, no longer defined by this war but by the moments we choose to share."

As the conversation drew to a close, Anna felt a profound sense of connection, a tether reaching through the digital ether, binding her to James in ways she had never anticipated. Outside, the city awakened, the first hints of sunlight piercing through the clouds, promising a day where anything seemed possible. Inside, Anna cherished the newfound warmth that had settled around her heart, a gentle reminder of the promise of a future filled with simple, yet profound, joys.

The morning progressed in Berlin, with the routine hustle that camouflaged the undercurrents of war threading through the city. In her office, amidst the soft whir of machines and the occasional distant rumble of military vehicles, Anna found herself increasingly absorbed by the personal element that had seeped into her correspondence with James. Each message felt like a thread pulling at the fabric of her carefully maintained boundaries between duty and desire.

Her latest message to James had been one of the most personal yet, promising future meetings filled with simple human pleasures, a stark contrast to their current reality surrounded by secrecy and war. Now, she waited anxiously for his response, each minute stretching out with palpable tension.

When the reply finally came, it was mid-morning, a time when the sun finally broke through the heavy Berlin clouds, casting a warm glow that filtered through Anna's window, bathing her workspace in a soft, comforting light.

"Anna," James's message began, "your words this morning have given me much to think about. It's strange to contemplate a future so normal when our present is anything but. Do you ever fear that these dreams we weave might remain just that—dreams?"

Anna paused before typing back, the click of her keys a steady punctuation in the quiet room. "I do fear that sometimes," she admitted. "But in our dreams, I find a strength I had forgotten. They remind us of why we fight and what we're fighting for—a chance at those very dreams."

"That's a hopeful way to see it," James responded quickly, his words echoing her thoughts. "And speaking of dreams, I've been considering your love of piano. I found an old recording of a piano concerto last night. I wish I could share it with you—it reminded me of our conversation."

Anna smiled faintly at the thought. "I would have loved to hear it. Music has a way of crossing barriers, doesn't it? It's like our messages—a form of connection that can transcend even the greatest of distances."

"Exactly," James typed back. "Perhaps, when all this is over, you can play, and I can bring my collection of old recordings. It would be an evening of shared melodies and memories."

"It sounds wonderful," Anna replied, allowing herself to indulge in the imagery. "An evening away from the shadow of war, filled with the sounds of a past we both hold dear."

Their conversation shifted slightly as James asked, "How do you keep up with your music? Do you still find time to practice, even now?"

"Not as much as I'd like," Anna confessed. "There's little time, and frankly, little heart for it. The world has grown too quiet for music, or perhaps too loud with other, harsher sounds."

"I understand," James replied. "Maybe our promised meeting can also be a rebirth of sorts—for your music and for both of our spirits."

"I'd like that," Anna typed, feeling a surge of optimism. "A rebirth. After all, isn't that what the end of a war should bring? A chance for new beginnings?"

"Yes, a chance for new beginnings," James echoed in his next message. "For music, for laughter, for coffee shared over tales of the past and plans for the future."

As their exchange drew to a close for the morning, Anna leaned back in her chair, her eyes drifting to the window where the sun had finally established its presence in the sky. The conversation had woven a new layer into the tapestry of their relationship, intertwining their hopes for the future with the ongoing rhythm of their daily responsibilities.

Outside, the city moved with the weight of the morning, unaware of the small oasis of hope that had blossomed in a quiet office, where dreams of peace and music momentarily overcame the thunder of war.

The afternoon had settled over Berlin with a quietude that belied the underlying tension of the city. In her office, Anna sat reviewing the transcript of her and James's morning conversation, a slight smile playing at the corners of her mouth. The dialogue had ventured into realms of hope and future possibilities, a rare luxury in their current existence.

Her machine chirped, signaling another incoming message. Quickly, she set to decoding, eager to continue their exchange.

"Anna, this morning's conversation has lingered with me," James's message read as it came to life on the screen. "It's rare to find a kindred spirit even in times of peace. More so now."

"It has stayed with me as well," Anna replied, her fingers deftly tapping the keys. "It's comforting to know there's someone out there who shares my hopes."

"Do you ever think about the first thing you'll do once the war is over?" James asked, his question floating across the digital divide.

"Often," Anna responded. "I think I'd like to see the ocean. I've missed it—the sense of infinity it gives. What about you?"

"I'd go for a long walk in the countryside," he typed back. "Somewhere far from any reminders of the war. Just fields, trees, and the sky above. Perhaps, one day, you could join me."

"That sounds perfect," she typed, allowing herself to imagine such a scene. "No echoes of conflict, just the peace of nature. It's a nice dream."

"More than nice, I hope," James wrote. "Let's agree to make it a reality. A walk in the countryside and a trip to the ocean. We can take a day to celebrate peace."

"I would like that," Anna replied, her heart lightening at the thought. "A day to reclaim the beauty of the world."

Their conversation drifted to more immediate concerns, sharing updates on their respective work and the general state of their cities, but always circling back to the personal connection that had deepened between them.

"Anna, these talks, they mean a great deal to me," James confessed. "You've become a part of my day that I look forward to."

"And you to mine," Anna admitted. "It's strange, isn't it? How important someone can become when you've never even met them?"

"Not strange at all," he reassured her. "Perhaps it's the most human thing of all—finding connection, however unlikely the circumstances."

"Yes, the human need to find a ray of light, no matter how dark the skies," she mused. "James, do you think when we finally meet, it will change things between us?"

"I hope it only adds another layer," he responded thoughtfully. "I don't want to lose this… whatever this is."

"Nor do I," she agreed. "Let's promise that no matter what, this—our conversations, our hopes—doesn't get lost."

"It's a promise, Anna. From the fields and skies to the depths of the ocean, we keep this alive."

As the afternoon waned into evening, Anna found herself reluctant to end their conversation. Each message seemed to weave them closer, threads of shared dreams and promises stretching across the war-torn divide.

Outside her window, the last light of day gave way to the twilight, a visual echo of their conversation—light persisting in the presence of encroaching darkness. In the quiet of her office, with the promise of the ocean and fields and a peace shared, Anna felt a rare peace settle around her.

As the night wrapped its quiet veil over Berlin, Anna found herself once again at her station, waiting for the familiar ping from her machine that signaled a new message from James. The city outside buzzed with a muted tension, a stark contrast to the intimate world she and James had carved out through their communications.

Her screen flickered to life, casting a soft glow in the dim light of her office. James's message appeared, weaving through the digital ether to find her, as always, eagerly awaiting his words.

"Anna, as the day closes, I find myself reluctant to end our conversation," James's message began, echoing her own thoughts. "It feels as if there's still so much left unsaid between us."

"James, I feel the same," Anna replied quickly. "It's as if each night, when we stop typing, a part of our connection pauses, left to wait until the morrow."

"It's a strange sort of friendship we've formed, isn't it?" James typed back. "Built on words and hopes, cast across the expanse of a war that seeks to divide us."

"Yet, it's a friendship that has become a cornerstone of my days," Anna typed, her fingers moving across the keyboard with practiced ease. "Do you think we'll remember these nights, these conversations, after the war?"

"I think these nights are what we'll remember most," James responded. "Not the battles, nor the chaos, but the moments we shared hope and dreams, despite everything."

"That's a comforting thought," Anna mused. "That amidst the darkest times, we found light in each other's words."

"Exactly," James agreed. "And speaking of light, have you ever watched the stars, Anna? Really watched them, not as a cryptographer, but as someone searching for beauty?"

"Sometimes," she admitted. "On clearer nights, when the curfew and clouds allow. They remind me that the world is so much larger than our current confines."

"I like to think of those stars as not just balls of gas burning billions of miles away, but as beacons of the future," James wrote. "Maybe one day, we could watch them together, without the shadow of war, just two people under the vast universe."

"I would like that very much," Anna replied, her heart lighter with the image. "A night where our conversations aren't coded, but as open and infinite as the sky itself."

"As would I," James sent back. "For now, though, these messages will have to suffice. But Anna, promise me something?"

"Anything," she responded, curious.

"Promise me that no matter how this war turns, you'll keep looking at the stars. Keep dreaming of music, of oceans, and of fields. And know that somewhere, I'm doing the same."

"It's a promise, James. And you must promise me the same. That you'll hold on to the thought of coffee, of laughter, and of books. And that you'll keep a piece of tonight with you, always."

"Agreed," James replied. "It's a deal, Anna. From one dreamer to another, under the same stars."

As their conversation dwindled down for the night, Anna leaned back in her chair, her eyes drifting to the small window that looked out over the night-shrouded city. There, the stars flickered faintly, distant yet present— much like the connection she felt with James. With a soft sigh, she turned off her machine, the promise of starlit skies and shared dreams echoing in her mind as she stepped out into the cool night air, her thoughts adrift in possibilities.

Chapter 4
Double Lives

In the dim glow of early dawn, Anna and James sat in the safe house, the map of Europe spread across the table between them. Their eyes scanned the intricate lines and dots that represented borders, roads, and potential threats. The final leg of their escape was planned meticulously, but the shadow of uncertainty loomed large.

"Do you think it's safe to trust Sophie Muller's contact?" James asked, his voice low but filled with concern. His eyes, sharp and alert, studied Anna's face for any sign of doubt.

"We have no choice," Anna replied, her voice steady despite the tension. "We've come this far, and we can't turn back now. Sophie has never steered us wrong."

James nodded, his mind already calculating the risks and strategies. "Alright, let's move out. We'll follow the route Sophie marked for us. It's risky, but it's our best shot."

Their preparations were swift but thorough. Anna packed their remaining supplies, ensuring nothing essential was left behind. James double-checked the perimeter, making sure no one had followed them to this secluded hideout. The early morning air was crisp, the silence only broken by the rustle of leaves and the distant call of birds.

As they stepped out into the pre-dawn light, the weight of their journey pressed heavily upon them. The forest path ahead was shrouded in mist, each step forward a leap into the unknown. They moved with practiced stealth, their senses heightened, every sound scrutinized for potential danger.

"We're almost there," Anna whispered, her breath visible in the chilly air. "Once we cross the border into Italy, we can blend in more easily."

James gave a grim smile, his hand tightening around hers. "Just a little longer. We can do this."

Their journey was punctuated by moments of tension and relief. At one point, they heard the distant sound of a patrol car, its engine rumbling through the stillness of the forest. They ducked behind a cluster of trees, holding their breath as the vehicle passed by, oblivious to their presence.

"That was too close," James muttered once the danger had passed. "We need to be more careful."

Anna nodded, her heart pounding in her chest. "We will be. Let's keep moving."

As they neared the border, the landscape began to change. The dense forest gave way to rolling hills and open fields. They could see the distant outline of a small village, its buildings bathed in the soft light of dawn.

"That's it," Anna said, pointing towards the village. "We make it through there, and we're in Italy."

James scanned the area, looking for any signs of danger. "It looks quiet. But let's not take any chances. We'll stick to the plan."

They moved cautiously, keeping to the shadows, their senses alert for any sign of trouble. The village was still waking up, the streets mostly empty save for a few early risers going about their morning routines.

"We need to find the contact," Anna whispered. "Sophie said they'd be in the café on the main square."

They approached the café, its windows glowing with warm light. Inside, a few patrons sipped their coffee, unaware of the drama unfolding just outside their doors. Anna and James exchanged a glance, their silent communication clear. This was it.

As they stepped inside, a figure in the corner caught their attention. A man, middle-aged with a worn but kind face, nodded subtly at them. They approached cautiously, their hearts pounding.

"Sophie's friends?" the man asked quietly, his eyes scanning the room for any eavesdroppers.

Anna nodded. "Yes. Are you our guide?"

The man smiled, a glimmer of hope in his eyes. "I am. Follow me. We don't have much time."

With that, they followed the man out of the café and into the next phase of their escape. The road ahead was uncertain, but for the first time in days, they felt a glimmer of hope. Together, they could face whatever lay ahead, their bond stronger than ever in the face of adversity.

The small, dimly lit café seemed an unlikely place for the pivotal moment in their escape, but here they were, following the middle-aged man out the back door into a narrow alley. The sound of their footsteps echoed softly against the cobblestones, mingling with the distant hum of the waking village.

"We need to move quickly," the man whispered, his voice urgent but calm. "There's a safe house on the outskirts where you can rest and regroup. We'll head there first."

Anna nodded, glancing at James, who gave her a reassuring squeeze on the shoulder. "Lead the way," James said, his tone steady.

As they navigated through the twisting alleys and narrow streets, the man filled them in on the plan. "My name is Marco," he began, keeping his voice low. "I've been helping people cross the border for years. The key is to stay invisible. Blend in with the locals. Don't attract attention."

"How far is the safe house?" Anna asked, scanning the surroundings for any signs of danger.

"Not far. Just a ten-minute walk," Marco replied. "From there, we'll arrange transportation to get you further south, away from the border patrols."

They continued in silence, the weight of their situation pressing heavily on their shoulders. The morning light grew stronger, casting long shadows across the village streets. Marco led them through a series of back alleys and hidden pathways, his familiarity with the area evident in his confident strides.

Finally, they arrived at a modest house on the edge of the village. Marco knocked on the door in a specific pattern, and moments later, it opened to reveal a young woman with a kind smile. "This is Elena," Marco introduced. "She'll take care of you from here."

"Welcome," Elena said warmly, stepping aside to let them in. "You must be exhausted. Come in, we have food and a place for you to rest."

Anna and James followed her inside, relief washing over them as they entered the cozy, welcoming space. The aroma of freshly baked bread filled the air, and a small table was set with simple but hearty food.

"Sit, eat," Elena urged. "You need your strength for the journey ahead."

As they settled at the table, Marco laid out the next steps. "We'll wait here until nightfall. It's safer to travel under the cover of darkness. From here, we have a driver who will take you to a more secure location further south. There, you'll find another contact who will guide you the rest of the way."

"Thank you," James said sincerely, looking from Marco to Elena. "We couldn't have made it this far without your help."

Elena smiled, her eyes full of empathy. "We're happy to help. Everyone deserves a chance at freedom."

Anna looked at Marco, a question lingering in her mind. "Why do you do this? Risking so much for people you don't even know?"

Marco's expression softened. "Because it's the right thing to do. My family was once in a similar situation, and strangers helped us. I'm just paying it forward."

The conversation turned to lighter topics as they ate, each of them savoring the brief respite from the constant fear and tension. Anna felt a sense of camaraderie growing among them, a shared bond forged in the crucible of their struggle.

After the meal, Elena showed them to a small room with a couple of beds. "Rest now. You need it. We'll wake you when it's time to go."

Anna and James lay down, exhaustion finally catching up with them. As they drifted off to sleep, Anna felt a flicker of hope. They had allies, a plan, and for the first time in days, a sense of safety.

Hours later, as the sun began to set, Marco and Elena gently woke them. "It's time," Marco said softly. "We need to move."

Anna and James gathered their belongings, ready to face the next leg of their journey. With Marco and Elena's help, they stepped out into the twilight, determined to reach freedom no matter what lay ahead.

As the sun dipped below the horizon, casting long shadows across the landscape, Anna and James prepared for the next phase of their escape. Marco had arranged for a driver, a trusted ally named Lorenzo, who would take them to a more secure location further south. The twilight provided the perfect cover for their departure.

Marco and Elena saw them off at the back door of the safe house. "Lorenzo will take you to a safe haven where you can rest and plan your next move," Marco explained. "It's a long drive, but he knows the safest routes."

Anna embraced Elena, grateful for her kindness. "Thank you for everything. We couldn't have done this without your help."

"Stay safe," Elena replied, her voice full of warmth and concern. "We'll be thinking of you."

James shook Marco's hand firmly. "We owe you our lives."

"Just keep moving," Marco said with a determined nod. "Don't look back."

Lorenzo, a man in his fifties with a weathered face and calm demeanor, led them to an old but well-maintained van parked discreetly behind the house. "Hop in," he said, opening the door for them. "We have a long journey ahead."

As they settled into the van, Lorenzo started the engine and pulled away from the safe house, navigating through the narrow, winding streets with practiced ease. The hum of the engine and the rhythmic motion of the vehicle had a soothing effect, momentarily easing the tension that had gripped Anna and James for days.

Lorenzo glanced at them in the rearview mirror. "Marco told me about your situation. You're brave to take this journey."

"We don't have much choice," James replied, his voice reflecting the weariness and determination that had become their constant companions.

Anna added, "We're just trying to survive. To find a place where we can be safe."

Lorenzo nodded understandingly. "I've helped many like you. Everyone deserves a chance at freedom. We'll get you there."

The drive continued in silence for a while, the dark countryside rolling past outside the windows. Anna couldn't help but feel a mix of apprehension and hope. The road ahead was uncertain, but each mile put more distance between them and the danger they were fleeing.

"How far until the next safe house?" Anna asked, breaking the silence.

"About three hours," Lorenzo replied. "We'll be traveling through some remote areas, which should keep us off the radar. I know a place where we can stop for a break if needed."

James leaned back, closing his eyes briefly. "Three hours isn't so bad. We've been through worse."

"True," Anna agreed, squeezing his hand. "We can handle this."

As they drove on, the conversation turned to lighter topics. Lorenzo shared stories of his own experiences helping others escape, tales filled with danger, close calls, and the occasional triumph. His stories brought a sense of normalcy and even humor to their journey, a welcome distraction from the constant tension.

At one point, Lorenzo pulled off the main road onto a secluded path, stopping in front of a small, rustic cabin. "This is a good place to stretch your legs," he said. "We have a bit of time before we need to move on."

They stepped out of the van, the cool night air refreshing against their skin. The cabin was quiet and peaceful, a stark contrast to the turmoil they had left behind.

Anna looked around, taking in the serene surroundings. "It's beautiful here. Hard to believe what's happening in the world."

"Sometimes, these little pockets of peace are what keep us going," Lorenzo said, leaning against the van. "Take a moment to breathe. We'll be back on the road soon."

James and Anna walked a short distance, finding a spot where they could sit and rest. They didn't speak much, simply enjoying the brief respite and the sense of safety the cabin offered. For a moment, the world seemed to pause, giving them a precious few minutes of calm.

When it was time to leave, they returned to the van, feeling a bit more refreshed and ready to continue. As they resumed their journey, the road ahead seemed a little less daunting, and the hope of reaching their destination felt a bit closer.

With Lorenzo's guidance and their unwavering determination, Anna and James knew they had the strength to face whatever challenges lay ahead. They were not alone in this journey, and with each mile they traveled, the promise of freedom grew stronger.

The cabin faded into the distance as Lorenzo's van rumbled back onto the road, the night growing darker with each passing mile. The hum of the engine and the occasional rustle of the trees were the only sounds breaking the stillness. Anna and James sat in the back, their hands intertwined, drawing strength from each other.

Lorenzo glanced at them in the rearview mirror, his expression thoughtful. "You know, every journey like this has its own challenges. But you two, you've got the right spirit. You remind me of a couple I helped last year."

"Were they trying to escape too?" Anna asked, her curiosity piqued.

"Yes," Lorenzo replied, his voice steady. "They were journalists, had uncovered some truths that powerful people didn't want exposed. It was a tough journey, but they made it. Found safety in a new country."

"That gives us hope," James said, his grip on Anna's hand tightening. "It's stories like that which keep us going."

Lorenzo nodded, keeping his eyes on the road. "Hope is essential. Without it, this journey would be impossible. But remember, staying alert is just as important. Danger can come from anywhere."

As if on cue, the van's headlights illuminated a checkpoint up ahead, a stark reminder of the peril they faced. Lorenzo's expression hardened. "Stay calm. Let me do the talking."

Anna and James exchanged a tense glance but nodded, trusting Lorenzo's experience. The van slowed as they approached the barrier, manned by a few guards with stern expressions.

One of the guards stepped forward, his flashlight sweeping over the van. "Where are you headed at this hour?" he asked, his voice authoritative.

Lorenzo responded smoothly, "Just delivering some goods to a friend's farm down south. Got delayed by some car trouble."

The guard's eyes narrowed, suspicion evident. "Mind if we take a look inside?"

Lorenzo's heart pounded, but he maintained his composure. "Of course, officer. Just some supplies in the back."

The guard gestured, and another approached the back of the van. Anna and James held their breath, their hearts racing. The guard opened the door, peering inside. Anna quickly grabbed a blanket, draping it over herself and James to appear as inconspicuous as possible.

The guard's flashlight flickered over the supplies and the bundled figures. After a tense moment, he seemed satisfied. "Alright," he said, stepping back. "You can go. Be careful on the road."

"Thank you, officer," Lorenzo replied, his voice steady. He drove away slowly, maintaining the façade of calm until they were out of sight. Once they were clear, he let out a breath he hadn't realized he was holding.

"That was close," Anna whispered, her heart still pounding.

James exhaled deeply. "Too close. We need to stay on guard."

Lorenzo nodded. "You handled it well. Just a bit further now. We'll reach the next safe house soon."

They drove in silence for a while, the tension slowly easing but not disappearing entirely. As they neared their destination, Lorenzo spoke again. "You've got a long road ahead, but you're not alone. There are more people out there willing to help than you might think."

Anna smiled, though it was tinged with exhaustion. "We've been incredibly lucky to find people like you, Marco, and Elena. It gives us the strength to keep going."

James added, "We owe you more than we can ever repay."

Lorenzo shook his head. "You don't owe me anything. Just promise me one thing—when you find your safe place, don't forget where you came from. Use your freedom to help others find theirs."

Anna and James exchanged a determined look. "We promise," they said in unison.

Soon, the van pulled up to a secluded farmhouse nestled among rolling hills. The lights inside were dim, a sign of caution and safety. Lorenzo turned to face them. "This is it. You'll be safe here for a while. The next contact will take you further south."

Anna and James thanked Lorenzo once more, their gratitude evident in their eyes. "Take care of yourselves," Lorenzo said as they stepped out of the van. "And remember, stay hopeful and stay alert."

With those parting words, Anna and James watched as Lorenzo drove away, disappearing into the night. They turned toward the farmhouse, ready to face whatever came next, their resolve strengthened by the kindness and bravery of those who had helped them along the way.

Chapter 5
A Risky Proposal

As dawn painted the skies over Berlin with strokes of pale orange and pink, Anna sat before her station, her thoughts tinged with the residual warmth of her and James's recent conversations. The office was quiet in the early hours, with only the soft hum of machinery and the distant sounds of the awakening city to accompany her.

Today, however, there was a palpable tension in the air. It was the day before an important operation, one that required her to encode messages of great strategic importance. Her task was clear, yet her mind wandered, caught between duty and the burgeoning fear of what the future might hold.

Her terminal pinged, signaling the arrival of a new message. It was James, punctual in his morning greeting, which had become something of a ritual between them.

"Good morning, Anna. How are you on this fine day?" James's words flickered onto the screen, bringing a small, involuntary smile to Anna's lips despite her anxieties.

"Good morning, James," she typed back. "I'm well, though today is laden with preparations. How are things on your end?"

"Busy as ever," James replied. "The war waits for no one, it seems. But I've been thinking about our last conversation, about making choices that aren't dictated by this conflict."

"It's a pleasant thought," Anna responded, her fingers hesitating slightly as she contemplated her next words. "Making choices that are truly our own... it seems like a luxury now."

"It does," James agreed. "But I hold onto the hope that one day it won't be. Speaking of choices, have you given any thought to what you'll do when the war ends? I mean, beyond the dreams we've shared?"

Anna paused, considering her response. The reality of life after the war was a mosaic of hope and uncertainty. "I have, though it feels almost daring to plan too far ahead. I would like to continue my work in cryptography, but in a peaceful capacity. And you?"

"I've thought about it quite a bit," James typed. "I'd like to teach, perhaps. Share some of what I've learned, not about war, but about the mathematics and strategies behind codes and ciphers."

"That sounds like you," Anna replied warmly. "Educating the next generation to use knowledge for building rather than destruction."

"It's an optimistic outlook," James admitted. "But then, I've found myself more optimistic since our conversations began."

Their exchange drifted then to the specifics of their work, the details of which were veiled even in their coded language. Yet, beneath the technical talk, there was a current of shared understanding, a connection forged not just by shared interests but by the shared burden of their roles in the war.

"As we prepare for tomorrow's operation, I find myself wishing for a swift end to all this," Anna confessed, her words heavy with the weight of responsibility.

"I share that wish," James responded. "Every operation feels like a step closer to an end, though whether it's the end we hope for remains to be seen."

"Indeed," Anna agreed. "But let's promise to focus on the future we desire, not just the end of the war but what comes after."

"A future where our meetings aren't just exchanges through screens," James suggested.

"Exactly," Anna typed, a note of determination in her digital voice. "A future where our discussions can be about possibilities and achievements, not just strategies and survival."

As the sky lightened further, signaling the start of another day governed by war, Anna felt a renewed sense of purpose. The conversation with

James had not only bolstered her spirits but also reinforced her resolve to see the conflict through to its conclusion, whatever it might be.

Turning her attention back to the tasks at hand, she carried with her the comforting thought of future possibilities—a world where her interactions with James could transcend the circumstances of war and flourish in the light of peace. The room filled gradually with the morning light, blending the digital and real worlds in a soft glow, as Anna continued her work, fortified by the promise of tomorrow.

In the labyrinth of corridors that constituted the German intelligence office, the morning bustle escalated into the frantic pace of midday. As Anna navigated through her responsibilities, the weight of the upcoming operation pressed heavily upon her. The once tranquil sanctuary of her office had transformed into a hub of strategic activity, with papers strewn about her desk and the constant clatter of teletype machines echoing through the air.

Outside, the streets of Berlin hummed with the subdued rhythms of a city at war, the sounds of commerce and conversation undercut by the distant, yet ever-present, roar of engines and the sporadic drum of boots on pavement. These were the sounds of readiness, of a population braced against the storm of conflict, mirroring the storm within Anna herself.

Her focus was absolute as she encoded vital messages, each one a thread in the vast tapestry of wartime communication. The precision required was immense; a single error could misdirect battalions or misinform commanders, potentially altering the course of battles. Yet, through the window of her cramped office, the sight of a clear blue sky offered a stark contrast to the gravity of her tasks, reminding her of the world beyond war, the world she often discussed with James.

As the day wore on, the brief exchanges with her distant confidant were not just a respite but a lifeline, pulling her back from the edge of a professional precipice. The intellectual intimacy they shared provided a counterbalance to the tactical coldness of her daily duties. Yet, today, there was little time for such exchanges. The operation demanded all her attention, and she granted it fully, aware of the lives that might depend on her proficiency.

Late in the afternoon, a momentary lull gave her pause. She leaned back in her chair, closing her eyes briefly, allowing herself a few seconds of reprieve. Her thoughts drifted inevitably to James. His words from their morning conversation echoed in her mind, a soothing balm amid the cacophony of war. They spoke of a future filled with hope, a stark contrast to the present filled with strategic maneuvers and coded directives.

Opening her eyes, Anna gazed out the window, the cityscape bathed in the golden light of the setting sun. The beauty of the moment was poignant, a reminder of the world's persistence despite the chaos of human conflicts. It reinforced her resolve, strengthening her determination to push through the current turmoil, to reach the peace they both envisioned.

With renewed vigor, Anna returned to her work, her fingers moving deftly over the keys as she finalized the preparations for the operation. The messages she sent were crafted with meticulous care, designed to convey critical information under layers of security. Each keystroke was a step toward the completion of her mission, each message sent a ripple in the waters of the war.

As the day shifted into evening, the pace of activity in the office gradually slowed. The earlier tension subsided, giving way to a cautious optimism as the preparations concluded. Anna's role was pivotal, and as she shut down her station, she felt a mixture of relief and apprehension. The operation would unfold the following day, its outcomes uncertain but its execution a testament to the efforts of countless individuals like herself.

Stepping out of her office, Anna took a deep breath, the cool evening air refreshing after the stuffiness of the cramped space. The stars were beginning to emerge, specks of light in the deepening twilight, each one a silent witness to the world's unfolding dramas. For a moment, she allowed herself to just be, a single soul amidst the vastness of the universe, connected by starlight to the hopeful dreams she shared with James. As she walked home, the stars overhead were a reminder of the promises made and the future they hoped to build, a future where war was just a memory, and peace was a tangible reality.

The night draped over Berlin like a somber cloak, shadows weaving through the streets as the city settled under the weight of anticipation. Inside her modest apartment, Anna sat at a small, cluttered desk, bathed in the soft light of a single lamp. The day's efforts had left her feeling drained, yet her mind raced with thoughts of the upcoming operation and its implications. Her focus was interrupted by the faint hum of her communication device activating—a late-night message from James, seeking her out in the quiet hours when thoughts grew deep and reflective.

"Anna, as the operation approaches, I find myself concerned for your safety," James's words appeared on the screen, his concern palpable even through the digital medium.

"Thank you, James," she replied, her fingers hesitating slightly over the keys. "I share your concern, but we've prepared as much as we can. How are things on your end?"

"Preparations are ongoing. It's all hands on deck," he typed back. "But tonight, I wanted to reach beyond the operation, to remind you—and perhaps myself—of the world beyond this conflict."

Anna smiled faintly, touched by his thoughtfulness. "That's a welcome respite, James. It's easy to get caught up in the immediacy of war, to forget the quiet moments we've shared discussing a future filled with peace."

"Yes, those conversations have become a sanctuary for me," James responded. "Speaking of sanctuaries, have you thought about where you might want to go when the war is over? A place to find peace?"

"I have," Anna typed, her gaze drifting towards the window where the city lights flickered like distant stars. "I've always dreamed of visiting the mountains—somewhere far from the reminders of war. A place where the air is clear and you can hear the wind in the trees. What about you?"

"The countryside for me," James replied. "A quiet village where life moves at a slower pace, where one can appreciate the simple joys of nature and community."

"It sounds perfect," Anna said. "A place to heal and rebuild. It's funny, isn't it? How we find ourselves dreaming of the simplest things."

"Perhaps it's those simple things that are most important," James mused. "Those dreams keep us grounded when the world around us seems to spiral out of control."

"They do," Anna agreed, feeling a sense of solace in their shared aspirations. "And it's these dreams that fuel our resolve to push forward, to make it through to see them realized."

"Exactly," James typed, a sense of resolve in his digital voice. "Anna, whatever tomorrow brings, remember that these dreams, our conversations—they matter. They're a reminder of what we're fighting for, not just against."

"I'll remember," Anna assured him, her heart strengthened by his words. "And I'll hold onto our promise of a future where we can pursue those dreams together."

As their conversation drew to a close, Anna felt a renewed sense of purpose. The operation loomed large, but so too did her hopes for the future—a future where dreams of peace could become reality. She glanced once more at the city outside her window, its quiet darkness a canvas for her thoughts.

Stepping away from the desk, Anna prepared for bed, the night's exchange with James echoing in her mind. It was a balm to the soul, a beacon through the darkness, reminding her that even in war, connections could be forged and dreams could thrive. As she lay down, the silent promise of tomorrow, of mountains and countryside, of peace and healing, lulled her toward sleep, a gentle reminder of the enduring power of hope.

As the morning sun breached the horizon, casting long shadows across the cobbled streets of Berlin, Anna found herself at her station earlier than usual. The operation was set to commence within hours, and the tension was palpable, not just in the air but in the hurried exchanges between her colleagues. Amidst the pre-dawn rush, her device signaled an incoming message from James, a now familiar beacon in her routine of preparations.

"Anna, it's the morning of. How are you holding up?" James's words appeared on the screen, his concern evident even through the cold digital text.

"I'm here, ready as I'll ever be," Anna typed back quickly, her eyes darting around the room to ensure her privacy. "It's a big day. The office is buzzing already."

"I can imagine," James replied. "Just remember, whatever happens today, stay safe. That's the most important thing."

"Thank you, James. I will," she responded, taking a deep breath. "And you too, whatever part you play today, be careful."

"The odd thing about being careful in our line of work is that so much is out of our hands," James typed, his message carrying a weight that matched the gravity of the day.

"That's true," Anna acknowledged. "But we make our moves and hope for the best. That's all we can do."

"In a way, it's like our conversations," James mused. "We send out our words and hope they find their mark, that they bring some comfort, or joy, or even just a moment's respite from the chaos."

"Exactly," Anna replied, smiling faintly at the comparison. "Speaking of which, these early morning chats have become something of a ritual for me. A moment of calm before the storm."

"They have for me as well," James confessed. "Knowing you're out there, thinking similar thoughts, facing similar challenges—it helps, more than I probably let on."

"I feel the same," Anna said, her fingers hesitating over the keyboard as a rush of emotion threatened her composure. "It's a connection I didn't expect to find in all this madness."

"A happy surprise, then, amidst the less welcome ones," James noted. "Anna, when this is all over, and we're living those dreams we talked about—mountains for you, the countryside for me—I hope we can look back on these days as a strange, dark time that brought something beautiful into our lives."

"I hope so too, James," Anna typed, her heart aching with the hopefulness of his words. "It's something to hold onto, a reminder that not all unforeseen things in life are to be feared or dreaded."

"And maybe one day, we can meet and share these stories in person, laugh about how we kept sanity through messages in the dead of night and plans for peaceful days," James suggested.

"That would be a conversation worth having," Anna replied warmly. "I look forward to it."

"As do I," James typed. "But for now, let's focus on today. Do what you need to do, and we'll talk again when it's all settled."

"Agreed," Anna responded. "Stay safe, James."

"You too, Anna."

With a final glance at the screen, Anna turned her attention back to the tasks at hand. The operation was imminent, and her role was crucial. Yet, James's words lingered in her mind, a gentle echo in the back of her thoughts, providing a subtle strength as she navigated the complexities of her day.

As she worked, the city awoke fully around her, the sounds of routine gradually drowning out the night's stillness. Anna felt a part of something much larger than herself—a network of hopes and duties, fears and aspirations, all intertwined on this significant day. Her fingers moved deftly, encoding the final messages, her thoughts intermittently returning to the mountains and countryside, to a future of peace and a meeting under different circumstances, her spirit buoyed by the promise of what lay beyond.

Chapter 6
Preparation and Paranoia

As dawn broke over Berlin, the aftermath of the previous day's operations hung heavy in the air. The city, though outwardly calm, thrummed with the undercurrents of tension and relief that followed significant military engagements. Inside the dimly lit intelligence office, Anna, with her usual composed demeanor, reviewed the outcomes and prepared her reports. Her workstation buzzed with the incoming transmission from James, breaking the early morning silence that had settled over her office.

"Anna, how did everything go on your end yesterday?" James's words appeared on her screen, concern lacing his typed message.

"It was intense, but we managed through," Anna replied, her fingers pausing as she reflected on the day's events. "There were moments when I wasn't sure we'd pull through without significant setbacks."

"I understand," James responded. "We had our share of challenges here too. It's never easy, but hearing from you now, knowing you're alright, it helps."

"Thank you, James," she typed back, the warmth of his words offering comfort. "Knowing there's someone who understands, who's waiting for my message—it makes all the difference."

"It does," James agreed. "It's strange how much our daily communications have become a cornerstone of stability in this chaos."

"Indeed," Anna continued, "it's more than just exchanging updates or strategic input. It's about maintaining a thread of normalcy in an otherwise tumultuous existence."

"Do you ever think about how things will change when the war is over? When these messages aren't filled with the weight of war but with the lighter tales of our day-to-day lives?" James asked, his question threading through the digital space between them.

"All the time," Anna admitted. "I look forward to the day when our conversations can revolve around mundane things like the weather or what we had for lunch, rather than reports and reconnaissance."

"That sounds perfect," James typed, a hint of amusement in his message. "Speaking of mundane, I had the most unremarkable breakfast today, yet somehow I think I'd enjoy even the most ordinary meals if I were sharing them with you."

Anna chuckled softly, the sound absorbed by the quiet of her office. "I agree. It's the company that makes meals memorable, not the cuisine. And I'd much rather discuss the weather with you than war strategies."

"Let's promise then," James suggested, "that our first meeting in peace will involve a thoroughly ordinary meal, where we can complain about the weather and share stories about trivial things."

"It's a promise," Anna replied, the corners of her lips curling up in a smile. "An ordinary meal, with extraordinary company."

"As for today," James's message continued, shifting back to the present, "what's on your agenda? More decoding, or do you have a moment to breathe?"

"A bit of both," Anna responded. "The aftermath of an operation always involves detailed reporting and analysis, but I'm hoping for a few quiet moments this afternoon."

"Make sure you take those moments," James advised. "They're as important as any part of your day. And if you find a minute or two, tell me something trivial—like the view from your window."

"I will," Anna promised. "And James, don't forget to look up from your work today too. Remember, there's a world outside that needs our attention just as much as our tasks do."

"Understood," he replied. "I'll keep that in mind."

As their conversation drew to a close, Anna felt a renewed sense of connection and purpose. The digital space between them was filled with the promise of future normalcy and shared trivialities, a stark contrast to the complexities of their current roles. She turned her attention back to her reports, fortified by the knowledge that beyond the war, ordinary moments awaited them, ready to be cherished and shared.

Late morning light filtered through the windows of Anna's office, casting long shadows across the floor. Outside, the city moved slowly, still recovering from the intensity of yesterday's operations. Inside, Anna sat at her desk, immersed in her tasks, when her communication device signaled an incoming message from James. She welcomed the break, eager for the distraction and the connection it promised.

"Anna, I took your advice and stepped away from my desk for a moment," James's message read. "I found myself at a small park nearby, watching the world go by. It made me think of our promise to share the trivial after the war. What's outside your window right now?"

Anna smiled and glanced out her window. "Right now, there's a group of children playing in the street, seemingly oblivious to the broader tensions around them. It's refreshing to see such innocence and joy amidst everything else."

"That must be a comforting sight," James responded. "Here, the park is filled with people trying to capture a slice of normalcy, much like those children. There's an old man feeding pigeons, which reminds me of a quieter, more peaceful time."

"It sounds lovely," Anna typed back. "It's these snapshots of everyday life that remind us what we're fighting for, isn't it? For the chance to enjoy simple, peaceful moments without the backdrop of war."

"Exactly," James replied. "Speaking of which, how are you managing today, after everything that's happened? Are you finding time to breathe?"

"I am, now," Anna said, allowing herself a moment to relax into their conversation. "This morning was busy with debriefings and reports, but talking to you now, I feel more at ease. It helps to share these moments."

"I feel the same," James typed, his words flowing easily. "Sharing with you makes the weight of my responsibilities a bit lighter. Sometimes I wonder how different my days would be without our chats."

"I wonder that too," Anna admitted. "Our conversations are a respite from the chaos, a connection that goes beyond the professional and touches on something deeply personal."

"As we continue to navigate through these challenging times, I hold onto the thought of our future mundane chats. Imagine us discussing our day over coffee, without a care about encrypting our words," James mused.

"I look forward to that," Anna replied, her heart lighter with the thought. "No codes, no hidden meanings, just straightforward conversation."

"And when that day comes, what do you hope we'll talk about?" James asked, curious.

"Everything and anything," Anna responded. "From books and music to our dreams and perhaps reflections on how we made it through these trying times."

"That sounds perfect," James said. "A future where our discussions are dictated by curiosity and interest, not necessity and duty."

As their conversation drew to a close, Anna felt a mix of nostalgia for the future they envisioned and gratitude for the present connection. "Until our next chat, take care of yourself, James. And keep finding those moments of peace."

"I will, Anna. And you do the same. Remember, there's a world of ordinary waiting for us on the other side of this."

With a final glance at the messages, Anna turned her attention back to her work, the promise of future trivial conversations providing a subtle but profound comfort. Outside, the children's laughter echoed faintly through her window, a poignant reminder of the stakes at play and the simple joys that awaited them once the war was over. As she focused on her reports, her thoughts occasionally drifted to the park where James found his moment of peace, and to the ordinary future they both cherished in their hearts.

As the afternoon stretched across Berlin, a calm yet persistent wind rustled through the leaves, whispering of change and resilience. Inside her office, Anna reviewed her day's work, ensuring every detail was precise, a crucial task that served as the foundation for their strategic communications. Her concentration was broken by the familiar chime of an incoming message from James, a welcomed interruption that always seemed to arrive just when she needed it most.

"Anna, as we face these daily challenges, I find myself increasingly grateful for our exchanges," James began, his words conveying a warmth that transcended the digital divide.

"James, I share that gratitude," Anna replied, her fingers swiftly navigating the keyboard. "It's strange how such a routine part of our day can bring so much comfort and perspective."

"It is," James agreed. "Today, I've been thinking about the resilience of the human spirit. Despite everything, people find ways to adapt and persevere. It's inspiring, really."

"It truly is," Anna responded thoughtfully. "Seeing the resilience around me, in the streets, in this office—it helps me keep going. It reminds me that there's a strength within all of us that sometimes only hardship can reveal."

"That's a powerful observation," James typed back. "It makes me wonder about the stories we'll tell when this is all over. The tales of resilience and perhaps, even of unexpected friendships like ours."

"I look forward to sharing those stories," Anna said. "Especially ours. To think that amidst a global conflict, we found a friendship that provides such strength and solace—it's something quite remarkable."

"Indeed," James replied. "Speaking of stories, have you thought about what you might like to do once the war is over? I mean, beyond the immediate return to normalcy?"

Anna paused, considering his question. "I've always had a passion for writing. Perhaps I'll finally write that book I've been dreaming about.

Maybe a story of war, not just the battles, but the human connections that endure and evolve because of, or perhaps in spite of, the chaos."

"That sounds incredible, Anna. I'd be first in line to read it," James encouraged. "And you've already got a compelling chapter to start with— our correspondence."

"Thank you, James," Anna smiled, touched by his support. "What about you? Any post-war aspirations that go beyond your teaching dreams?"

"I've been thinking about traveling," James revealed. "Not just to escape but to explore. To see the places I've only read about or intercepted in coded messages during the war."

"That sounds like a wonderful pursuit," Anna replied. "To seek understanding and perhaps healing in new places. And maybe, our paths could cross during these travels."

"I'd like that very much," James typed, a note of hope threading through his words. "To meet not just in the context of our usual discussions but in new environments, sharing new stories."

As their conversation continued, the topic shifted towards more immediate tasks, yet the undercurrent of future plans remained a strong presence, weaving through their dialogue. They discussed their current projects and the day's challenges, but always with an undertone of the future, of hope, and of the shared dreams they nurtured.

"Anna, before we end our chat today, remember to take a moment for yourself," James advised as the conversation neared its close. "A moment to dream, to plan, or simply to breathe."

"I will, James. And you do the same," Anna responded, her heart lifted by the thoughtfulness of his words.

With a final exchange of well-wishes, Anna turned back to her work, the conversation with James lingering in her mind like a comforting melody. The rest of her day passed in a blend of routine tasks and reflective moments, each one colored by the thoughts of future possibilities and the strengthening bond that the war had unexpectedly deepened. As evening approached, she felt a profound connection not just to the tasks at hand but to the broader tapestry of human experience, enriched by the resilience and hopes shared with a once-distant friend.

As twilight descended upon Berlin, casting a soft, dusky glow over the city, Anna remained at her station, the faint hum of her equipment a constant backdrop to her thoughts. The room was bathed in the gentle light of her desk lamp, which flickered occasionally, reminding her of the fragility of the peace she longed for. Her communication device chimed, signaling another message from James, a now familiar and comforting routine that punctuated her evenings.

"Anna, as the day winds down, I find myself reflecting on our earlier conversations about resilience and the future," James's message read, his digital presence a steady anchor in the shifting tides of war.

"James, those reflections have become a crucial part of my day," Anna typed back, her fingers moving deftly over the keys. "They remind me that there is a future worth looking forward to, one that involves more than just conflict."

"It's that future I cling to on tougher days," James replied. "Speaking of which, how do you manage to stay so focused and optimistic? Your strength is something I've come to admire greatly."

"Thank you, James. It's not always easy," Anna admitted. "I draw a lot of strength from our chats, actually. Knowing there's someone who understands, who shares similar burdens and hopes, it makes all the difference."

"I feel the same," James typed, his words flowing with sincerity. "It's our shared moments that often pull me through. But tell me, outside of our conversations, what else gives you hope during these trying times?"

"Oddly enough, it's the small acts of kindness I see around me," Anna shared. "Even in the midst of war, people find ways to help each other, to offer comfort. It's a reminder that humanity endures."

"That's a beautiful observation," James responded. "It's those glimpses of humanity that reassure me that there is still good in the world, still something worth fighting for."

"Exactly," Anna replied. "And it's why I look forward to a time when we can leave behind the constraints of war and focus on rebuilding, on nurturing those glimpses into lasting peace."

"I share that hope," James said. "And speaking of nurturing, have you thought about what you might like to nurture in peace times? You mentioned writing, but is there anything else?"

Anna paused, considering his question. "I'd like to nurture relationships, James. Reconnect with old friends, strengthen new ones—like ours. Maybe even teach a bit, share what I've learned not just about cryptography, but about resilience and hope."

"That sounds wonderful, Anna," James replied warmly. "You'd be an excellent teacher. And you're right about relationships. They're the foundation of everything we do, aren't they?"

"They are," Anna agreed. "And on that note, I want to make sure that whatever happens, we continue this—our discussions, our sharing of hopes and dreams."

"I wouldn't have it any other way," James assured her. "Our connection is something I value deeply. It's one of the few good things this war has brought me."

"As it has for me," Anna said, a smile touching her lips as she typed. "James, let's promise to meet after the war, not just to talk about what we've been through, but to celebrate what lies ahead."

"It's a promise, Anna," James replied, the commitment clear in his words. "A celebration of peace, of friendship, and of all the mundane joys we've missed."

As their conversation drew to a close for the night, Anna felt a profound sense of gratitude and anticipation. The war still raged beyond the walls of her office, but within those digital exchanges, a future was taking shape—a future filled with promise and peace. She turned off her equipment, the silence of the room enveloping her, yet within her, a light remained—a light kindled by shared dreams and the promise of a new beginning.

Chapter 7
First Encounter

Morning light spilled across Berlin, casting a soft glow through the heavy curtains of Anna's office. The city was quietly bustling, a stark contrast to the high-tension atmosphere that had blanketed the area just days before. Anna sat at her desk, her mind a blend of focus and distant thought as she reviewed encrypted messages from the front lines. Her fingers paused over the keyboard, her thoughts interrupted by a persistent, nagging feeling of unease that had settled in her since the previous night's discussion with James.

As she sifted through her morning routine, her communication device pinged softly, signaling the arrival of James's daily correspondence. It was a part of her day she had come to rely on, a moment of connection that bridged the gap between duty and personal comfort.

"Good morning, Anna," James's message read, his words a simple yet powerful reminder of their ongoing support for each other. "How are you today? Anything unusual on your end?"

Anna typed back, a slight tension easing from her shoulders as she engaged in this familiar interaction. "Good morning, James. All is as well as can be expected here. The usual reports and data to sift through. How about you? How are things on your side?"

"It's much the same," James replied. "Though, there's a sense of anticipation building up, likely due to the upcoming strategic movements we're preparing for. It keeps us all on edge."

"I can imagine," Anna responded, her mind reflecting on her own similar experiences. "It's during these times of anticipation that I find myself thinking more about the future. About what we'll do when all this is over."

"It's important to hold on to those thoughts," James typed back, his words encouraging. "They remind us there's an end to this, a purpose to our efforts beyond the immediate chaos."

"Indeed," Anna agreed. "I find myself thinking about returning to normal life, about mundane things like attending a concert or walking through a market without fear."

"Those simple pleasures," James wrote, "they seem like luxuries now, don't they? But soon, they'll be our reality again. We just have to keep pushing forward."

"Yes, pushing forward," Anna echoed, her eyes scanning the horizon visible from her small window, where the city stretched under the morning sun. "Sometimes, I wonder how quickly we can adapt back to a peaceful existence. War changes a person, doesn't it?"

"It does," James affirmed. "But I believe it also shows us how much we can handle, and that resilience can help us appreciate peace even more when it comes."

Their conversation shifted towards the practical aspects of their respective duties for a moment, discussing updates and logistical challenges, but the underlying theme of hope and future plans remained a strong undercurrent.

"As we plan for the end of conflict, we should also plan for our first meeting," James suggested, bringing a more personal element back into their exchange.

"I look forward to that day," Anna replied, warmth seeping into her words. "To finally meet, not through coded messages or veiled conversations, but in person, where we can truly share our experiences and celebrate our resilience."

"Absolutely," James responded. "A meeting in peace, in a world where our discussions are no longer shadowed by war."

As the conversation ended, Anna leaned back in her chair, her gaze lost momentarily in the peaceful view outside her window. The city was slowly waking up, and with it, her heart held on to the hope of normalcy and the simple joys of life that awaited them. Her duties called her back to reality, but a part of her remained anchored in the promise of a future filled with peace and new beginnings. The morning continued, and Berlin moved under the watchful eyes of those who dared to dream of its peaceful days to come.

The day progressed steadily, the rhythm of Berlin's heart seeming to pulse just a little slower than usual, a city catching its breath after the relentless pace of wartime exigencies. Inside her office, Anna worked methodically through her tasks, her mind often wandering back to the conversation with James. Each task she completed brought her one step closer to the future they often spoke of—one filled with mundane joys and peaceful gatherings.

Late in the afternoon, as a gentle light bathed her desk, Anna received another coded message from James. This time, his words carried an air of reflection that matched the waning light of the day.

"Anna, as we approach what may be the final stages of conflict, I've been thinking about the lessons we've learned through all this. What do you think will stay with you the most?" James's inquiry appeared on her screen, pulling her thoughts from the immediate to the philosophical.

Taking a moment to gather her thoughts, Anna replied, "I think the resilience of the human spirit, as we discussed this morning. And also, the understanding of how deeply interconnected we all are. This war has shown that actions on one side of the world can impact everyone." Her fingers paused before she continued, "What about you, James?"

"I agree with you on the interconnectedness," James responded after a pause. "And I've learned about the capacity for compassion in the face of hardship. It's something I hope to carry forward in all my future endeavors."

"That's a valuable lesson," Anna typed back, her heart in agreement with his sentiment. "It's these lessons that I believe will help rebuild a better world after the war."

Their conversation briefly delved into more specific details about the current strategic movements, a necessary interlude to their more reflective discourse. But soon, the dialogue returned to their personal reflections and hopes.

"In a way, our roles have given us a unique perspective on the war," James noted. "Do you think this will change how you view your future career or life choices?"

"It might," Anna considered her answer carefully. "I feel a stronger commitment now to using my skills not just in service of national security but towards broader goals like peace and understanding."

"That's an admirable path," James encouraged her. "I hope to find a way to contribute similarly. Maybe through teaching, as I've mentioned, or even through volunteer work."

"I think you'd excel at that," Anna replied, genuinely. "You have a way of understanding and conveying complex ideas that can really make a difference."

As the light in her office dimmed with the setting sun, Anna found herself contemplating the near future. The city outside her window showed signs of life returning to normal, with people strolling in the late afternoon calm, a scene far removed from the chaos of just a few weeks ago.

Her thoughts were interrupted by James's next message, a sign-off for the day. "Anna, I'll let you get back to your evening. Remember to look for those moments of peace we talked about."

"I will, James. Take care," Anna responded, feeling a sense of completion for the day's work and conversations.

The day's end brought a soft silence to her office, a stark contrast to the usual hum of activity. Anna packed away her things, her mind rich with thoughts of future contributions and the peaceful world they both aspired to create. As she walked out of the building, the crisp evening air reminded her of the changing seasons, and with it, the hope for change in the world itself. She walked home with a lighter step, envisioning a future where the lessons learned from war shaped a lasting peace, and where her meetings with James were filled with laughter and shared stories, no longer overshadowed by conflict.

As evening draped its cool shadows over Berlin, Anna settled into a small cafe, a rare change from her usual evenings spent within the confines of her home or office. Her communicator buzzed softly beside her, a signal that James was reaching out, this time perhaps to share more casual evening thoughts.

"Anna, are you still at work, or have you found a moment for yourself today?" James's words scrolled across the screen, his concern for her well-being evident even through the digital medium.

"Actually, I'm at a cafe right now," Anna typed back, a smile touching her lips as she took in her surroundings. "It's nice to step out and see the city coming back to life. What about you?"

"I'm home, finally. Took a walk earlier. It's refreshing to see normal life slowly resuming," James replied. "I'm glad you're out. What's the cafe like?"

"It's quaint, quiet. A few people are here, mostly reading or working on laptops. It feels almost normal," Anna described, her eyes sweeping over the gentle hum of subdued conversations around her.

"That sounds wonderful. I miss that sort of atmosphere. I'm having a quiet evening too, just some music and a book," James shared. "What music is playing here?"

"Some classical pieces, soft and soothing. It's nice background music for reading or just thinking," Anna responded, letting herself relax into the chair. "What are you reading?"

"A history book, believe it or not. About the events leading up to the war. It's a bit heavy, but enlightening," James admitted. "I find understanding the past helps in making sense of our present."

"That's very true. Sometimes I think if more people understood history, we might avoid repeating the same mistakes," Anna mused, her thoughts aligning with his.

"Exactly my sentiment," James agreed. "Speaking of understanding, do you think our experiences have changed how we'll view the world after all this is over?"

"Definitely," Anna replied quickly. "I feel like I've gained a broader perspective, not just on war but on what it means to strive for peace. It's something I hope to carry forward in whatever I do next."

"That's a powerful outlook," James noted. "I hope to carry forward a similar perspective. Perhaps we can both contribute to building a more understanding world."

"I'd like that. Working towards something meaningful, something that can truly make a difference," Anna said, her voice firm with conviction.

"It's a goal worth pursuing," James responded. "And having a friend who shares that goal? It makes it even more achievable."

"It does," Anna smiled. "It's comforting to know there's someone else out there who understands, who shares the same hopes."

"And speaking of sharing, have you tried anything interesting at the cafe?" James's tone shifted slightly, lighter now.

"Just a cup of coffee so far, but there's a pastry display that's been tempting me since I arrived," Anna chuckled, glancing towards the counter. "Maybe I'll give in to the temptation before I leave."

"Go for it, Anna. Enjoy the little pleasures. After all, it's those small joys that can make a day special," James encouraged.

"I think I will," Anna agreed. "And you should find a small joy this evening too, James."

"I will," he promised. "Maybe another cup of tea, or perhaps I'll start a lighter book before bed."

"Sounds like a perfect evening," Anna concluded, feeling a sense of peace settle over her. "Let's catch up again tomorrow, share more of these simple joys."

"I look forward to it," James replied. "Enjoy your pastry and the rest of your evening, Anna."

"Thank you, James. Enjoy your tea and your book. Goodnight," Anna typed, her heart lighter than it had been all day.

As she set her communicator aside, Anna ordered the pastry, deciding to fully embrace the moment's simple pleasure. The cafe, with its soft music and ambient noise, provided a perfect backdrop to her thoughts. Outside, the city continued its slow dance towards normalcy, each step forward a testament to the resilience they had all learned. Inside, Anna allowed herself to dream, not just of peace, but of a future filled with evenings just like this one, shared with friends and filled with laughter.

As the evening deepened, the streets of Berlin slowly emptied, leaving a serene quietness that draped over the city like a soft blanket. Inside the cafe, the gentle murmur of conversation had dwindled to a near whisper, allowing the classical music playing softly in the background to take a more pronounced role in the atmosphere. Anna sat back in her chair, the remnants of the pastry she had indulged in a sweet memory on her palate. She savored the quiet moment, her mind wandering through the possibilities of the future she and James often discussed.

The soft ding of her communicator pulled her back from her reverie. It was a message from James, likely his final for the night. "Goodnight, Anna. Let the music inspire dreams of peace," it read. She smiled, typing back a quick, "Goodnight, James. May your dreams be peaceful too," before turning off the device. The brief exchange was a fitting end to their conversation, encapsulating the warmth and support that had become the foundation of their relationship.

Anna lingered in the cafe a while longer, her eyes tracing the patterns of light and shadow cast by the street lamps outside. Her thoughts were introspective, delving into the themes of resilience and interconnectedness that had characterized her discussions with James. These were not just idle musings; they were reflections on the profound changes she had undergone during the war. The conflict had sharpened her understanding of the world, deepening her appreciation for the peace she now actively longed to see restored.

As she finally stood to leave, the empty cafe seemed to echo with the remnants of the day's earlier vitality. Her walk home was quiet, the sound of her footsteps on the cobblestone streets a rhythmic accompaniment to her thoughts. She considered the transformation of the city around her, slowly recovering from the scars of war, much like its inhabitants. The resilience of Berlin was a mirror to her own, a testament to the enduring human spirit that refused to be quelled by adversity.

Upon reaching her apartment, Anna found herself pausing at the door, taking a moment to look back at the cityscape. The skyline was a silhouette against the night sky, the outlines of buildings stark, yet promising. She thought about the ordinary joys James had encouraged her to embrace— the simple act of enjoying a pastry, the quiet reflection in a nearly empty cafe, and the shared aspirations of a peaceful future.

Inside, her home welcomed her with the familiarity of a well-loved book. She moved through her evening routine with a calm efficiency, each step a progression towards the solitude of night. But instead of solitude, tonight, her mind was filled with a sense of connection—to James, to the city, to the world beyond her immediate experiences.

Before bed, Anna stood by her window, looking out at the quiet night. The stars were visible, a rare sight given the usual glow of the city lights. They twinkled, not unlike the way James had described in one of their conversations. It was as if each star was a note in a silent melody, a lullaby for the war-weary soul.

As she climbed into bed, her thoughts lingered on the day's conversations, on the music in the cafe, and on the stars above. These were the pieces of her life now, each a fragment of a larger mosaic of experiences. They were reminders of the past, markers of the present, and beacons for the future.

The night deepened around her, the city slept, and Anna found herself drifting into dreams where the melody of peace was no longer just a background tune in a quiet cafe, but the soundtrack to a world rebuilt on the resilience and hopes of those who dared to dream it into reality.

Chapter 8
Exploring Lisbon

As dawn broke over Berlin, painting the sky in hues of soft pink and gold, Anna found herself walking the quiet streets, enjoying the crisp morning air that hinted at the changing of seasons. The war had drawn to a close, leaving the city and its people in a state of cautious optimism, their routines slowly returning to normalcy. Anna's steps led her to a small park that had become a sanctuary for many seeking peace in the aftermath of conflict.

Seated on a bench, her eyes observed the gentle stirrings of the city as it awoke. Her communicator buzzed lightly, signaling a message from James. It had been a few days since their last conversation—a necessary pause as they both adjusted to the new pace of peacetime.

"Good morning, Anna," James's message appeared, the text a comforting sight. "How does the city look through your eyes today?"

"Good morning, James," Anna typed back, her fingers moving with ease. "The city seems hopeful, like a deep breath taken after a long sprint. People are out, there are more smiles, and the air feels different. What about you? How are things on your end?"

"It's much the same here," James replied. "There's a palpable sense of relief and a tentative step towards normalcy. It's refreshing and, admittedly, a bit disorienting after so long."

"I understand," Anna responded. "It's a strange transition, isn't it? From constant alertness to this... quiet. It takes some getting used to."

"It does," James agreed. "But it's a good change. Speaking of change, have you thought about what you'll do now? Will you continue your work in cryptography, or are you considering new paths?"

"I've been thinking about that a lot," Anna shared, her gaze drifting to a pair of children playing nearby. "Cryptography has been my life for so long, but I feel a pull towards something different now. Perhaps teaching or maybe even taking up that writing project I mentioned."

"That sounds like a wonderful idea," James encouraged. "You have a wealth of knowledge and experience that would benefit many. And your book, I'm sure it would offer unique insights into the war and its impacts."

"Thank you, James," Anna smiled slightly. "Your support means a lot. What about you? Any plans to venture into new territories?"

"I'm actually considering a few options," James typed, the hint of excitement palpable even through text. "Teaching is still on my list, but I'm also exploring the possibility of working with peacebuilding organizations. It feels like a natural extension of what we've been through."

"That's an admirable path," Anna replied, nodding slightly even though he couldn't see her. "Using your skills to build peace rather than strategize for war—it's a worthy transition."

"It feels right," James said. "And speaking of transitions, how are you adjusting to the everyday? Is it as challenging as you expected?"

"In some ways, yes, it's challenging," Anna admitted. "But it's also a relief. There's a certain joy in rediscovering the ordinary, in participating in the mundane activities that we took for granted before the war."

"I can imagine," James reflected. "It's these ordinary moments that now seem extraordinary."

As their conversation came to a close, Anna stood up from the bench, feeling more grounded and certain of her path forward. "I have to head to a meeting now, James. But let's keep this dialogue going. I want to hear more about your plans and thoughts on peacebuilding."

"Definitely, Anna," James replied. "Take care, and we'll talk soon."

Anna tucked away her communicator and walked on, her heart lighter with each step. The park around her buzzed with the early signs of recovery, a reminder of the resilience of life. The city, once shadowed by conflict, now shimmered with the promise of renewal and growth. As she moved through the streets, her thoughts were filled not just with plans for the future but with a deep appreciation for the present, a present that was slowly but surely weaving itself into a tapestry of peace.

In the vibrant heart of Berlin, Anna found herself at a small bookshop that had recently reopened, its windows displaying an array of literature that spoke of a world eager to remember and learn, not just endure. As she perused the shelves, her communicator vibrated softly in her pocket, a sign that James was reaching out.

"Anna, I've been thinking about our last conversation," James's message read, pulling her attention away from a collection of post-war poetry. "How is your day shaping up?"

"It's a day of small discoveries, James," Anna typed back, her fingers brushing against the spines of books as she spoke. "I'm currently in a bookshop, surrounded by thoughts bound in paper. It's quite inspiring. How about you? What are you up to?"

"I'm at a café, drafting ideas for a series of lectures I might give," James replied. "But I'm intrigued about your bookshop visit. Find anything interesting?"

"A few potential treasures," Anna responded, her gaze settling on a novel set in the aftermath of a historical conflict. "Books that remind us of the past but also help us imagine the future. Speaking of the future, how are your lecture plans coming along?"

"Slowly but surely," James typed. "I'm focusing on how communities rebuild after conflict, drawing from both historical examples and personal observations. It feels like a way to make sense of what we've experienced."

"That sounds incredibly valuable," Anna replied, her voice filled with genuine admiration. "Education really is a powerful tool for healing and understanding."

"It is," James agreed. "And I think it's something we need, now more than ever. But tell me more about your discoveries. Any book in particular that caught your eye?"

"There's one," Anna said, lifting a volume adorned with a peaceful landscape on the cover. "It's about how societies transition from war to peace, the psychological shifts that occur. It seems fitting, doesn't it?"

"Very fitting," James chuckled through text. "It sounds like a book I should read too. Maybe you can lend it to me once you're done?"

"I'd like that," Anna smiled, tucking the book under her arm. "It could be the first of many exchanges. I hope we can share not just books, but insights and reflections as well."

"I'm sure we will," James responded warmly. "And speaking of sharing, have you thought more about your writing project? I remember you mentioned starting it once things settled down."

"I have, actually," Anna replied, her enthusiasm evident. "I'm outlining a narrative that intertwines personal stories with historical events. It's daunting but exciting."

"That's brilliant, Anna. Your perspective is unique, and I believe your stories will resonate with many. If you ever need a sounding board or just want to share a draft, I'm here."

"Thank you, James. I just might take you up on that," Anna said, her heart buoyed by the support. "And what about you? Any new projects on the horizon besides your lectures?"

"I'm considering writing a piece on the role of communications in peacebuilding," James revealed. "Drawing from our own experiences, of course."

"That would be fascinating to read," Anna replied. "Communications, in our case, did more than relay messages; it built bridges."

"Exactly," James agreed. "Well, Anna, it seems we both have our paths charted out, intertwined with the past but looking forward to creating something meaningful."

"As always, James, our conversations leave me inspired," Anna typed, feeling a renewed sense of purpose. "I better get going now, though. This book won't read itself."

"Of course," James responded. "Enjoy your reading, and we'll catch up soon. Take care, Anna."

"You too, James. Until next time," Anna typed back, slipping the communicator into her pocket.

With new books in hand and a heart full of plans, Anna stepped out of the bookshop into the gentle afternoon light. The city around her buzzed with the quiet hum of life moving forward, a perfect symphony to accompany the new chapter she was about to begin. Each step she took was a step toward a future crafted with words, wisdom, and the hope of shared understanding, a future that, for the first time in a long while, seemed not just possible, but inevitable.

As the day meandered towards evening, Anna found herself in a quaint cafe, nestled among rows of revitalized boutiques and freshly painted townhouses that mirrored the city's recovery. With a steaming cup of coffee before her and the novel she had purchased tucked beside her, she reflected on the budding sense of renewal that seemed to permeate Berlin. The buzz of her communicator interrupted her thoughts, heralding another message from James, whose correspondence had become a cornerstone of her daily routine.

"Anna, I'm curious," James's message popped up, his inquisitive nature never far from the surface. "Have you found any inspiration in that book you mentioned earlier?"

"Yes, actually," Anna responded, her fingers tapping with a rhythmic cadence on the small table. "It's fascinating how the author intertwines personal narratives with broader historical events. It's given me ideas for my own writing. How's your lecture drafting going?"

"Progressing, thanks to our discussions," James typed back. "Your insights have been invaluable. Speaking of which, have you thought about incorporating our own experiences into your project? Our dialogue could provide a unique perspective on communication during conflict."

"That's an interesting idea," Anna mused aloud, her gaze drifting to the window as she considered the suggestion. "Our conversations have indeed been a lifeline, not just in a practical sense but in maintaining our morale. It could add a deeply personal layer to the narrative."

"It certainly could," James agreed. "And it would be a testament to the power of connection, even in the most unlikely circumstances."

"I'll definitely consider it," Anna replied, her mind already weaving the potential threads of such a story. "James, in your own work, how do you balance the need to educate with the desire to inspire?"

"That's a fine line," James admitted. "I aim to present facts in a way that not only informs but also engages and encourages reflection. I believe that education is most effective when it connects with personal experiences."

"That makes sense," Anna nodded, appreciating his approach. "It's about striking a balance between the intellectual and the emotional."

"Exactly," James responded. "On a different note, how are you finding the pace of life now that things are settling down? Is it easier to find time for yourself?"

"It's getting easier," Anna said, taking a sip of her coffee. "Though there's a part of me that still operates in 'war-time mode.' Slowing down feels almost unnatural."

"I understand that feeling," James typed back. "It's like learning how to breathe again, finding a new rhythm in a world that's no longer defined by urgency."

"It's a welcome challenge, though," Anna smiled, her eyes reflecting a quiet resolve. "James, through all the chaos, what's one thing you've rediscovered about yourself?"

James paused before responding, his message thoughtful. "I've rediscovered my capacity for hope. No matter how dire the situation, I've learned that looking forward is crucial."

"That's a powerful rediscovery," Anna replied warmly. "For me, it's resilience. I've learned that I'm stronger than I thought, and that strength comes not from avoiding challenges but from facing them head-on."

"As always, you inspire me, Anna," James's words glowed with genuine respect. "Let's continue to share these discoveries. They enrich our understanding of ourselves and each other."

"I agree," Anna responded, her heart lightened by their exchange. "Let's keep this dialogue open. It's one of the most rewarding parts of my day."

As their conversation drew to a close, Anna lingered in the cafe, surrounded by the soft murmur of other patrons and the gentle clink of coffee cups. Her thoughts were a blend of contemplation and creativity, spurred by her dialogue with James. With each passing day, she felt more anchored in the present, more hopeful about the future. She closed her book, her mind filled with ideas for her next chapter, both literary and personal. Outside, the city continued its steady march towards renewal, mirroring her own journey towards a new beginning.

Late in the afternoon, the sun began to dip low in the Berlin sky, casting long, dramatic shadows across the bustling streets. Anna sat at a small wooden table outside a different café, one that had become her favorite haunt for people-watching and for writing. Her communicator lit up, a welcome distraction from her intense focus on drafting a chapter of her book.

"Anna, how goes the writing today?" James's text read, always punctual and thoughtful in his inquiries.

"James, it's going well, actually," Anna typed back quickly, grateful for the break. "I'm working on a section about resilience, drawing from both our experiences and broader historical contexts. It's challenging but rewarding. How's your day shaping up?"

"It's been productive. I gave a small talk on peace efforts today, and it was well-received," James replied, his enthusiasm evident even through the text. "But tell me, what specific themes are you exploring in your section on resilience?"

"I'm focusing on the resilience of communities, how collective spirit can overcome even the most daunting challenges," Anna responded, her eyes scanning the crowd for a moment before returning to her screen. "I'm trying to weave in personal stories to highlight individual contributions to a larger narrative."

"That sounds compelling," James said. "Using personal stories makes the historical events more relatable. It personalizes the abstract. Do you include any specific examples that have touched you personally?"

"Actually, yes," Anna typed, her fingers hesitating as she considered how much to share. "One story involves a small group of citizens who banded together to save their neighborhood from destruction. Their courage and unity were incredibly inspiring."

"It's stories like those that really underscore the human capacity for strength and hope," James reflected. "It's important to remember and share these tales."

"Absolutely," Anna agreed. "And it's also about showing that resilience isn't just about enduring but about actively shaping outcomes. What about your talk? What aspects of peace efforts did you focus on?"

"I emphasized the role of communication in rebuilding trust," James responded. "How open dialogues can bridge divides that seem insurmountable. It's something I've come to appreciate even more through our conversations."

"That's a crucial point," Anna nodded, feeling a surge of pride for his work. "Open dialogue is foundational. It's something I've tried to echo in my writing. Speaking of which, how do you handle the emotional aspect of such discussions in your lectures?"

"It's a delicate balance," James admitted. "I try to be empathetic yet objective. It's important to engage the audience emotionally but also to provide them with clear, actionable insights."

"That's a wise approach," Anna replied. "Engaging the heart and the mind equally ensures a more lasting impact."

"It does," James agreed. "And speaking of impact, I believe your book will have a great one. You have a unique way of capturing the essence of human experience."

"Thank you, James," Anna said, genuinely moved. "Your support means a lot. I hope that my readers will find both solace and inspiration in these stories."

"I'm sure they will," James assured her. "And I can't wait to read the finished product. Perhaps over a cup of coffee in that café you love?"

"That sounds perfect," Anna smiled, typing the words with a sense of anticipation. "It's a date. And maybe by then, you'll have a draft of your work to share as well?"

"Indeed," James typed back, the promise of shared future endeavors warming his words. "It's a plan, then. For now, though, I'll let you get back to your writing. Inspired work shouldn't be interrupted for too long."

"Thanks, James," Anna responded, her heart light with the exchange. "Talk soon, and take care."

As their conversation ended, Anna set her communicator aside and returned to her manuscript, her thoughts enriched by their discussion. The cafe around her buzzed with the energy of the city, a harmonious backdrop to her focused writing. Each word she wrote was a step toward weaving the intricate tapestry of human resilience and hope, a narrative bolstered by her own experiences and those shared with James. As the sun set, casting a golden glow over her table, Anna felt a profound connection to her work, to James, and to the unfolding story of peace they were both helping to write.

Chapter 9
Complications Arise

The morning air was brisk as Anna made her way through the rejuvenated streets of Berlin, her steps echoing softly against the cobblestones. The city, alive with the bustling energy of renewal, provided a vivid backdrop to her reflective mood. As she entered a familiar cafe, her communicator buzzed with an incoming message from James, punctuating the start of her day with a hint of anticipation.

"Good morning, Anna. How are you feeling today?" James's message greeted her, a virtual smile in the form of words.

"Good morning, James. I'm feeling quite hopeful actually," Anna typed back, settling into a corner of the cafe with her coffee. "The city seems to be waking up from a long sleep. It's quite energizing. How about you? How are things on your end?"

"It's a similar feeling here," James responded. "There's a palpable sense of starting anew, which brings both challenges and excitement. Speaking of new beginnings, have you made any more progress on your book?"

"I have, indeed," Anna replied, her fingers tapping enthusiastically on the screen. "I've just finished a chapter on the resilience of urban communities. It's fascinating how much we can endure and adapt. What about your projects? Any new developments?"

"Yes, actually," James typed. "I've started collaborating with a local peace initiative. We're working on community reconciliation projects, trying to bridge the divides that the war left behind. It's rewarding work."

"That sounds wonderful, James," Anna said, genuinely pleased. "It must be quite fulfilling to be part of such direct and positive change."

"It is," James admitted. "And it's also challenging. Each community has its unique dynamics and issues. But tell me more about your chapter. What kind of resilience aspects did you explore?"

"I focused on the grassroots movements that sprang up during the war. People really came together in remarkable ways," Anna explained, her eyes lighting up with passion for her subject. "These movements not only addressed immediate needs but also fostered a sense of unity and purpose that endured beyond the conflict."

"That's incredibly powerful," James reflected. "It shows that resilience isn't just about surviving; it's about thriving and transforming adversity into a catalyst for community strength."

"Exactly," Anna agreed. "It's about finding light in the darkest of times. Speaking of which, have any particular stories from your work with the peace initiative stood out to you?"

"There are many," James shared, his tone tinged with both somberness and hope. "One story involves two neighboring families who were on opposite sides during the conflict. We facilitated a series of dialogues between them, and over time, they began to understand and forgive. They're now working together to rebuild their local park."

"That's incredible," Anna responded, inspired by his story. "It's amazing what understanding and communication can achieve. It's like what we've always discussed—dialogue is crucial."

"It really is," James affirmed. "And these personal stories of reconciliation are what I hope to bring into the public sphere. Maybe even include them in a book of my own someday."

"You should," Anna encouraged warmly. "Your experiences could offer so much insight and inspiration to others."

"Perhaps we could even collaborate on a piece," James suggested playfully. "A joint chapter or a series of essays."

"I would like that very much," Anna smiled, her heart warmed by the prospect. "A collaboration between friends, each bringing their unique perspectives to the table."

"Let's plan on that then," James concluded, the promise of future projects adding an extra layer of excitement to their conversation. "For now, though, I'll let you enjoy your morning. We'll talk more soon."

"Sounds perfect, James. Have a great day," Anna typed, feeling a surge of creativity and anticipation for the work ahead.

As the conversation ended, Anna sipped her coffee, her thoughts adrift in the potential of their joint endeavors. Around her, the cafe hummed with the quiet activity of the morning crowd, each person a participant in the city's ongoing story of recovery and growth. Anna felt deeply connected to this narrative, fueled by the exchange of ideas with James and driven by a shared commitment to fostering peace and understanding. As she opened her laptop to write, the words seemed to flow effortlessly, a testament to the power of collaboration and friendship in the face of rebuilding.

Berlin's landscape, marked by its stoic, war-scarred buildings gradually giving way to the hopeful signs of repair, reflected a city and its people in transition. Anna, walking through this transforming cityscape, felt a deep resonance with its recovery—a mirror to her own evolving narrative. Her morning conversations with James had stirred something within her, a renewed sense of purpose, blending her historical insights with present realities into her writing.

She headed towards a newly opened library, a symbol of the community's resilience and commitment to rebuilding intellectual and cultural life. The building stood bright and welcoming amid the remnants of older, more somber structures. As she entered, the smell of fresh paint mixed with the familiar scent of books was unexpectedly comforting, a sensory reminder of new beginnings.

Inside, Anna wandered through rows of shelves, her fingers tracing the spines of books that ranged from historical accounts to contemporary analyses of peace processes. Each title seemed to echo the collective yearning for understanding and reconciliation that had become the heartbeat of the city.

She chose a few books that promised deeper insights into the social dynamics of rebuilding communities after conflicts. As she settled into a corner with her selections, the quiet murmur of the library wrapped around her, providing a perfect backdrop for reflection.

Anna opened her notebook, her thoughts flowing freely. She sketched out the structure of her next chapter, which would delve into the interplay between individual resilience and community recovery. Her research in the library was not just about gathering facts; it was about understanding the underlying human experiences that shaped these facts.

As she wrote, her mind occasionally replayed her morning exchange with James. His work with the peace initiative and the stories of reconciliation he shared were not just inspiring; they were integral to the narrative she was crafting. They exemplified the personal impact of broader peace efforts, a theme she was eager to explore further.

Anna's writing was periodically punctuated by brief conversations with other library patrons. A local historian, recognizing her from a recent panel discussion, stopped by her table to offer insights into the city's post-war recovery efforts. Their exchange was brief but rich with shared understanding and mutual respect for the subject matter.

"Your work is essential to our understanding of ourselves in this post-conflict world," the historian remarked, a sentiment that resonated deeply with Anna.

"Thank you," Anna replied, appreciating the affirmation. "I believe in the power of shared stories to foster a deeper, more inclusive understanding of our past and present."

As the afternoon waned, Anna continued her work, the historian's words lingering in her mind. She felt a profound connection to her city and its people, a woven fabric of stories and histories that she was now a part of. Her task was more than academic; it was a personal journey intertwined with the collective narrative of her community.

Closing her notebook, Anna took a moment to look around the library. It was more than a collection of books and resources; it was a community sanctuary, a place of gathering and learning that symbolized the city's resilience and hope.

She packed up her belongings, her heart full of the day's productive solitude and the interactions that had enriched her understanding. As she stepped out of the library, the early evening light cast long shadows across the pavement, reminding her of the continuing passage of time and the ongoing journey of recovery.

Her walk home was reflective, her mind busy weaving the threads of her research and conversations into the broader tapestry of her book. Berlin, with its resilient pulse and rejuvenated spirit, provided endless narratives of struggle and triumph, each a testament to the enduring strength of the human spirit.

Anna spent the later part of the afternoon at a small, secluded park that had recently been restored, a quiet enclave that stood as a testament to the city's gradual rebirth. Sitting on a newly installed bench under the shade of young trees, she pulled out her notebook and a pen, ready to jot down thoughts that had been swirling in her mind since her visit to the library.

Her concentration was interrupted by the arrival of an old friend, Markus, who was also deeply involved in community restoration projects. He recognized her from a distance and approached with a warm smile.

"Anna, it's been too long," Markus greeted her, his voice filled with genuine pleasure. "I heard about your project. It sounds like a truly significant piece of work."

"Markus, thank you," Anna replied, closing her notebook and welcoming the conversation. "It's ambitious, but I hope it will contribute something meaningful to our understanding of this period. How have your projects been coming along?"

"Quite well, actually," Markus responded, sitting beside her on the bench. "We've just completed a community center that's meant to serve as a hub for various outreach programs. It's all about knitting the community back together."

"That's wonderful to hear," Anna said. "Integration and healing are so crucial right now. It must be rewarding to see tangible results from your efforts."

"It is," Markus agreed. "And it's projects like yours that help pave the way intellectually. Documenting our experiences, understanding the societal shifts—that's how we ensure this doesn't happen again."

"That's the hope," Anna nodded. "I'm trying to balance the narrative between the individual stories and the larger community dynamics. It's complex but fascinating."

"I can imagine," Markus said, his eyes reflecting a mix of admiration and understanding. "If there's any way I can assist, whether through providing data or connecting you with community leaders, just let me know."

"I appreciate that, Markus," Anna replied, grateful for the offer. "Actually, having access to some of your project outcomes might provide a valuable perspective. It's the practical side of theory, after all."

"Consider it done," Markus promised. "I'll send you some reports and analysis by tomorrow. It might give you a deeper insight into the community's recovery process."

"Thank you, that would be incredibly helpful," Anna said, her notebook momentarily forgotten as they delved deeper into discussion about potential collaboration.

As their conversation drew to a close, Markus stood, ready to continue his evening walk. "It's been great catching up, Anna. Let's make sure it doesn't take another year before we talk again."

"Definitely," Anna smiled, feeling invigorated by the exchange. "Take care, Markus."

"You too, Anna. Good luck with the book. I know it'll be enlightening," Markus said before walking away, leaving Anna to her thoughts.

She reopened her notebook, now with a renewed sense of purpose and a flurry of new ideas to incorporate into her manuscript. The shadows grew longer as the sun began to set, casting a golden hue over the park. Anna continued to write until the light faded, her pen moving steadily across the pages.

As she finally packed up to leave, the park was quiet, with only the gentle rustle of leaves and the distant sounds of the city as her companions. The day's interactions had enriched her perspective and deepened her connection to her work and her community. Walking back through the park, Anna felt a profound alignment with her surroundings—both were healing, both were rediscovering their rhythm, and both were moving towards a future that, while uncertain, held a promise of renewal and understanding. She left the park with her notebook full and her heart optimistic, ready to weave the day's insights into the broader narrative she was crafting.

The sun had set by the time Anna reached her apartment, the city lights beginning to twinkle against the twilight sky, mimicking stars obscured by the urban glow. The evening's cool air was a gentle reminder of the season's change, a natural progression that mirrored the transformation happening within her and around her.

Inside her home, Anna set her bag down and made herself a cup of tea, the ritual offering comfort and a moment to transition from the public world of her day's interactions to the private sphere of her evening reflections. She took her tea to the small balcony overlooking her neighborhood, a space that had become a sanctuary for thought and relaxation.

As she sipped her tea, she pondered the discussions of the day, particularly her conversation with Markus. His projects and insights were invaluable, providing a real-world anchor to the themes she explored in her writing. The opportunity to integrate such tangible examples into her work excited her, adding depth and authenticity to her narrative.

She thought about how to weave these elements into her next chapter, considering the balance of personal stories with broader community impacts. Her phone buzzed gently on the table next to her, a message from James breaking into her thoughts.

"Evening, Anna. How was your day?" his message read, always timely, always considerate.

"It was full of inspiration," Anna typed back, a smile crossing her face. "Met with an old friend working on community projects. It's given me a lot of material to think about for my book. How was your day?"

"Productive. Spent it at a workshop on community healing. It's always enlightening to hear different perspectives on peacebuilding," James replied.

"That sounds like a perfect complement to what I've been exploring today," Anna responded, her fingers typing quickly. "It's amazing how our separate experiences still tend to weave together in this tapestry we're creating."

"It really is," James agreed. "It's these overlaps that enrich both our individual understandings and our collective narrative."

Anna nodded to herself, appreciating the truth in James's words. "I'll have to incorporate some of today's insights into the book. They're too valuable to leave out."

"Looking forward to reading it," James messaged back. "I'm sure it'll be insightful."

"Thanks, James," Anna typed, setting her phone aside to finish her tea. The city below her balcony was quiet, the bustling noise of the day settling into the peaceful hum of evening.

She stayed outside a little longer, enjoying the cool breeze and the quiet of the night. Her mind was alive with ideas, each one sparking the next, like a chain reaction that fueled her passion and dedication to her work. The stories she planned to tell were not just narratives of past events but beacons for future understanding and growth.

Eventually, she went back inside, feeling refreshed and ready to tackle her writing with renewed vigor. The evening stretched out before her, filled with potential. Anna opened her laptop, a blank document ready to be filled with the words and ideas that had been forming throughout the day.

She began to type, the clicking of the keys a steady rhythm in the quiet apartment. The words flowed easily now, each sentence building on the last, her thoughts clear and focused. She wrote about resilience, about community, about the interplay of individual actions and collective memory.

As she wrote, the line between past and present blurred, the lessons of history intertwining with the hopes for the future. Anna was crafting more than just a book; she was documenting a journey of recovery, a testament to the strength and spirit of a city and its people.

Long into the night, she wrote, her narrative growing, a story of pain and triumph, of destruction and rebuilding, of despair and hope. When she finally paused, the clock showed the early hours of a new day. Satisfied with her progress, Anna closed her laptop, her mind still racing but her heart content. The journey was far from over, but each word she wrote was a step toward understanding, a step toward peace.

Chapter 10
A Lover's Quarrel

The chill of early morning was still in the air as Anna walked through the streets of Berlin, her breath visible in the crisp autumn air. The city was quietly awakening, the early risers appearing like shadows against the soft light of dawn. Anna felt a deep connection to this city, its resilience mirroring her own, each step through its streets reinforcing her sense of purpose and belonging.

Today, she was on her way to a local university where she had been invited to speak about her upcoming book and to share her insights on the role of personal narratives in understanding historical events. The opportunity to discuss her work, to engage with an audience about the themes so close to her heart, was both exhilarating and daunting.

Arriving at the university, Anna was greeted by Professor Klein, a history scholar who had taken a keen interest in her work.

"Anna, it's wonderful to have you here," Professor Klein said warmly, leading her into the lecture hall where students were already gathering. "Your perspective on the intersection of personal and communal resilience in historical narratives is quite revolutionary."

"Thank you, Professor Klein," Anna replied, her nerves settling with the familiar comfort of academic discussion. "I'm eager to share and hopefully to inspire these students to appreciate the depths of our recent history, not just as a series of events but as lived experiences."

"I have no doubt that you will," the professor assured her as they reached the podium.

As the hall filled, Anna arranged her notes, each page a testament to her journey through the process of writing and reflection. The room buzzed with the murmur of students, their youth and energy palpable, a stark contrast to the often somber subjects of her book.

"Good morning, everyone," Anna began, her voice steady, projecting a calm authority as the room quieted. "Today, I want to discuss not only the historical significance of personal narratives in our understanding of events but also the emotional and psychological impacts these narratives can have on both the individual and the community."

The students listened intently, their faces a mix of curiosity and contemplation. Anna spoke of the challenges of weaving personal stories into a broader historical context, the responsibility of honoring those stories while presenting an analytical perspective.

"As we explore these narratives, we begin to see history not as a distant past but as a living, breathing entity that shapes and is shaped by individual experiences," Anna explained, her passion for the subject evident in her animated gestures and expressive face.

A student raised a hand, a thoughtful expression on his face. "How do you ensure the authenticity of these personal narratives without allowing them to be overshadowed by larger historical events?" he asked.

"That's an excellent question," Anna responded, appreciating the depth of inquiry. "It's about balance and respect. Each narrative must be approached with the understanding that it is part of a larger tapestry. We must give it space to speak its truth while also placing it within the wider context of history."

The lecture continued, with Anna discussing various methodologies for research and narrative construction, sharing examples from her own work that highlighted the emotional and social impact of historical events on individual lives.

As the session drew to a close, the students' engagement and thoughtful questions reaffirmed Anna's belief in the importance of her work. Their interest and feedback were invigorating, providing new perspectives and reinforcing the relevance of her research.

"Thank you, Anna, for a truly enlightening session," Professor Klein concluded as the students began to applaud. "We look forward to seeing your book in print."

"Thank you for having me," Anna replied, her heart full with the exchange of ideas and the evident impact of her words.

Stepping out of the lecture hall, Anna felt a renewed commitment to her project. The interaction with the students had not only enhanced her understanding but also deepened her connection to her own narrative. She walked back through the university campus, the early morning now giving way to a bright, clear day. Her path, much like the discussions of the morning, was illuminated with the promise of insight and understanding, her every step a narrative in its own right, weaving through the fabric of history and personal growth.

Invigorated by the morning's lecture and the engagement with the students, Anna decided to visit the newly opened city archive to continue her research. The archive, a repository of the city's history, offered a tangible connection to the past, its shelves laden with documents that had witnessed the ebb and flow of generations.

Upon entering, Anna was greeted by the archivist, Mr. Weber, a man whose life's work had been the preservation of history. His face lit up with recognition and respect as he approached her.

"Ms. Richter, what a pleasure to see you here," Mr. Weber exclaimed, extending a hand. "I heard about your upcoming book. It's the talk of the historical community here."

"Thank you, Mr. Weber," Anna replied, shaking his hand. "I'm hoping to uncover some documents today that can provide deeper insights into the personal experiences during the war. Anything you could recommend would be immensely helpful."

"Of course! Follow me, please," Mr. Weber said, leading her deeper into the archive. "We recently received a donation of personal letters written during the war. They're uncatalogued but might offer exactly what you're looking for."

"That sounds perfect," Anna responded, her eyes reflecting her excitement. They walked between towering shelves, the air thick with the musk of old paper.

Reaching a less frequented section of the archive, Mr. Weber pulled out several boxes filled with letters, setting them on a reading table. "These are from a local family. The correspondence spans several years, detailing daily life, struggles, and hopes. It's quite touching and very raw."

Anna carefully opened one of the boxes, her hands respectfully sifting through the contents. "This is incredible, Mr. Weber. Each of these letters is a window into the past, a narrative thread in the fabric of our city's history."

"As you read them, you'll find the resilience of the human spirit quite evident," Mr. Weber noted, watching her reaction. "It's what these letters breathe through every word."

Anna picked up a letter, its edges worn, the handwriting elegant yet hurried. She read aloud, "'Despite the shadows that fall around us, our hope is the light we cannot extinguish.' It's profoundly beautiful," she remarked, deeply moved.

"Indeed," Mr. Weber agreed. "It's documents like these that remind us why we do what we do here. Preserving these voices gives us perspective and, I believe, guidance for the future."

"Absolutely," Anna said, continuing to explore the contents of the box. "The personal stories behind these wars are what truly tell us about our society, about our collective and individual journeys through adversity."

"These documents are at your disposal, Ms. Richter. Take all the time you need," Mr. Weber offered, his voice a blend of professionalism and genuine support.

"Thank you, Mr. Weber. This means a lot to me, and it will certainly enrich my book," Anna said, grateful for the access to such valuable resources. "It's important that these personal stories are heard and integrated into the broader historical narrative."

"Indeed, it is," Mr. Weber nodded in agreement. "And it's writers like you who ensure these stories find their audience."

Anna spent the next several hours immersed in the letters, each one a treasure trove of emotion and history. Mr. Weber left her to her research, returning occasionally to ensure she had everything she needed.

As the afternoon light began to wane, casting long shadows across the archive's reading room, Anna gathered her notes, her mind filled with the poignant stories she had uncovered. She thanked Mr. Weber again for his assistance and made her way out of the archive, the weight of the letters' narratives adding gravity to her step.

These stories, woven with pain, love, and hope, were not just remnants of the past; they were lessons and legacies that Anna was determined to share. Her walk home was reflective, the day's discoveries filling her with a sense of responsibility and renewed purpose. Each step took her closer not just to her home, but to the completion of a project that she knew would offer both remembrance and insight.

Anna spent the remainder of her week delving deeper into the letters she had discovered at the city archive, each correspondence revealing layers of personal triumph and turmoil that painted a vivid picture of the city's past. Her work had not gone unnoticed, and an invitation to participate in a panel discussion about personal narratives in historical documentation soon followed.

The panel was to be held at a local cultural center, a place that had become a hub for discussions and exhibitions that aimed to bridge historical understanding with contemporary insights. As she prepared for the event, Anna felt a blend of excitement and responsibility. This was her chance to share the profound connections she had uncovered, not just as academic exercises but as living, breathing testimonies of human resilience.

Upon arrival, Anna was greeted by other panelists, each a respected figure in their respective fields of history, psychology, and literature. The moderator for the panel was an old acquaintance, Dr. Emil Hoffmann, a professor of modern history known for his dynamic approach to teaching and his deep appreciation for the nuances of personal histories.

"Anna, it's wonderful to see you," Dr. Hoffmann greeted her warmly as she approached the stage set for the panel. "Your work on the integration of personal narratives into the broader historical context is quite groundbreaking. I'm eager to hear your thoughts today."

"Thank you, Emil," Anna responded, appreciative of his words. "It's an honor to be here. I believe that personal narratives are essential to understanding the full scope of history. They bring depth and emotion to what might otherwise be just dates and events."

"Absolutely," Dr. Hoffmann agreed, adjusting his glasses. "Let's take our seats, shall we? The audience is filling up quickly."

As they settled into their chairs, the room buzzed with anticipation. The audience was a diverse mix of academics, students, and community members, all eager to engage with the panel's theme.

"Welcome, everyone," Dr. Hoffmann began, addressing the crowd once everyone was seated. "Today, we delve into the power and importance of personal narratives in shaping our understanding of history. Anna, perhaps you could start by telling us about how you came across the collection of letters that inspired your current project?"

"Certainly," Anna started, her voice clear and confident. "I discovered the letters in a donation to our city archive, completely uncatalogued. They were from a family that lived through the war right here in Berlin. Each letter was a piece of history, not just of the war but of human emotions— fear, hope, love, despair."

"How do you go about weaving these deeply personal experiences into a narrative that also needs to maintain historical accuracy and relevance?" another panelist, a historian named Dr. Lara Schmidt, inquired.

"It's a delicate balance," Anna admitted. "The key is to respect the authenticity of these personal accounts while contextualizing them within the larger historical framework. I aim to let the voices in the letters speak for themselves, enhancing rather than overshadowing the historical facts."

"That's a fascinating approach," Dr. Schmidt noted. "Do you think this method changes the audience's engagement with history?"

"I believe it does," Anna replied. "Personal stories invite the audience to connect on an emotional level. It makes history relatable. When people see the past through the eyes of those who lived it, they gain a deeper, more empathetic understanding of history."

The discussion continued, each question from the audience and each response from the panel weaving a richer tapestry of dialogue about the significance of personal narratives. Anna shared insights from her research, drawing on specific examples from the letters that highlighted the universal themes of human endurance and adaptability.

As the panel concluded, the audience applauded, a sign of their appreciation and engagement. Dr. Hoffmann thanked the panelists, particularly highlighting Anna's contributions.

"Thank you, Anna, for sharing your insights and your remarkable research," he said as the panelists stood to leave the stage.

"It was my pleasure," Anna responded, feeling gratified by the exchange of ideas.

As the crowd dispersed, many attendees stayed to ask questions or to express their thanks. Anna felt a sense of accomplishment, knowing her work resonated so deeply with others. Her journey through the past, guided by the personal stories of those who had lived it, was not just an academic pursuit but a mission to enrich the collective memory of her city and beyond.

As she left the cultural center, the evening air was cool and refreshing. The successful panel had reaffirmed her commitment to her project, each step forward a validation of her belief in the power of personal narratives to illuminate the corners of history often left in shadow.

The following week, as Berlin basked in the soft light of an autumn afternoon, Anna found herself at a local cafe, meeting with a young journalist, Lena, who was interested in discussing her upcoming book. The cafe was bustling with the quiet energy of late afternoon patrons, providing a lively backdrop for their conversation.

Lena, eager and notebook ready, greeted Anna with an enthusiastic smile. "Ms. Richter, thank you so much for meeting with me. I've been following your work closely, and I'm really excited about your book."

"It's my pleasure, Lena," Anna responded warmly, settling into her seat. "I'm glad to hear you're interested in the project. It's been a labor of love and a real journey into the heart of our city's past."

"I can imagine," Lena said, opening her notebook. "What inspired you to focus on personal narratives specifically?"

Anna sipped her coffee before answering. "I've always believed that history is not just about events, but about the people who live through them. When I stumbled upon a collection of personal letters at the city archive, I knew I had found a unique window into the lived experiences of the war. These stories bring history alive in a way that traditional narratives often miss."

"That's fascinating," Lena noted, her pen poised. "How do you think these personal stories will change the way people view the history of the war?"

"I hope they'll make it more relatable," Anna explained. "By weaving individual stories into the broader historical context, I want to show that history is made up of real people, not just names in a textbook. It's about the choices they made, the hardships they endured, and the hopes they harbored."

"Absolutely," Lena agreed. "Do you find that there's a particular story that resonates more deeply with you?"

"There are many, but one that stands out is the story of a young woman who kept a diary throughout the war. Her entries reflect not only the fear and uncertainty of the time but also moments of joy and resilience. It's incredibly moving."

"That sounds powerful," Lena remarked, clearly moved. "In your research, how do you handle the emotional impact of such intense stories?"

"It can be challenging," Anna admitted. "There are days when the weight of these stories is overwhelming. But I also feel a deep responsibility to tell them with the dignity and respect they deserve. It's important to me that these voices are heard."

"That's a significant burden to bear," Lena said, her expression thoughtful. "With the book nearing completion, what do you hope your readers take away from it?"

"I hope they gain a deeper understanding of the human aspects of history," Anna replied. "I want them to see that history affects everyone differently and that these personal narratives are essential to understanding the full impact of historical events."

"That's a powerful goal," Lena said, jotting down notes. "And once the book is published, what's next for you? Any new projects on the horizon?"

Anna laughed lightly. "I think I'll take a little break first. But I do have ideas brewing. Perhaps another book, maybe focusing on a different aspect of Berlin's history. There's no shortage of stories to tell."

"I'll look forward to that," Lena said, her eyes bright with anticipation. "And finally, if there's one message you'd like your readers to remember, what would it be?"

Anna paused, considering the question. "That history is not just about learning what happened, but about understanding how those events shaped the lives of individuals just like us. We must remember the past with empathy and a commitment to learning from it."

"Thank you, Ms. Richter," Lena concluded, closing her notebook. "Your insights are truly inspiring. I can't wait to share them with our readers."

"Thank you, Lena," Anna said, pleased with the thoughtful exchange. "It was a pleasure to discuss the project with someone so genuinely interested."

As Lena left, Anna remained at the cafe, reflecting on their conversation. She felt a sense of accomplishment and anticipation, eager to see her book in the hands of readers. The discussions, like the one with Lena, reinforced the relevance of her work, encouraging her to continue exploring and narrating the rich tapestry of human experiences that shaped the city's, and her own, history.

Chapter 11
Codes and Confrontations

The morning was draped in a cool mist that clung to the streets of Berlin, softening the edges of the city as it awakened. Anna stood by her window, watching the gentle bustle below, a daily ritual that grounded her thoughts and prepared her for the day ahead. Today, however, was not just any day. It was the launch of her book, a compilation of narratives that wove together the personal and historical into a tapestry of resilience and recovery.

The local bookstore, a quaint, warmly lit space nestled on a busy corner of her neighborhood, was hosting the event. As Anna approached, she could see the display through the front window, her book prominently featured among the autumn releases. The sight stirred a complex brew of excitement and nerves within her, each step towards the entrance feeling increasingly significant.

Inside, the familiar scent of coffee and books welcomed her, mingling with the subtle fragrance of the fall decorations adorning the store. The owner, Mr. Adler, spotted her immediately, his face breaking into a broad smile.

"Anna, it's wonderful to see you," he greeted her, extending his hand. "We're all set up. There's quite a buzz about your book. I think we're going to see a good turnout today."

"Thank you, Mr. Adler," Anna replied, shaking his hand. "I appreciate all the effort you've put into this. It means a lot to me."

As they spoke, early attendees began to filter in, their expressions curious and expectant. Anna took her place near the display, her heart buoyed by the sight of people holding copies of her book, flipping through the pages with interest.

The event began with Mr. Adler introducing Anna, highlighting her dedication to capturing the nuanced experiences of those who lived through the war and the aftermath that shaped Berlin. As applause filled the small space, Anna stepped forward, her nerves steadying as she addressed the audience.

"Thank you all for being here," she began, her voice clear and steady. "This book is not just my work; it's a tribute to the city of Berlin and its inhabitants. It's about the stories that don't often make it into the history books, yet are integral to understanding our past and shaping our future."

Her talk was brief but impactful, focusing on the importance of personal stories in historical narratives. She read excerpts from her book, each chosen to illustrate the depth and variety of experiences detailed in the pages.

After the reading, Anna engaged with the audience, answering questions and sharing insights into her research process. The interaction was rich with shared reflections and thoughtful inquiries, making the event not just a book launch, but a forum for dialogue and community connection.

As the formal part of the event concluded, Anna signed books, each inscription personalized with a message of hope and remembrance. Her conversations with readers were heartfelt, many expressing gratitude for her work in bringing these stories to light.

The afternoon waned, and the crowd thinned, leaving Anna with a moment to reflect on the day's successes. She felt a profound connection to each person who had shared their thoughts with her, reinforcing her belief in the power of storytelling to unite and heal.

Mr. Adler approached her as she prepared to leave, his expression one of genuine satisfaction. "Anna, that was a wonderful event. Your book is going to make waves, I'm sure of it."

"I hope so, Mr. Adler," Anna replied, smiling. "If it encourages even a few people to see history through a more personal lens, then it will have done its job."

As she stepped out of the bookstore, the evening air crisp and invigorating, Anna felt a sense of accomplishment and anticipation. Her book was now part of the world, its stories set to ripple through the fabric of understanding and memory. She walked home slowly, savoring the quiet streets and the sense of fulfillment that came from sharing her passion with the world. The city around her was a testament to the resilience and renewal she had chronicled, and as the day closed, she felt an enduring kinship with the spirit of Berlin, its past, present, and future forever interwoven in her work and her heart.

In the days following the book launch, Anna found herself immersed in the busy whirlwind of promotional activities. Interviews, guest blog posts, and public readings filled her calendar, each event threading her deeper into the fabric of the city's cultural and intellectual life. Yet, despite the flurry of engagements, a particular invitation stood out—a request to speak at a historical society meeting, where the focus would be the impact of personal histories on collective memory.

As Anna prepared for the meeting, she considered the deeper implications of her work. It wasn't just about recounting events; it was about understanding how those events affected individuals and communities, how the personal and the historical were irrevocably intertwined. This understanding was what she hoped to convey in her discussion, emphasizing the importance of recognizing personal narratives in the study of history.

The evening of the meeting was marked by a gentle rain that seemed to cleanse the city streets, leaving the air fresh and invigorating. Anna arrived at the venue, a stately building that housed decades of historical archives, its walls lined with books that whispered tales of yesteryear.

The room was filled with an attentive audience, their faces reflecting a shared passion for history and a keen interest in Anna's perspective. She was introduced by the society's chairperson, an elderly historian whose life's work had been dedicated to preserving Berlin's intricate past.

"We are honored to have Ms. Anna Richter with us tonight," the chairperson announced, his voice resonant in the quiet room. "Her recent publication has brought a new dimension to our understanding of historical impacts, reminding us that history is not only about what happened, but also about how it was experienced by those who lived through it."

Anna took the podium with a slight nod of thanks, her presence commanding yet approachable. "Thank you for that warm introduction. It's a privilege to be here among fellow historians and enthusiasts. Tonight, I hope to discuss not just the events that shape our history, but the personal stories that give color and depth to those events."

She proceeded to outline her approach to historical research, describing how personal letters, diaries, and interviews played a crucial role in her work. She shared anecdotes from her book, each story illustrating the profound effect of historical events on individual lives and how these effects rippled through generations.

"As we delve into history," Anna explained, "we must remember that behind every event are people—ordinary people whose lives are transformed in extraordinary ways. By incorporating their stories into our understanding, we ensure a more complete and empathetic view of our past."

The audience listened intently, occasionally nodding in agreement or jotting down notes. Anna's talk sparked a lively question-and-answer session, where she engaged with the audience, appreciating their insights and addressing their queries with thoughtfulness and expertise.

As the meeting concluded, many attendees lingered, eager to discuss further or to express their appreciation for her work. Anna felt a profound connection with this community of historians, a bond forged by a mutual commitment to uncovering and understanding the nuanced layers of history.

After the last of the guests had departed, Anna stepped outside. The rain had stopped, and the city lay before her, its streets glistening under the streetlights, a silent testament to the enduring nature of its history. She walked slowly, lost in thought, her mind replaying the evening's discussions.

Her journey through the past had not only changed her perception of history but had also altered her understanding of her role as a historian. It was not just about documenting what happened but about interpreting those events through the lens of human experience.

As Anna continued her walk, the cool night air felt invigorating, clearing her mind and reaffirming her dedication to her craft. The city around her was alive with its own stories, each corner a reminder of the depths of history she had vowed to explore. With each step, she felt more connected to her mission, driven by a desire to illuminate the shadows of the past with the light of personal truth.

One afternoon, as the golden light of autumn bathed the streets of Berlin, Anna found herself at a local university, invited to lead a seminar with students studying modern history. The classroom was filled with eager young minds, a testament to the next generation's interest in the past and its implications for the future. Anna set her notes on the podium, ready to engage in what promised to be a stimulating discussion.

"Welcome, everyone," Anna began, her voice echoing slightly in the spacious room. "Today, we're going to explore the importance of personal narratives in understanding historical events. I believe that history is not just about what happened; it's also about the people who lived through those events. Let's start with your thoughts on this. What do you think makes personal stories significant in historical studies?"

A young woman in the front row raised her hand immediately. "I think personal stories add a human element to history. They provide emotions and experiences that statistics and general accounts can't convey."

"That's a great point," Anna responded, nodding appreciatively. "Personal narratives allow us to connect emotionally with the past, which can make the events more real and impactful. How about others? Any different thoughts?"

A young man from the back spoke up. "While I see the value in personal narratives, I sometimes worry they may introduce bias. How do we balance these personal perspectives with the need for objectivity in history?"

"That's an excellent question," Anna acknowledged. "The key is to use personal narratives as a complement to more traditional historical sources. By integrating personal accounts with other data, we can provide a fuller, more balanced view of history. It's about weaving these stories into the larger fabric without letting them overshadow the broader events."

The students nodded, some jotting down notes, their engagement palpable. Another student, a young woman with keen eyes, added, "In my studies, I've found that personal stories sometimes challenge the established narratives. They can bring to light aspects of history that are overlooked or sanitized in mainstream accounts."

"Absolutely," Anna agreed, her tone enthusiastic. "This is one of the most powerful aspects of including personal narratives in historical studies. They can challenge and enrich our understanding. This is particularly important in contexts where history has been used to serve specific ideologies."

The discussion shifted as another student asked, "Could you share an example from your book where a personal narrative changed your understanding of an event?"

Anna smiled, recalling a vivid memory from her research. "Certainly. While working on my book, I came across a diary written by a young nurse during the war. Her accounts of daily life and the challenges she faced provided a stark contrast to the official records of the war efforts in her city. Her narrative brought a deeply personal, often painful perspective that was absent from public records. It reminded me that behind every large event, there are countless individual stories, each deserving recognition."

The students listened intently, visibly moved by the example. The conversation continued with discussions about methodology and the ethics of using personal documents in historical research.

As the seminar came to a close, a student in the middle row asked, "What advice would you give to us, as aspiring historians, when approaching personal narratives?"

"Be respectful and meticulous," Anna advised. "Approach each narrative as a valuable piece of the historical puzzle. Seek to understand the context in which it was created, and always consider how it fits into the larger picture. Most importantly, let empathy and a commitment to truth guide your work."

The students clapped appreciatively as the session ended, many staying behind to ask further questions or to express their gratitude for the insights Anna had provided.

As she gathered her notes and prepared to leave, Anna felt a deep satisfaction. Sharing her passion and knowledge with the next generation was not just a duty but a privilege, one that reaffirmed her commitment to her field. The discussions had not only enlightened the students but had also reinvigorated her own dedication to uncovering and sharing the personal dimensions of history.

Stepping out of the university, Anna walked through the autumn-lit streets, her mind abuzz with the day's exchanges, each student's question and each thoughtful response weaving yet another layer into her ongoing engagement with history.

As the promotional tour for her book continued, Anna found herself at a cozy neighborhood library for an evening discussion with local book club members. The group, comprised mostly of avid readers and amateur historians, gathered around in a semi-circle, each with a copy of her book in hand. The warmth of the library, with its shelves brimming with books, created an intimate atmosphere conducive to a deep and personal discussion.

Anna was introduced by the book club leader, Marlene, a retired schoolteacher whose enthusiasm for history was infectious. "We are so honored to have Anna Richter with us tonight. Her book has given us so much to think about, and we're eager to dive deeper into her insights on personal narratives," Marlene announced to the group.

"Thank you, Marlene," Anna began, smiling warmly at the group. "I'm thrilled to be here. This book is a passion project for me, and I'm excited to discuss it with people who share a love for history and storytelling."

A gentleman in the front, his hair peppered with gray, raised his hand. "Ms. Richter, your book brilliantly captures the essence of what it was like to live through the events you describe. How did you go about selecting which personal stories to include?"

"That's a great question," Anna replied. "The selection process was both challenging and deeply personal. I looked for stories that not only provided unique insights into historical events but also highlighted the diverse human experiences during those times. It was important that the stories resonated on a personal level, not just historically."

A younger woman on the right, clutching her copy of the book, chimed in. "I was particularly moved by the diary entries of the young nurse you included. What impact did her story have on you personally?"

Anna paused thoughtfully before answering. "Her story was one of the most impactful for me. It illustrated the resilience and vulnerability of those living through the war. Her perspective challenged my own understanding of the events and emphasized the importance of personal courage and sacrifice. It's stories like hers that remind us of the human cost of historical events."

The discussion shifted as another member, a middle-aged man with keen eyes, asked, "How do you ensure that these personal narratives are represented accurately and respectfully?"

"Respect and accuracy are my top priorities," Anna explained. "I meticulously cross-reference personal accounts with historical records. It's also vital to approach each narrative with sensitivity and an ethical responsibility, acknowledging that these are not just stories, but real experiences of real people."

The room nodded in agreement, the importance of ethical storytelling resonating with the group. Marlene then steered the conversation toward a broader perspective. "How do you think your work contributes to our collective understanding of history?"

"My hope," Anna began, "is that by weaving personal narratives into the broader historical tapestry, my work helps humanize history. I want readers to understand that history is not made up of faceless names in textbooks but of individuals with families, dreams, and fears—much like all of us here."

A lively discussion ensued, with members sharing their thoughts on how the book changed their views on history and personal narratives. The evening passed quickly, filled with rich dialogue and shared reflections.

As the meeting concluded, the club members expressed their appreciation for Anna's insights and the depth of her research. "Thank you, Anna, for such an engaging discussion," Marlene said as the group began to disperse. "Your book has added a valuable dimension to our understanding of history."

"It was my pleasure," Anna responded, feeling a deep sense of fulfillment. "Thank you all for such thoughtful questions and for a wonderful evening."

Leaving the library, Anna felt connected to her audience in a way that went beyond just a shared interest in history. The discussion had reinforced the importance of her work and the impact it had on its readers. As she walked home under the starlit sky, her heart was full, knowing that her efforts to illuminate the personal sides of history had resonated so profoundly with others. Her journey as an author had not only brought the past to life but had also fostered a community of readers eager to understand and appreciate the depth of human experiences.

Chapter 12
The Setup

The brisk morning air of Berlin was alive with the whisper of falling leaves, signaling the deepening of autumn. Anna, her spirits lifted by the successful interactions of her recent book discussions, decided to spend the morning at a public garden she had often frequented during her years of research. The garden, a mosaic of vibrant colors framed by ancient trees, served as a living metaphor for the narratives she had woven—each plant and pathway telling a story of survival and renewal.

As Anna strolled along the winding paths, she reflected on the journey her book had initiated, not just for herself but for her readers. The garden was mostly quiet, save for the occasional chatter of early visitors and the distant laughter of children. It was here, among the whispering trees and the soft rustle of leaves, that she felt most connected to the pulse of the city and its historical tapestry.

Her thoughts were interrupted by the soft ding of her phone. James had sent a message, checking in as he often did during these reflective days. "How are you this beautiful morning?" his message read, bringing a smile to Anna's face.

"I'm at the old public garden, taking in the peace and thinking about new projects," she typed back. "How about you?"

"Just heading into a meeting. But I wanted to hear how you're doing. Any new inspirations?" James replied quickly, always keen to keep abreast of her thoughts.

"Perhaps," Anna responded, her eyes tracing the path ahead. "Walking here, where so many have walked before, makes me think about the layers of history under our feet. Maybe that's something I could explore next."

"That sounds fascinating," James messaged back. "History beneath us, history around us—there's no end to the stories waiting to be told."

Anna pocketed her phone and continued her walk, her mind alive with potential ideas. The garden was more than just a place of natural beauty; it was a sanctuary where the past met the present, where every corner held memories etched into its landscapes.

She paused by a bench overlooking a small pond, where ducks glided across the still water, undisturbed by the world beyond the garden walls. Anna sat, taking out her notebook and pen. She began to jot down the thoughts swirling through her mind, each idea flowing into the next like the water before her.

As she wrote, an elderly couple approached and took a seat at the other end of the bench. They exchanged quiet words, their conversation a soft murmur blending with the rustle of the trees. Anna noticed their hands, gently clasped together, a silent testament to shared years and shared stories.

"Beautiful day, isn't it?" the woman said, turning slightly towards Anna with a friendly smile.

"It is indeed," Anna replied, returning the smile. "I find this garden always gives back a bit of what the city takes away. It's a good place to reflect."

"We've been coming here for years," the man added. "Seen it change, seen it grow. Like us, I suppose."

"That's a beautiful way to put it," Anna remarked. "I often think about how places like this hold memories, not just our own but those of everyone who has passed through."

"It's true," the woman nodded. "And each time we come, it seems both familiar and new. There's always something different to notice, something new to see."

Their conversation drifted naturally, the couple sharing snippets of their lives and Anna listening intently, absorbing the subtle wisdom in their words. Here was living history, embodied in two lives intertwined with the garden's own chronicles.

After some time, the couple bid Anna farewell, continuing their walk hand in hand. Anna watched them go, their presence a gentle reminder of the enduring human connections that thread through the fabric of time.

She remained on the bench a while longer, her notes now filled with fresh inspirations. The garden had offered her more than just a respite; it had provided new avenues for exploration, new stories to uncover. The city, with all its layers and lives, was an unending source of discovery, and Anna felt an invigorating surge of purpose as she considered her next project.

Gathering her things, Anna left the bench, her steps light with anticipation. The garden, with its blend of past and present, had once again stirred the storyteller within her, promising new journeys into the heart of the city's—and her own—ever-unfolding history.

The days began to shorten as autumn deepened its hold on Berlin, painting the city in hues of orange and red. Anna spent her afternoons wrapped in the cozy confines of her study, where maps and old photographs now lay scattered across her desk—a visual mosaic of her next project, which aimed to explore the layered histories hidden beneath the city's modern facade.

As she delved deeper into her research, she discovered tales of forgotten locales and lost artifacts, each story offering a glimpse into the lives that had pulsed through Berlin's streets in bygone eras. These discoveries were more than mere historical curiosities; they were portals to the past, beckoning Anna to step through and bring their stories to light.

One afternoon, her focus was particularly drawn to an old map detailing the city's layout before the bombings of the Second World War. She traced the streets with her finger, noting how many had vanished or transformed over the decades. Her phone rang, pulling her momentarily from her reverie. It was James, checking in as he often did during these solitary research sessions.

"Anna, how's the historical excavation going?" James's voice was light, tinged with curiosity.

"It's fascinating, James," Anna replied, her eyes not leaving the map. "Every document, every map tells a story. It's like piecing together a giant puzzle where some pieces are lost to time."

"I can imagine it's quite the detective work," James said, his interest evident. "Anything particular that's caught your eye today?"

"There's a section of the old city that seems to have completely disappeared in the modern layout," Anna shared, her enthusiasm growing. "It's near the old cathedral, and apparently, it was once a bustling marketplace."

"That does sound intriguing," James mused. "A hidden chapter of the city's life, waiting to be told."

"Exactly," Anna agreed. "I'm thinking of visiting the archives tomorrow to see if I can unearth anything more about it. Who knows what stories are waiting there?"

"Keep me posted," James said warmly. "Your discoveries always make for the best tales."

"I will," Anna promised, her mind already racing with possibilities.

Returning to her research, Anna's attention was next captured by a series of photographs from the early 1900s, showing a vibrant neighborhood festival. The images were black and white, but the vitality of the scene transcended the monochrome, conveying the laughter and camaraderie of a community now largely forgotten.

The photographs inspired a sense of urgency in Anna. It was not just about chronicling history; it was about reviving the essence of these lost moments, rekindling the spirits that had once animated these spaces. She felt a deep responsibility to weave these fragmented histories into a narrative that honored their legacy, a narrative that would resonate not just with historians but with anyone who walked the streets of Berlin.

As evening fell, Anna organized her notes and planned her visit to the archives. The prospect of uncovering further ties to the past energized her, and she looked forward to the tactile connection of handling documents that were nearly as old as the city itself.

Her study was quiet, save for the soft ticking of the clock and the occasional rustle of paper. Outside, the city continued its never-ending dance, modern and bustling, largely unaware of the layers upon layers of history that lay beneath its surface. Anna felt a kinship with these hidden stories, a duty to bring them into the light.

With a contented sigh, she stepped away from her desk, her mind filled with plans for the next day. The past was alive, woven into the fabric of the present, and Anna was its diligent weaver, crafting a tapestry that would tell the story of a city known and unknown. As she turned off the light in her study, the shadows of the day gave way to the possibilities of tomorrow, each waiting to be explored and understood in the unfolding narrative of history.

Early the next morning, Anna arrived at the city archives, her heart set on uncovering more about the vanished section of Berlin near the old cathedral. The archives, a repository of the city's memory, were quiet, save for the soft murmur of a few dedicated researchers and the occasional creak of the old wooden floors.

As she settled at a research table, the archivist, Mr. Henning, approached with a stack of dusty ledgers and maps. "Good morning, Ms. Richter. I found some materials that might be of interest to your project on the old city sectors," he announced, laying them out before her with care.

"Thank you, Mr. Henning," Anna said, her eyes lighting up as she surveyed the documents. "This is wonderful. Do any of these specifically cover the marketplace area near the cathedral?"

"Yes, actually," Mr. Henning replied, pulling a particularly worn map from the stack. "This one from the early 1900s shows the marketplace in great detail. It was a vibrant area, bustling with traders and local festivals until the war."

Anna leaned over the map, tracing the lines with her finger. "It's incredible how much has changed. Do we have any personal accounts or photographs from this area?"

"We do have a collection of personal letters from a family that lived in that marketplace area," Mr. Henning informed her. "And there are some photographs in the municipal collection. Would you like to see them?"

"That would be fantastic," Anna replied eagerly. "Personal accounts are invaluable. They bring the past to life in ways that maps and records can't."

Mr. Henning nodded and went off to retrieve the additional materials. While she waited, Anna continued to examine the map, imagining the lively exchanges that once filled the now-quiet area.

Returning with a box of photographs and a folder of letters, Mr. Henning set them down gently on the table. "Here are the photographs and the family letters. I hope they help illuminate the character of the marketplace."

Anna began sifting through the photographs, each image a snapshot of a time long past. "These are incredible," she murmured, holding up a photo of a crowded festival in the marketplace. "Look at the vitality of these gatherings."

"It's quite a contrast to the present state of that area, isn't it?" Mr. Henning remarked, peering over her shoulder.

"It really is," Anna agreed. "These letters—are they from the family in these photographs?"

"Yes, they belonged to the Müller family," Mr. Henning explained. "They were quite prominent in the area. The letters detail daily life, the challenges they faced during the wars, and their deep connection to the community."

Anna opened the folder, her fingers gently flipping through the pages. As she read, the voices of the past seemed to echo through the letters, each word adding depth to the images in the photographs.

"This is a treasure trove, Mr. Henning. It's exactly what I needed to bring the narrative of this area to life," Anna said, her voice filled with gratitude. "These personal stories are what make history resonate on a human level."

"I'm glad to hear they're of value to your research," Mr. Henning responded, pleased to assist. "If there's anything more you need, just let me know."

"Thank you, I certainly will," Anna said. She spent the next few hours engrossed in the materials, taking notes and making copies of the photographs.

As the afternoon waned, Anna packed up her research, her mind brimming with ideas and narratives for her project. She thanked Mr. Henning again and left the archives, stepping back into the modern city with a renewed sense of connection to its past.

Walking through the streets, Anna felt as though she carried the stories of the old marketplace with her, each step a link in the chain of history that connected the past to the present. The voices of the Müller family and the images of the bustling festivals enriched her understanding of the city, weaving new threads into the fabric of her ongoing exploration of Berlin's layered history.

After a productive day at the archives, Anna decided to share her new findings with James, who had been a consistent source of encouragement and intellectual engagement throughout her project. She called him as she walked through a quiet park, the sun casting long shadows across her path.

"James, you won't believe the treasures I uncovered today at the archives," Anna began, her voice brimming with excitement as he answered the call.

"Tell me everything," James responded, his interest piqued. "What did you find?"

"There was a map of the old city, specifically showing the marketplace area near the cathedral. It's fascinating to see the layout before the war reshaped everything. But even more exciting, I found a collection of personal letters and photographs from a family who lived there," Anna shared enthusiastically.

"Photographs too? That sounds like a goldmine for your project," James remarked. "What do the letters reveal?"

"They paint a vivid picture of daily life in the marketplace. The family, the Müllers, were quite involved in their community. The letters are filled with details about local festivals, the challenges of wartime, and the close-knit relationships among the residents," Anna explained, her words quick with the thrill of her discoveries.

"How does it feel to read those personal accounts, to get such an intimate glimpse into their lives?" James asked, genuinely curious about her emotional response to the materials.

"It's incredibly moving. There's a letter where the father describes a festival night, the square aglow with lanterns, music floating in the air, children running around. It's so lively, so human. It makes the history tangible, real," Anna described, her voice softening as she visualized the scene.

"That's what makes your work so powerful, Anna. You bring these forgotten moments back to life," James said, his tone full of admiration. "Do you think you'll use these details directly in your book?"

"Absolutely. These narratives provide the human connection that statistics and broad historical accounts often lack. They remind us that history isn't just about dates and events; it's about people living through those times, with all their complexities and joys," Anna affirmed.

"I can't wait to read how you weave these stories into the broader tapestry of Berlin's history. It's like you're reconstructing the soul of the city," James commented, his words encouraging.

"That's exactly what I aim to do. And hearing their stories, I feel a responsibility to convey them with the dignity they deserve," Anna added, feeling the weight and privilege of her role as a storyteller.

"Speaking of stories, how are you planning to integrate these new findings into your current project? Are they changing your narrative approach at all?" James inquired, always interested in her process.

"They are indeed. These documents have introduced a new layer of depth to my narrative. I'm planning to expand the chapter on community life to include these firsthand accounts. It will highlight the vibrancy of the marketplace before it was lost to war," Anna detailed, already outlining the chapter in her mind.

"It sounds like you're on the brink of something really special, Anna. This kind of work—it's more than just writing; it's a form of cultural preservation," James noted thoughtfully.

"It feels that way," Anna agreed. "Sometimes I feel like an archaeologist, unearthing these buried stories and bringing them into the light."

"As you should," James concluded warmly. "Keep digging, Anna. The stories you uncover are the pieces of history that too often go missing."

"Thank you, James. I'll keep you updated on how the chapters are shaping up," Anna said, grateful for the conversation and the continual support.

"I look forward to it. Take care, Anna, and say hello to the past for me," James joked lightly.

"I will," Anna laughed, ending the call with a smile. As she continued her walk through the park, her mind was alive with the voices of the past, each step forward fueling her resolve to honor their stories in her work. The park around her was quiet, but in her thoughts, she could hear the faint echoes of music and laughter from the marketplace festivals long gone, a reminder of the vibrant life that once filled the streets of Berlin.

Chapter 13
Doubts and Decisions

As winter approached, the chill in the Berlin air became more pronounced, carrying with it the whisper of approaching snow. Anna, wrapped warmly against the cold, made her way to a local community center where she was scheduled to give a talk about the importance of preserving personal histories. The center, a hub for cultural and historical exchange, buzzed with activity as people from various backgrounds gathered, all united by a common interest in the past and its relevance to their lives today.

Inside, Anna was greeted by Klaus, the coordinator of the event, a man whose passion for community engagement was evident in his enthusiastic welcome. "Anna, we are so delighted to have you with us tonight. There's a real buzz about your talk. People are eager to hear about your work and the forgotten narratives you've brought to light," he said, leading her to a small auditorium that was filling up quickly.

"Thank you, Klaus. I'm just as excited to share these stories," Anna replied, setting up her notes at the podium. "It's heartening to see such a diverse group interested in our city's history."

As the audience settled, Anna began her presentation with a slide of an old, faded photograph depicting a bustling market scene from the early 1900s. "This image," she started, pointing to the screen, "captures more than just a moment in time; it captures the spirit of a community that no longer exists in the same form today. It's these personal, everyday experiences that I believe are crucial to understanding our history."

A hand went up in the crowd, belonging to a young woman in the front row. "How do you find these personal stories, and how do you verify their authenticity?" she asked, her voice curious.

"That's a great question," Anna responded. "Finding these stories often starts in archives, through letters, diaries, and sometimes photos like this one. Verifying them involves cross-referencing with other historical documents, public records, and sometimes even reaching out to families or descendants if possible."

A middle-aged man in the back spoke next. "Why do you think it's important to bring these personal histories into the light? What value do they add to our understanding of the past?"

Anna nodded thoughtfully. "Personal histories provide depth and context to the broader events we learn about in history books. They offer insights into how individuals and communities experienced and influenced historical events, giving us a more complete picture of the past. They teach us about resilience, adaptation, and the human condition, which are incredibly relevant to our lives today."

The discussion turned more interactive, with audience members sharing their thoughts and engaging with Anna's points. "Do you think there's a risk that personal narratives might be overly romanticized, losing the factual rigor necessary for historical accuracy?" another audience member inquired.

"That is indeed a risk," Anna conceded, "and it's something historians must be cautious of. However, by maintaining rigorous research standards and contextualizing these stories within broader historical facts, we can mitigate that risk. It's about balance and responsible storytelling."

As the talk drew to a close, the final question came from a young man near the center. "How can we, as ordinary citizens, contribute to the preservation of these kinds of histories?"

"Everyone can contribute by documenting their own histories and those of their families," Anna explained. "Keep records, write down stories, preserve photographs, and share them. Participate in community history projects. It's about keeping the dialogue open and passing down these stories to future generations."

The audience applauded warmly as Anna thanked them for their engagement and thoughtful questions. Klaus approached her as the room began to clear, a smile of satisfaction on his face. "That was inspiring, Anna. I think you've sparked a lot of interest in personal history tonight."

"I hope so, Klaus," Anna said as they walked toward the exit together. "Every person's story adds a thread to the larger historical tapestry. It's vital we keep weaving."

Stepping out into the cool night, Anna felt a sense of accomplishment and connection. Her discussions had not only illuminated the past but had also inspired others to see themselves as part of an ongoing historical narrative. As she walked home, her thoughts were on the stories yet to be told, each step a reminder of the paths that intersect in the journey of history.

With the success of her recent community center talk still fresh, Anna arranged to meet with a group of local historians and documentarians at a café known for its quiet atmosphere and rich history, ideal for in-depth discussions. The group was eager to explore collaborative opportunities that could further illuminate the city's past through various media.

As they gathered around a rustic wooden table, Anna was greeted by an enthusiastic filmmaker, Eric, who had been particularly keen on discussing her approach to narrative history.

"Anna, it's great to finally meet you," Eric began, shaking her hand. "I've been following your work closely, and I think there's a lot we can do together. Your focus on personal narratives is exactly what documentary filmmaking needs to make history come alive."

"Thank you, Eric," Anna replied, settling into her chair. "I'm excited about the possibilities. Combining our disciplines could really enhance the way people engage with history."

Across from her, a historian named Marta chimed in, her eyes bright with ideas. "I've been thinking about an interactive exhibit that pairs personal stories with artifacts from the era. Anna, your research could provide the narrative backbone for such an exhibit."

"That sounds fascinating, Marta," Anna responded enthusiastically. "Personal stories can indeed give context to artifacts that otherwise might seem just like old objects to many viewers. They tell us how these items were used, cherished, or even lost."

Eric nodded in agreement, then leaned forward, his voice animated. "And imagine if we could bring those stories to life through film, using your research and Marta's exhibit as a basis. We could create a documentary series that travels through time, exploring different eras through the eyes of the people who lived them."

"I love that idea," Anna said, her mind racing with the narrative possibilities. "Each episode could focus on a different story or artifact, drawing viewers into the personal experiences behind historical events."

Marta added, "And with each story, we could provide viewers with the historical background, using archival footage, photographs, and your research, Anna. It would be a holistic approach to history."

The conversation turned to logistics, with each member of the group contributing their expertise. "What about funding?" Anna asked, knowing that such projects could be costly.

"I have some contacts at cultural foundations that might be interested," Eric offered. "And there's always the possibility of crowd-funding for such a unique project. People love engaging with history in new ways."

"That's true," Marta agreed. "I'll start drafting a proposal. Anna, could you provide some outlines of stories from your research that might work well for our first few episodes?"

"Absolutely," Anna confirmed. "I can also reach out to the university. They might be interested in supporting a project that highlights innovative ways to teach history."

As the meeting drew to a close, the group was invigorated by the collaborative spirit that had marked their discussion. "Let's keep the momentum going," Eric said as they gathered their notes and laptops. "We have the potential to create something truly impactful."

"I'll send everyone an email summary of our discussion and next steps tonight," Marta offered, always organized.

"Perfect," Anna said, feeling a surge of anticipation for the project ahead. "Thank you all for such a productive meeting. I'm looking forward to seeing where we can take this."

With their plans set in motion, they left the café, each member of the group energized by the collaborative venture they were about to undertake. Anna felt a deep satisfaction knowing her research would not only be preserved in books but would also come alive on screen and in exhibits, reaching a broader audience in compelling new ways.

Walking back through the streets, Anna's steps were light, her heart full of possibilities. The city around her, with its layers of history both hidden and visible, seemed more alive than ever, each corner whispering stories waiting to be told. As she blended into the flow of the city, her thoughts were already on her next visit to the archives, fueled by the exciting new direction her work was taking.

The collaborative project began to take shape over the following weeks, and Anna found herself back at the café for another crucial meeting with Eric and Marta. This time, they were joined by Claudia, a graphic designer who specialized in digital exhibitions, to help visualize the interactive elements of their proposed exhibit.

As they settled around the same rustic table, laden with laptops and various papers, Eric opened the discussion. "I've spoken with the documentary team, and they're all in about integrating Anna's research into the series. Claudia, we're hoping you can bring these stories to life in the exhibit as well."

Claudia nodded, her eyes scanning the material spread out before her. "I've looked over the narratives you sent, Anna. They're compelling. I can create interactive displays that allow visitors to delve deeper into each story, maybe even interact with digital versions of the artifacts."

"That sounds amazing," Anna responded, clearly excited. "Each artifact has its own story that resonated through time—like the diary of the nurse from the war. It's more than just paper and ink; it's a window into her life."

Marta, who had been sketching out potential layouts for the exhibit, looked up. "For the diary, we could set up a listening station where visitors can hear portions of it read aloud, perhaps even view images of the actual pages on a touchscreen."

"Exactly," Claudia agreed, tapping a few notes into her laptop. "And for broader context, Anna, could you provide us with short narratives that connect the personal stories to larger historical events?"

"Of course," Anna said. "I can also include quotes from the letters and diaries that visitors can interact with—select a quote and learn more about the person who wrote it, and the circumstances they were living through."

Eric, who had been listening intently, chimed in. "This is going to be a powerful experience. I think we can engage a much wider audience by making history this accessible and personal. Anna, how do you see these narratives being adapted for the documentary?"

"We could start each episode with a personal story that introduces the episode's theme," Anna suggested. "For instance, the story of a soldier on the front lines could lead into an episode about the war's impact on families. His letters home could serve as the narrative thread."

"That's a strong start," Eric nodded appreciatively. "It ties the personal directly to the historical, making each episode compelling and relatable."

Marta looked up from her sketches. "I think integrating visual elements from the exhibit into the documentary could also create a cohesive experience. Perhaps we could film parts of the exhibit as interactive scenes for the documentary."

"Brilliant idea," Claudia added. "It would visually tie the exhibit and the documentary together, reinforcing the connection between the formats."

As their plans solidified, the group discussed timelines and logistics, their conversation a lively back and forth of ideas and confirmations. "I'll start drafting the first set of interactive scripts," Claudia offered, her fingers poised over her keyboard ready to begin work.

"And I'll coordinate with the documentary team to ensure our narratives align perfectly," Eric added, his role as a connector vital to the project's cohesion.

Anna, feeling a deep sense of fulfillment, smiled at her colleagues. "This is more than I had hoped for when I started my research. It's not just about writing history; it's about bringing it to life and making it matter."

As the meeting drew to a close, each person knew they were part of something significant. The blend of history, personal narrative, and modern technology was a potent formula for educating and engaging people in new and meaningful ways.

Leaving the café, the cool air greeted them with a refreshing touch, as if to underscore the new energy they were bringing into their work. They parted ways, each tasked with a piece of the project, ready to transform how people interacted with history. As Anna walked home, her mind buzzed with the possibilities—not just for the project, but for the many other stories still waiting to be told.

As the collaborative project progressed, Anna devoted an afternoon to visiting the venue where the exhibit would be hosted. The space was an old industrial building that had been transformed into a cultural hub, with high ceilings and large windows that bathed the interior in natural light. Here, the histories Anna had unearthed would soon be shared with the public, bridged beautifully with modern technology to create a deeply immersive experience.

Upon her arrival, Anna met with Marta and Claudia to discuss the final arrangements for the exhibit layout. The walls were already marked with placeholders for digital installations and interactive stations.

"This space is perfect," Anna remarked, looking around appreciatively. "It really brings a sense of history itself, doesn't it?"

"It does," Marta agreed, unrolling a large blueprint across a table. "We've allocated this central area for the main interactive timeline. It'll guide visitors through the different eras, with branches leading off to more detailed explorations based on your narratives."

Claudia, adjusting her glasses, pointed to a corner of the blueprint. "Over here, we're planning a special section for the diary entries you provided. We're integrating voice-overs and touchscreens that will allow visitors to explore the entries in depth."

"That's fantastic," Anna said, leaning closer to examine the plan. "It's important that visitors can connect with these personal stories on multiple sensory levels. Hearing the entries read aloud will really bring them to life."

"Exactly," Claudia replied. "We want the emotional impact to be as powerful as the intellectual understanding."

As they walked through the space, discussing the placement of various elements, Eric joined them, his enthusiasm evident. "How's everything looking?" he asked, greeting Anna with a warm handshake.

"We're just going through the layout," Marta explained. "Anna was just commenting on how the voice-overs for the diary entries will enhance the experience."

"It's all coming together," Eric said, looking around. "And the documentary team is excited too. They've started editing the first episode, incorporating some of the footage we shot right here last week."

"That's wonderful to hear," Anna responded, pleased with the synergy between the exhibit and the documentary. "Seeing this project evolve from ideas and discussions into something tangible is truly rewarding."

"I agree," Eric said. "It's a testament to the power of collaboration. Your research has inspired not only us but will soon inspire our visitors and viewers."

They continued their tour, discussing technical requirements and visitor flow. The afternoon passed quickly, filled with constructive discussions and creative planning. As the sun began to set, casting long shadows through the large windows, the team felt a collective sense of accomplishment.

"This is going to be more than just an exhibit," Anna mused aloud as they prepared to leave. "It's going to be an educational journey, one that I hope will resonate with people for a long time."

"I have no doubt that it will," Marta said, gathering her plans and notes. "Your stories, Anna, they're not just histories; they're lessons in humanity."

As they parted ways, Anna felt a surge of anticipation for the exhibit's opening. The next few weeks would be crucial, but she was confident that the final result would be a profound exploration of history's personal dimensions.

Walking back through the quiet streets, Anna reflected on the project's scope and its potential impact. Each step took her closer to the realization of a vision that had started with her first discovery of those dusty letters in the archive. Now, those stories were about to be shared in a way that honored their origins while embracing the possibilities of the present.

The project was more than just a culmination of her work; it was a bridge connecting the past with the future, crafted through the collaborative efforts of those who believed in the power of history to enlighten and inspire. As the city's evening lights flickered to life, Anna felt deeply connected to the unfolding story, a narrative that continued to grow with each passing moment.

Chapter 14
A Night of Revelations

Winter had settled over Berlin, cloaking the city in a crisp, white blanket of snow that softened its usual sharp edges. Inside the warmth of a bustling coffee shop near the heart of the city, Anna met with James to discuss the final preparations for the upcoming exhibit and documentary series launch. They chose a corner table, a secluded spot where the murmur of other patrons created a comforting backdrop for conversation.

James greeted Anna with a broad smile as he arrived, brushing snowflakes from his coat. "Anna, this weather makes the city look like a scene from one of those old films, doesn't it?"

"It really does," Anna replied, sharing his smile as she sipped her coffee. "It adds a bit of magic to the air, perfect for setting the mood for our launch."

"How are the final preparations going?" James asked, his eyes reflecting genuine interest as he settled into his chair.

"We're nearly there," Anna began, her voice mixing excitement with a hint of nerves. "The interactive displays are set up, and Claudia did a fantastic job with the digital installations. They're truly immersive. I think they'll give visitors a profound sense of connection to the stories."

"That sounds amazing," James said. "And how about the documentary? Last time we talked, you mentioned that the editing was almost complete."

"Yes, Eric sent over the final cuts yesterday. They've done a remarkable job weaving the narratives together with the historical footage and interviews. It tells a cohesive story that's both informative and deeply moving," Anna explained, her enthusiasm evident.

James nodded appreciatively. "It must be satisfying to see all these pieces coming together after so much hard work."

"It is," Anna agreed. "There's a part of me that's anxious about how it will all be received, but mostly, I'm excited. We've all poured so much into this project."

"And rightfully so," James said. "The way you've managed to link personal stories with broader historical contexts is going to offer people a new way to understand history. It's not just about the past; it's about the narrative threads that connect us to it."

"That's exactly what I hope people will take away from it," Anna replied. "Especially with the personal stories—like the nurse's diary entries. When you hear her words, it's almost like she's right there with you."

"How are you planning to introduce the exhibit and the series at the launch?" James asked, shifting the topic to the logistics of the opening night.

"We're starting with a small reception, then moving into a guided tour of the exhibit. Marta will lead that, highlighting key stories and the technology behind the displays," Anna detailed. "Afterward, we'll have the screening of the first episode of the documentary series, followed by a Q&A session."

"That will give the audience a chance to dive right into the experience and discuss it while it's fresh in their minds," James noted, clearly impressed with the setup.

"Exactly," Anna said. "We want to engage them right from the start, make them feel a part of the history they're walking through."

"As they should be," James added. "History is living, after all. It's all around us, in the air we breathe, in the streets we walk, and in the stories we share."

Their conversation drifted to other topics, but the project remained the central theme, weaving its way through their dialogue like the narrative threads of Anna's exhibit. As they parted ways, with the snow still gently falling outside, Anna felt a surge of anticipation and a slight nervous thrill. The launch was more than just the culmination of her project; it was the beginning of a new dialogue about history, one that she had crafted and was now ready to share.

Stepping back into the cold, Anna's breath visible in the air, she felt connected to the city and its stories in a way she never had before. Each step through the snow carried her closer to the launch, to the night when the past would come alive under the lights of the exhibit, and the voices of history would speak again through the channels of modern technology.

The day of the exhibit and documentary launch arrived, bringing with it a flurry of activity as final touches were added to the displays. Inside the cultural hub, the air was charged with anticipation, the exhibit space transformed into an immersive portal to the past, where echoes of Berlin's history awaited the influx of visitors.

Anna was inspecting the final setup when Marta approached, her expression a mix of excitement and last-minute nerves. "Anna, everything looks fantastic. Claudia's interactive designs really bring your narratives to life," she said, gesturing toward the installations that were now buzzing softly as their screens flickered to life.

Anna smiled, her eyes taking in the scene. "I'm thrilled to hear that, Marta. How are things in the reception area?"

"Everything's set," Marta replied. "The catering team is ready, and the media folks have just finished setting up. We're expecting the first guests in about thirty minutes."

"That's great," Anna said, checking her watch. "Do you think we're ready for the guided tours after the reception?"

"Absolutely," Marta assured her. "I've briefed the tour guides again this morning. They're all well-versed in the key stories and the technological aspects of the exhibits. They're really excited to share this with the audience."

"Perfect," Anna responded, her gaze lingering on a display featuring the diary of the wartime nurse. "This diary... it's the heart of the exhibit for me. I hope it touches the visitors as much as it touched us."

"It will," Marta said confidently. "It's one of the most powerful pieces. The way you've woven her words into the broader context of the war is incredibly moving."

As they were talking, Eric joined them, his face beaming. "Ladies, tonight is the night! The documentary team is all set up for the screening. The first episode looks amazing on the big screen."

"That's wonderful to hear, Eric," Anna replied. "The integration of the documentary with the exhibit pieces will really set this apart from a traditional viewing experience."

"I think so too," Eric agreed. "The narrative flows beautifully from what people will experience walking through here into what they'll see on screen. It's a seamless transition that keeps the story alive."

Anna nodded, her mind briefly caught in the myriad details of her research that had led to this moment. "I'm curious, how has the feedback been from your team? Are they as excited as we are?"

"They're over the moon," Eric chuckled. "Most of them have never worked on a project that intertwines so many elements—history, technology, personal stories. They feel like they're part of something groundbreaking."

"I'm glad to hear that," Anna said, her heart swelling with pride. "This is a collective effort, and every part of this team has added something unique to the project."

Marta checked her phone, then looked up. "We should get ready to greet the guests. Anna, you should probably take a moment before everything kicks off."

"You're right," Anna agreed, taking a deep breath. "Let's go make history come alive."

As they parted ways to prepare for the arrival of the guests, the space hummed with the quiet buzz of the exhibits and the soft murmur of the staff making final preparations. Anna walked through the exhibit one last time, each display a chapter of the city's history that she had helped uncover and narrate. She felt a deep connection to each story, a bond formed through months of research and emotional investment.

Tonight, those stories would be shared, not just as echoes of the past, but as vibrant, living narratives that continued to shape the present. As she mingled among the arriving guests, her role shifted from historian to host, eager to see the impact of her work reflected in the eyes of the viewers. The evening stretched before her, filled with promise, as the past and present merged under the soft lighting of the exhibit hall.

The launch evening unfolded with a seamless grace, the exhibit rooms filling with an eager audience whose murmurs of anticipation resonated through the high-ceilinged hall. Each guest was greeted by the glow of interactive displays and the subtle ambience of historical soundscapes designed to transport them back through decades. Anna watched from the sidelines, her heart thrumming with a mixture of pride and nervous excitement as she observed the visitors engaging deeply with the installations.

The central piece of the exhibit—the interactive timeline—drew a particularly attentive crowd. Guests moved from one era to another, touching screens to delve deeper into personal stories that highlighted each period's human experience. Anna's meticulous research had breathed life into these narratives, and now they stood as testaments to the lived realities of those who had shaped the city's history.

Midway through the evening, as guests transitioned from the exhibits to the documentary screening area, Anna found herself standing next to Claudia, who was observing the crowd's reactions with satisfaction. "It's working, Anna," Claudia said softly. "Look at how engaged everyone is. Your stories have really struck a chord."

Anna nodded, her gaze following a young couple as they paused at a display about the Berlin Wall. "It's one thing to write these stories, quite another to see them come alive like this. It feels like we're not just sharing history but re-living it with them."

Claudia smiled, her eyes reflecting the flickering lights from a nearby display. "This is just the beginning. The feedback we collect tonight will help us refine the experience even further."

Grateful for Claudia's partnership and vision, Anna turned her attention back to the guests, pleased to see the rapt attention they paid to each exhibit. The documentary screening was about to begin, and the atmosphere buzzed with the audience's heightened curiosity.

As people settled into their seats, Eric approached Anna, a clipboard in hand. "Everything's ready for the screening. I think the audience will be especially impressed with how we've woven the personal narratives into the broader historical context."

"I hope so," Anna responded, watching as the lights dimmed and the first frames flickered onto the screen. "This is the story of our city, told through the voices of its people."

The documentary began with the story of a young man in post-war Berlin, his diary entries reflecting the chaos and hope of the era. The film skillfully transitioned between his writings and archival footage, with narrations drawn directly from Anna's research. The audience was captivated, drawn into the narrative by the power of personal testimony intertwined with historical events.

As the screening progressed, Anna felt a deep sense of fulfillment watching the audience react. Their expressions of empathy, their nods of understanding, and their silent reflections during poignant moments spoke volumes about the impact of the narrative.

After the screening, while guests mingled and discussed their impressions, Anna had a quiet conversation with Marta, who was beaming with pride. "Anna, you've done something remarkable here," Marta said, her voice earnest. "You've turned history into a shared experience, not just a lesson."

"It was a collective effort," Anna replied, her eyes scanning the room. "Seeing everyone so engaged, it's more than I could have hoped for."

The evening wound down with guests reluctant to leave, lingering around their favorite displays, discussing insights, and sharing their thoughts with the team. Anna found herself answering questions, discussing potential future projects, and receiving heartfelt thanks from those who felt a personal connection to the stories shared.

As the last guests departed, Anna, Claudia, Eric, and Marta gathered to debrief. The success of the evening was undeniable, and there was enthusiastic talk of expanding the project, perhaps even taking it to other cities.

Stepping out into the cool night air, Anna felt a profound connection not only to the past but to the community that had embraced her work. The city around her was quiet, its history just a little more alive thanks to the stories that had been shared. Walking home, the streets seemed different, each corner holding a whisper of the past, each shadow a reminder of the stories still left to tell.

As the success of the exhibit and documentary continued to resonate throughout the community, Anna found herself invited to a local university to discuss the impact of the project with students studying documentary filmmaking and history. The seminar room was filled with eager young minds, notebooks at the ready, as Anna set up her presentation, her slides a collage of images from the exhibit, snippets from the documentary, and quotes from the personal stories that had been featured.

The professor, Dr. Weber, who had organized the seminar, introduced Anna with high praise. "We are privileged today to have Ms. Anna Richter with us, whose innovative approach to historical storytelling has opened new doors in both the fields of history and documentary filmmaking."

"Thank you, Dr. Weber," Anna began, acknowledging the introduction. "I'm thrilled to be here and share some insights into how we can bridge the gap between historical research and media to engage wider audiences."

A student in the front row raised her hand immediately, her expression curious. "Ms. Richter, what was your main goal when you started this project? Did you anticipate the kind of impact it would eventually have?"

"My main goal was to make history accessible and relevant," Anna explained. "I wanted to move beyond traditional academic boundaries and present historical narratives in a way that people could not only understand but feel. The impact has exceeded my expectations, largely because of the personal connections people have made with the stories."

Another student, a young man with a thoughtful demeanor, asked, "How did you choose which personal stories to include? What criteria did you use?"

"That's a great question," Anna replied. "We looked for stories that not only had historical significance but also emotional depth. We wanted narratives that reflected broader societal changes and personal resilience. Each story needed to add a unique perspective to the historical events we were covering."

A third student chimed in, her voice tinged with enthusiasm. "The integration of interactive technology was really impressive. How did you decide on the specific technologies to use in the exhibit?"

"We collaborated closely with digital artists and tech experts," Anna answered. "We discussed what technologies could best enhance the storytelling without overshadowing the narratives themselves. Augmented reality and interactive touchscreens were chosen because they allowed visitors to engage directly with the stories, making the history feel alive."

Dr. Weber, nodding along, added his own question to the mix. "Could you talk a bit about the challenges you faced in balancing historical accuracy with narrative engagement?"

"Balancing accuracy with engagement is always challenging," Anna acknowledged. "We had to be meticulous in our research to ensure factual correctness. Yet, we also had to tell the stories in a way that resonated on an emotional level. This meant choosing the right words, the right images, and the right medium for each part of the story. It was a constant process of adjustment and fine-tuning."

The discussion evolved into a broader conversation about the future of historical documentation and storytelling. "Where do you see this field heading in the next decade?" asked Dr. Weber, inviting Anna to speculate based on her experiences.

"I see a growing trend towards multimedia and multidisciplinary approaches in historical documentation," Anna projected. "The future lies in collaborations across fields—history, technology, art—to create more dynamic and immersive ways to experience the past. We're just scratching the surface of what's possible."

As the seminar concluded, the students gathered around Anna, eager to discuss their own project ideas and seek her advice. Her willingness to engage with each question and provide thoughtful feedback left a lasting impression.

Leaving the university, Anna felt inspired by the interaction with the students. Their energy and innovative ideas reassured her that the future of historical storytelling was vibrant and full of potential. Each question they had asked opened up new avenues for exploration, reminding her that history was not a static field but a living, evolving narrative.

Walking back through the campus, with the late afternoon sun casting long shadows, Anna reflected on the profound connections that her project had forged. What began as a quest to bring history to life had evolved into a continuing dialogue about how we understand and interact with our past. The stories she had helped tell were now part of a larger conversation, one that would continue to grow and reshape itself just like the city around her.

Chapter 15
Escape Plans

As the leaves began to unfurl and the grip of winter loosened, Berlin awakened to the brisk beginnings of spring. The city, ever a canvas of historical juxtapositions, now glistened under a gentle sun that promised new beginnings. For Anna, this change of seasons was a mirror to her own evolving journey, as she prepared to embark on a new chapter in her project: a series of lectures and workshops aimed at engaging a broader audience with the lessons gleaned from her exhibit.

Her first engagement was at a well-known cultural center in the heart of the city. Here, surrounded by walls that echoed with decades of artistic expressions and political debates, Anna set up her presentation. The room was arranged to foster an intimate atmosphere, with chairs gathered in a semi-circle and the soft light of the morning sun filtering through high windows.

Today's session was titled "History through Personal Stories: Bridging the Past and Present." Anna had prepared a collection of artifacts and copies of personal letters, which were displayed on a table at the front, inviting early attendees to peruse them as they waited for the talk to begin.

As the room filled, Anna could sense the palpable curiosity of the audience. These were people from diverse backgrounds—students, educators, history enthusiasts, and even a few local historians. Her heart swelled with a mix of pride and responsibility, knowing that each person was here to connect, learn, and perhaps carry forward the torch of historical inquiry.

With the chime of the clock marking the start of the session, Anna took her place at the front. "Good morning, everyone. Thank you for joining me today," she began, her voice steady and welcoming. "We gather here in a place steeped in history, to explore how personal narratives can transform our understanding of the past."

She clicked to the first slide—a photograph of the old marketplace, vibrant and bustling in the early 1900s. "This image," Anna continued, "is not just a photograph. It's a portal to countless stories—of traders, families, celebrations, and the everyday life that colored this city's history."

Anna moved through her slides, each one a thread in the rich tapestry of Berlin's past. She shared excerpts from diaries and letters, each piece a testament to the resilience and complexity of the human spirit. The audience listened intently, moved by the personal accounts that illustrated larger historical events, making the abstract tangible and relatable.

Midway through the presentation, Anna paused at a slide showing a series of personal items—a worn doll, a set of military medals, a hand-written recipe book. "Each of these items," she explained, "carries a story. Imagine the hands that sewed the doll's dress, the chest that bore these medals, the family meals that this recipe book helped prepare. These are not mere relics; they are echoes of lives lived, of struggles and joys."

The talk concluded with a discussion session, where Anna encouraged the audience to share their thoughts and ask questions. "How can we, as a community, contribute to preserving such personal histories?" she posed to the group, sparking a lively conversation about local history projects and personal archiving.

As the session drew to a close, many attendees lingered, eager to discuss their own family histories or to get advice on how to preserve their personal narratives. Anna engaged with each query with genuine interest and encouragement, knowing that every interaction was a seed planted for future historical exploration.

After the last of the participants had left, Anna began to pack up her materials, her mind already on the next workshop. She felt a profound satisfaction in having shared her passion for history and in having ignited similar enthusiasm in others. Her project, initially a solitary endeavor, had grown into a communal journey, enriching not only her understanding of the past but also that of others.

Stepping out into the spring air, Anna took a deep breath, feeling invigorated. The city around her was alive with the buzz of the present, but beneath its surface ran the undercurrents of the past, now a little more understood and appreciated thanks to the narratives she had helped bring to light. Her steps echoed softly on the cobblestone streets, each one a testament to the ongoing dialogue between the past and the present, a dialogue she was honored to facilitate.

In the wake of her successful lecture at the cultural center, Anna arranged to host a workshop at a local library, focusing on practical methods for preserving personal histories. The library, a quaint building nestled within a quieter district of Berlin, was a repository of both books and local lore, making it the perfect venue for such an event.

As Anna set up her materials—a mixture of digital recorders, archival storage solutions, and a small exhibit of successfully preserved items—she was greeted by the librarian, Mr. Schneider, a man with a keen interest in community heritage.

"Ms. Richter, it's wonderful to have you here," Mr. Schneider said, extending a hand. "Your workshop is quite the talk of the town. We've had numerous inquiries over the past week."

"I'm delighted to hear that, Mr. Schneider," Anna replied, shaking his hand warmly. "I hope today's session will empower people to begin preserving their own family histories."

"I'm sure it will," he affirmed. "Many of our patrons have expressed a desire to capture their family stories but are unsure where to start. Your expertise will certainly guide them."

As the participants began to arrive, Anna greeted each with a smile, pleased to see a diverse group ranging from young adults to the elderly, all united by a shared interest in safeguarding their histories. Once everyone had settled, Anna began the workshop.

"Good morning, everyone. Thank you for joining me today," Anna started, her voice echoing slightly in the quiet room. "This workshop is designed to give you practical tools and techniques to preserve your own personal histories."

A young woman raised her hand, her expression eager. "Ms. Richter, what's the most important aspect of starting a personal history project?"

"Great question," Anna responded. "The most important aspect is simply to start. Begin with interviews of family members, if possible. Record their memories, their stories, and even the mundane details of daily life, as these are often the most telling about an era."

A middle-aged man in the back, who had been taking meticulous notes, asked, "What about the technical side? What kind of equipment would we need?"

"For recording, a simple digital recorder or even a smartphone app can work well," Anna explained. "For preserving physical items like letters, photographs, or artifacts, it's important to use archival-quality materials. Acid-free boxes and folders can protect these items from deterioration."

An elderly lady, her eyes twinkling with curiosity, chimed in. "And once we have these recordings and items, how should we store them to ensure they last?"

"Digital recordings should be backed up in multiple locations if possible," Anna advised. "For physical items, store them in a cool, dry place away from direct sunlight. Humidity and temperature control are crucial to avoid damage."

The group listened intently, some jotting down every word, others nodding in understanding. The workshop continued with a practical demonstration, where Anna showed how to use a digital recorder and how to handle and store physical items properly.

As the session neared its end, a young man asked, "How often should we revisit and maintain these archives?"

"It's good practice to check on them at least once a year," Anna suggested. "Make sure the storage conditions are stable, and consider transferring digital records to new formats every few years to keep up with technology changes."

The participants gathered around the demonstration tables, discussing their plans to start their projects, inspired by the tools and knowledge they had gained. Anna moved among them, offering advice, encouraging their efforts, and sharing in their enthusiasm.

The workshop concluded with a round of applause for Anna, as participants began to leave, chatting animatedly about their plans to preserve their family stories. Mr. Schneider approached Anna, a smile of satisfaction on his face.

"Thank you, Ms. Richter. I believe you've started something wonderful here today," he said, shaking her hand.

"It was my pleasure," Anna replied, packing up her materials. "I look forward to seeing how their projects develop."

Leaving the library, Anna felt a deep sense of fulfillment. The workshop had not only imparted practical skills but had also sparked a passion for preservation among the participants, ensuring that the stories of today would become part of the fabric of tomorrow's history. As she walked through the library's doors, the crisp air of the emerging spring seemed to whisper of stories yet to be told, each waiting for someone to listen and preserve.

Buoyed by the success of her recent workshop, Anna was invited to speak at a local history club's monthly meeting. The venue was a small community hall adorned with historical photos and artifacts from the neighborhood, providing a fitting backdrop for a discussion about preserving personal histories.

As people began to filter in, carrying notebooks and cameras, Anna set up her projector and laid out some of her own collected items—letters, photographs, and small personal artifacts. The attendees were a mix of amateur historians, local residents, and students, all eager to learn more about integrating personal narratives into the broader tapestry of history.

The club president, Mr. Hoffman, a retired history teacher with a deep voice and an infectious enthusiasm for historical preservation, introduced Anna to the group. "Ladies and gentlemen, we are very fortunate tonight to have Ms. Anna Richter with us. She has done remarkable work in the field of historical preservation, particularly in capturing and maintaining personal histories."

"Thank you, Mr. Hoffman," Anna began, smiling warmly at the audience. "It's wonderful to be here tonight. I believe that everyone has a story, and these stories are the threads that connect us not only to our past but also to future generations."

A woman in the second row raised her hand. "Ms. Richter, could you share with us one of your favorite stories that you've preserved?"

"Of course," Anna replied, clicking to a slide showing a series of worn letters and a faded photograph of a smiling couple. "This is one of the most touching stories I've worked on. These letters were exchanged between a soldier on the front and his wife during the war. Despite the hardships, their correspondence is full of hope and love. Preserving these letters involved careful digital scanning and protective storage, but sharing their story has touched many people."

"That's beautiful," another member commented. "How do you approach people about sharing these personal items and stories?"

Anna nodded thoughtfully. "It's all about respect and sensitivity. I explain the importance of preserving their history and assure them of how it will be handled. Most are eager to share once they understand the value of their contributions to our collective history."

A young man at the back asked, "Once you have these stories, how do you decide the best way to present them to the public?"

"That's a great question," Anna responded. "It depends on the story. Some are best told through exhibitions, where people can interact with the artifacts. Others might be more impactful through documentaries or written publications. The key is to honor the story and present it in a way that resonates with people."

Mr. Hoffman interjected, "What are some challenges you've faced in this work?"

"One major challenge is ensuring the accuracy and authenticity of the stories," Anna explained. "It requires meticulous research and sometimes detective work to verify details. Another challenge is the physical preservation of fragile items, which can be quite complex and costly."

A woman towards the front spoke up, "Do you have any tips for us, as amateur historians, on how to start our own projects?"

"Start small," Anna advised. "Focus on a specific family or a small community. Use local archives and talk to elders. Document everything and back it up in multiple formats. Most importantly, share your findings. Whether it's a blog, a local exhibit, or a community presentation, getting your stories out there is what really keeps history alive."

The discussion continued, with members sharing their own experiences and seeking advice on specific challenges. Anna engaged each question with enthusiasm, providing insights and encouragement.

As the meeting came to a close, Mr. Hoffman thanked her again. "Ms. Richter, you've given us not only valuable knowledge but also inspiration to keep pursuing our passion for history."

"It was my pleasure," Anna said, as the members clapped warmly. Packing up her projector, she felt a renewed sense of purpose. Each interaction, each shared story, was a step toward preserving the intricate mosaic of personal histories that would otherwise be lost to time.

Leaving the community hall, Anna's thoughts were filled with the discussions of the evening. The engagement and passion of the local history enthusiasts reaffirmed her belief in the power of shared stories to enrich understanding and foster community connections. As she walked under the starlit sky, the echoes of the past mingled with the promise of future discoveries, each step a continuation of her journey through the living history all around her.

Spring deepened its hold on Berlin, the city parks ablaze with the colors of tulips and the fresh green of new leaves. The change of seasons seemed to mirror the closing of one chapter and the beginning of another in Anna's journey. With the success of her various talks and workshops, she found herself reflecting on the broader impact of her work, contemplating her next steps.

On a clear morning, Anna decided to visit one of the city's oldest cemeteries, a place where history was etched into stone and whispered through the leafy avenues. She walked along the paths, her steps slow, her mind occupied with thoughts of the countless stories that lay untold beneath her feet. It was here, amidst the quietude of resting lives, that she often found clarity and inspiration.

As she paused by a particularly ornate gravestone, marking the final resting place of a forgotten poet from the city's vibrant Weimar era, her phone rang. It was Marta, calling to discuss the feedback they had received from the recent community history projects.

"Anna, the response has been overwhelmingly positive," Marta's voice came through, vibrant and full of excitement. "People are really connecting with the stories we've helped bring to light. There's a real appetite for more."

"That's wonderful to hear, Marta," Anna replied, a smile spreading across her face. "It feels like we've started something that's taken on a life of its own."

"Exactly," Marta agreed. "And there's something else. A few educational institutions have reached out. They're interested in incorporating our approach into their history curricula. They think it could really engage students in a meaningful way."

"That's incredible," Anna said, genuinely moved by the potential to influence future generations. "It's more than I hoped for. History, when told through the lens of personal narrative, becomes more than just facts and dates—it becomes a living, breathing thing."

"Exactly my thoughts," Marta replied. "I think this could be our next big venture—shaping how history is taught, making it accessible and relatable."

"I'd love that," Anna said, her mind already racing with ideas. "Let's set up a meeting to discuss this further. There's a lot we could do here."

"I'll arrange that," Marta confirmed. "Talk soon, Anna."

As the call ended, Anna continued her walk, her heart light with the new possibilities that Marta had brought to her attention. The idea of influencing educational approaches to history was both a daunting and an exhilarating prospect.

Turning her thoughts back to her surroundings, Anna let the serenity of the cemetery guide her reflections. Each headstone in the cemetery was a marker of a life, each life a potential story that contributed to the fabric of the city's history. It was a tangible reminder of her mission to uncover and preserve these personal narratives, not just for the sake of the past but for the enrichment of the future.

Lost in her thoughts, she didn't notice the time passing, the sun moving across the sky, casting long shadows over the graves. Her connection to the city and its past had never felt more profound.

Leaving the cemetery, Anna felt renewed and inspired, ready to take on the challenges of expanding her project into educational realms. The stories she had helped to preserve were already changing the way people viewed history, and now they had the potential to inspire new ways of learning and understanding.

As she walked back through the city, each street and building seemed to hold a whisper of the past, a call to remember and honor those who had walked these paths before. Her role as a chronicler of these stories was evolving, just like the city itself, continually shaped by the people who lived in it and loved it. The past was not static, and neither was her journey through it. Each step was a continuation, each breath a commitment to the living history all around her.

Chapter 16
The Chase Begins

As the lush vibrancy of spring gave way to the warm embrace of summer, Berlin buzzed with life, its streets a testament to the city's enduring spirit and resilience. For Anna, this transition marked the beginning of a new phase in her project—shifting her focus from public exhibitions and talks to collaborating on educational initiatives that would integrate her research into school curriculums.

One bright morning, Anna visited a local high school where she had been invited to pilot a workshop based on her work. The school, situated in a historic district, had a longstanding commitment to innovative educational programs. Its red brick facade and sprawling courtyard spoke of a richness of history, mirroring the depth and complexity of the narratives Anna was eager to share.

As she set up in a spacious classroom, overlooking a garden where students often read or sketched, Anna arranged her materials: digital tablets loaded with interactive timelines, copies of primary sources, and small artifacts that had once been mere footnotes in the larger historical narrative. She was preparing to introduce a group of students to a hands-on approach to history that encouraged exploration and connection.

The students filed in, their youthful energy and curiosity filling the room with a palpable excitement. They gathered around the tables, eyes wide at the sight of the artifacts laid out before them. Anna greeted them with a warm smile, ready to guide them through the past with a focus on the personal stories that had shaped their city.

"Good morning, everyone," Anna began, capturing their attention. "Today, we're going to do something a little different. We're not just going to talk about history; we're going to interact with it, explore it, and see how the lives of people not so different from you and me have woven the fabric of the city around us."

She walked the students through the use of the digital tablets, showing them how to access detailed accounts of historical events through the lens of personal narratives. "These stories," she explained, "are from people who lived through these events. They are voices from the past that still have much to tell us."

The workshop emphasized critical thinking and empathy. Anna encouraged the students to ask questions, to delve into the 'why' and 'how' of history. "What can these stories tell us about resilience? About community? About the impact of decisions made during times of crisis?" she posed to the group.

The students engaged eagerly, discussing among themselves and with Anna. They examined the artifacts, touching the pages of diaries carefully preserved in protective sleeves, tracing the lines written by hands long gone. They debated the motivations behind the choices people had made, guided by Anna's insightful prompts.

As the session drew to a close, the students' feedback was overwhelmingly positive. They expressed a newfound appreciation for the personal aspects of history, noting how these stories made the past feel more relevant and alive.

"History feels different when you see it through the eyes of someone who actually lived it," one student remarked, a sentiment echoed by nods from the group.

Anna packed up her materials, her heart full of hope. This workshop had been a test, a first step toward bringing her project into educational settings, and the response confirmed she was on the right path.

Leaving the classroom, Anna paused to look back at the garden, now lively with students returning to their day. The session had not only introduced them to a new way of looking at history but had also reminded her why she had started this journey.

As she walked through the school gates, the city stretched out before her, its history interwoven with the vibrancy of the present. Anna felt a deep connection to her work, energized by the potential of these educational endeavors to shape how history would be taught and understood in the future. Each step forward was a step into new possibilities, each narrative shared a bridge connecting the past with the future, ensuring that the voices of history would continue to resonate and teach.

As the lush vibrancy of spring gave way to the warm embrace of summer, Berlin buzzed with life, its streets a testament to the city's enduring spirit and resilience. For Anna, this transition marked the beginning of a new phase in her project—shifting her focus from public exhibitions and talks to collaborating on educational initiatives that would integrate her research into school curriculums.

One bright morning, Anna visited a local high school where she had been invited to pilot a workshop based on her work. The school, situated in a historic district, had a longstanding commitment to innovative educational programs. Its red brick facade and sprawling courtyard spoke of a richness of history, mirroring the depth and complexity of the narratives Anna was eager to share.

As she set up in a spacious classroom, overlooking a garden where students often read or sketched, Anna arranged her materials: digital tablets loaded with interactive timelines, copies of primary sources, and small artifacts that had once been mere footnotes in the larger historical narrative. She was preparing to introduce a group of students to a hands-on approach to history that encouraged exploration and connection.

The students filed in, their youthful energy and curiosity filling the room with a palpable excitement. They gathered around the tables, eyes wide at the sight of the artifacts laid out before them. Anna greeted them with a warm smile, ready to guide them through the past with a focus on the personal stories that had shaped their city.

"Good morning, everyone," Anna began, capturing their attention. "Today, we're going to do something a little different. We're not just going to talk about history; we're going to interact with it, explore it, and see how the lives of people not so different from you and me have woven the fabric of the city around us."

She walked the students through the use of the digital tablets, showing them how to access detailed accounts of historical events through the lens of personal narratives. "These stories," she explained, "are from people who lived through these events. They are voices from the past that still have much to tell us."

The workshop emphasized critical thinking and empathy. Anna encouraged the students to ask questions, to delve into the 'why' and 'how' of history. "What can these stories tell us about resilience? About community? About the impact of decisions made during times of crisis?" she posed to the group.

The students engaged eagerly, discussing among themselves and with Anna. They examined the artifacts, touching the pages of diaries carefully preserved in protective sleeves, tracing the lines written by hands long gone. They debated the motivations behind the choices people had made, guided by Anna's insightful prompts.

As the session drew to a close, the students' feedback was overwhelmingly positive. They expressed a newfound appreciation for the personal aspects of history, noting how these stories made the past feel more relevant and alive.

"History feels different when you see it through the eyes of someone who actually lived it," one student remarked, a sentiment echoed by nods from the group.

Anna packed up her materials, her heart full of hope. This workshop had been a test, a first step toward bringing her project into educational settings, and the response confirmed she was on the right path.

Leaving the classroom, Anna paused to look back at the garden, now lively with students returning to their day. The session had not only introduced them to a new way of looking at history but had also reminded her why she had started this journey.

As she walked through the school gates, the city stretched out before her, its history interwoven with the vibrancy of the present. Anna felt a deep connection to her work, energized by the potential of these educational endeavors to shape how history would be taught and understood in the future. Each step forward was a step into new possibilities, each narrative shared a bridge connecting the past with the future, ensuring that the voices of history would continue to resonate and teach.

The success of Anna's initial workshop at the local high school ignited a series of opportunities to expand her educational outreach. She found herself in dialogue with several educational institutions, each expressing keen interest in adopting her methods to enrich their history curriculums. This shift towards educational integration marked a new chapter in Anna's journey, one that promised to extend the reach of her research into the roots of community and history.

On a crisp morning, Anna sat down for a meeting with representatives from a coalition of city schools. The conference room, located within an old school building that had been renovated to serve as a district education office, was lined with tall windows that looked out over a playground where children played decades ago. Now, it was a place where the future of education was being shaped.

As she laid out her presentation materials, Anna felt a familiar mix of excitement and responsibility. She knew that the work ahead would involve not just sharing knowledge but also training educators on how to make history come alive for their students.

Dr. Lenz, the head of the district's curriculum development team, opened the meeting with enthusiastic introductions. "Ms. Richter, we've heard a lot about your work and are intrigued by the potential it has to transform how we teach history. Can you tell us more about your approach?"

"Certainly, Dr. Lenz," Anna began, clicking to the first slide of her presentation. "My approach focuses on the integration of personal stories into the historical narrative. It's about making history tangible and relatable by showing students that history is not just about dates and events but about real people who lived through these times."

She progressed through the slides, each illustrating key components of her methodology—interactive timelines, primary source analyses, and the use of digital tools to explore historical events through personal perspectives.

"The goal," Anna explained, "is to engage students on a deeper level, encouraging them to understand the complexities of history and its impact on real lives. This method not only increases engagement but also fosters empathy and critical thinking."

The representatives listened intently, occasionally nodding or jotting down notes. Ms. Bauer, a seasoned teacher and member of the curriculum team, asked, "How adaptable is your program for different age groups? We need to be able to scale this across various educational levels."

"That's a great question," Anna responded. "The program is designed to be flexible. For younger students, we might focus more on storytelling and simple artifact interaction. For older students, we can incorporate more critical analysis and deeper research opportunities."

As the meeting continued, they discussed potential pilot programs, training for teachers, and the logistics of integrating new materials into existing curriculums. The conversation was collaborative and productive, with a clear mutual interest in bringing a more narrative-driven approach to history education.

By the end of the meeting, there was a palpable sense of excitement about the potential impact of this initiative. Dr. Lenz concluded, "Anna, your insights have been invaluable. We believe this could be the start of a significant shift in our educational approach, and we're eager to start the pilot program."

"Thank you, Dr. Lenz," Anna replied, feeling both honored and motivated by the trust placed in her vision. "I'm looking forward to seeing how these stories will inspire both teachers and students."

As she left the meeting, the weight of her new responsibility was tempered by the exhilaration of seeing her work evolve in such a meaningful direction. Walking through the schoolyard, where echoes of the past played out in the laughter of children, Anna felt deeply connected to her mission. Her project was no longer just about preserving history; it was about passing it on, about ensuring that the lessons of the past would enrich the minds of the future.

Stepping into the sunlight, Anna's thoughts turned to the work ahead. Each step forward was a step toward realizing her vision of making history a living, breathing part of contemporary education.

Following the successful meeting with the education district representatives, Anna embarked on a series of school visits across Berlin. These visits were designed to directly engage with both students and teachers, to better understand their historical interests and needs, and to provide a hands-on demonstration of her interactive historical approach.

On one bright morning, Anna visited an older, well-respected high school nestled within a busy neighborhood that resonated with history. The school's architecture was a blend of old and new, much like the city itself, making it a fitting backdrop for Anna's mission to blend historical narratives with modern educational techniques.

As she set up her presentation in the school's library—a spacious room lined with books that whispered tales of the past—Anna was greeted by Mr. Grothe, a history teacher known for his innovative teaching methods.

"Ms. Richter, it's a pleasure to have you here," Mr. Grothe said, offering a firm handshake. "The students are quite excited about your workshop. There's a buzz about it all over the school."

"I'm thrilled to be here, Mr. Grothe," Anna replied, her eyes sweeping across the rows of eager faces. "I hope today's session will help students see history in a new light, as a story of real people, not just dates and facts."

The room filled quickly, students clustering around the tables set up with digital devices and replicas of historical artifacts. As Anna began her workshop, her voice filled the room with the life and color of the past.

"Today, we'll explore how personal stories can change our understanding of major historical events," Anna started, projecting images of personal letters and diaries onto the screen. "These are not just pieces of paper; they are windows into the lives of people who experienced history firsthand."

A student in the front, a young girl with a keen interest in history, raised her hand. "Ms. Richter, how do you find these personal stories? Are they just in big archives, or can they be found in other places?"

"Great question," Anna responded, clicking to a slide showing various sources. "While many documents are indeed found in archives, others come from family collections, attic finds, and sometimes even flea markets. Each story requires a bit of detective work."

As the workshop progressed, Anna guided the students through an interactive timeline she had developed. "When you click on this date, you see the personal account of a Berliner during the blockade. You can hear his voice, see photos, and read his diary. It's about making the connection between the personal and the political."

Mr. Grothe watched the engagement of his students with a growing sense of appreciation. "This is remarkable, Anna. Seeing history through personal narratives really brings it to life. It's much more engaging than the traditional way we teach history."

"I believe it makes history more relatable," Anna explained, helping a student navigate the digital timeline. "When students can connect emotionally with the people in the past, they gain a deeper understanding of history's impact."

The workshop concluded with a group discussion, where students shared their thoughts on what they had learned. "It makes history feel more real," one student noted. "Like, these were actual people, not just names in a textbook."

As the students filed out, many lingered to ask Anna additional questions or to thank her for the session. Mr. Grothe approached her again, a smile of genuine satisfaction on his face.

"Thank you, Anna. This was an enlightening experience for both the students and myself. I hope we can incorporate more of this approach into our curriculum."

"I'd love to see that happen," Anna said, packing up her equipment. "And I'm always here to help or provide materials."

Leaving the school, Anna felt a renewed sense of purpose. Each visit, each workshop added layers to her understanding of how her work affected others. The dialogue with students and educators not only validated her methods but also provided insights on how to refine and expand her approach.

As she walked down the tree-lined street away from the school, the sound of students in the distance, Anna was more convinced than ever of the power of personal narratives to transform historical education. She was not just recounting history; she was helping to shape its future narrators.

As the academic year drew to a close, Anna's initiative to integrate personal histories into school curricula had taken root. The pilot programs she had helped launch were flourishing, prompting her to organize a capstone event that brought together students, teachers, and local historians. The venue chosen was a historic hall in Berlin, its walls lined with portraits of figures who had witnessed the city's transformations—appropriate custodians for a celebration of living history.

Anna arrived early to set up the space, arranging displays of student projects that ranged from digital storybooks to small documentaries, each a reflection of their engagement with the personal narratives she had introduced them to. As guests began to arrive, the hall filled with an atmosphere of anticipation and pride.

Dr. Lenz, who had been instrumental in supporting Anna's program, approached her as she was arranging the last of the displays. "Anna, this is quite impressive. The students have really taken to this approach," he remarked, looking around at the bustling room.

"Thank you, Dr. Lenz," Anna responded, her eyes bright with enthusiasm. "It's been amazing to see how they've embraced these stories, making them their own. It feels like we're not just teaching history but fostering historians."

"I couldn't agree more," Dr. Lenz said. "The depth of understanding they're showing, and the creativity in how they present it—it's beyond what I had envisioned when we first discussed your ideas."

As the event officially began, Anna took a moment to address the gathering. "Thank you all for joining us tonight," she started, her voice carrying over the chatter. "This event is a showcase not just of what these students have learned, but how they have learned. Each project here is a testament to the power of personal stories in bringing history to life."

The audience listened intently, many nodding in agreement as they surveyed the room filled with the students' work. The evening progressed with presentations from several students who shared their experiences and the personal impact of the project.

A young girl, perhaps fourteen, stood confidently by her project, a detailed scrapbook of a local family's history spanning three generations. "Working on this project, I learned that history isn't just about big events. It's also about ordinary people, like my great-grandmother, who lived through those times," she explained to a small crowd gathered around her display.

"Seeing it through her eyes," the girl continued, "made me realize how these events affected her daily life, her choices, and ultimately, her future. It made me think about how I would have felt in her place."

The feedback from the attendees, especially the educators, was overwhelmingly positive. They discussed the students' displays with interest, asking questions and offering words of encouragement. The projects sparked conversations about the broader implications of teaching history through personal narratives and the potential for expanding this approach further.

As the evening wound down, Anna spoke with a group of teachers who were eager to take her workshop materials back to their schools. "Your methods have opened a new dimension in teaching history," one teacher said. "We're seeing students connect with the material in ways we hadn't seen before."

"I'm so glad to hear that," Anna replied. "If there's anything more I can do to support your programs, please let me know. I believe every student has the potential to learn deeply from this approach."

With the hall slowly emptying, Anna took a moment to reflect on the journey that had led her here. From the archives to classrooms, and now back into the community, her work had come full circle. Each step had been guided by her belief in the importance of personal narratives in understanding our past.

Packing up her materials, Anna felt a sense of accomplishment and anticipation for the next steps. The success of tonight's event was not just a personal victory but a beacon for future educational endeavors. As she stepped out into the night, the city's history seemed to walk beside her, a constant companion on a path that continued to unfold with each new project, each new story brought to light.

Chapter 17
Across Borders

The air was crisp with the onset of autumn as Anna prepared for a new venture: a series of community-based workshops aimed at further integrating personal narratives into the broader public understanding of history. Her project had gained traction, and with the backing of a local cultural foundation, she was now set to expand her influence across various districts in Berlin.

On a bright September morning, Anna met with Henrik, the coordinator for the cultural foundation, at a small café nestled in a historic part of the city. The café was a favorite local haunt with walls adorned with photographs and memorabilia from the city's past, providing a fitting ambiance for their discussion.

"Anna, I must say, the proposal you submitted was quite compelling," Henrik began, stirring his coffee. "We're excited to see how you can bring this project to different communities around Berlin."

"Thank you, Henrik," Anna replied, her notebook open on the table to her project outlines. "I believe that by reaching out directly to these communities, we can make history feel more relevant and personal. Each neighborhood in Berlin has its own story, and I want to help people discover and share those stories."

Henrik nodded, visibly pleased with her enthusiasm. "That's exactly why we think this project is important. There's a lot of history hidden in plain sight in our city, and you have a unique way of bringing that to the surface."

Anna smiled, encouraged by his words. "I plan to start in the Marzahn district. It has a rich, albeit complex history that many residents are unaware of. We'll hold workshops there to teach people how to research and document their own histories."

"That sounds like a great starting point," Henrik responded. "How will you engage the residents? It can be challenging to get people interested in history, especially if they think it doesn't relate to them directly."

"I've found that storytelling can bridge that gap," Anna explained. "We'll use local archives and collaborate with neighborhood elders to gather initial stories. Then, I hope to host storytelling evenings where these histories can be shared. It's about creating a space where history is seen as a living, communal asset."

Henrik considered this, his expression thoughtful. "Engaging the elders is a smart move. They're often keepers of a community's history. What support will you need from us to get this off the ground?"

"I'll need access to local archives and possibly some help in organizing the events," Anna said. "Any assistance with outreach would be invaluable to ensure the community knows about and feels welcome to participate in the project."

"We can definitely help with that," Henrik assured her. "We can use our networks to promote your workshops and help coordinate with the local community centers."

Pleased with the productive meeting, Anna felt a renewed sense of purpose. "Thank you, Henrik. I'm confident that with the foundation's support, we can make a significant impact."

As they concluded their meeting, Anna felt invigorated by the path ahead. She spent the rest of the day visiting the Marzahn district, walking its streets, and speaking with some local residents who expressed interest in her project. Each conversation added layers to her understanding of the community and reinforced the importance of her work.

Leaving Marzahn as the afternoon waned into evening, Anna was filled with ideas and plans. The upcoming workshops promised new challenges and opportunities, and she was ready to meet them head-on. Each step through the district had strengthened her resolve to illuminate the rich tapestry of personal histories waiting to be uncovered and celebrated. With the city's history as her canvas, Anna was eager to draw out the colors of individual stories that could inspire and educate, knitting the past with the present in the ever-evolving narrative of Berlin.

As autumn deepened, casting a golden hue over Berlin, Anna's community workshops began to take shape. The first series was scheduled in Marzahn, a district rich with untold stories and a complex history often overshadowed by the city's more central narratives. Anna chose a local community center for these sessions, a place embedded within the heart of the neighborhood, accessible and familiar to its residents.

On the day of the first workshop, Anna arrived early to set up. She arranged chairs into a circle to foster an open and inclusive atmosphere, and displayed some historical photographs and documents on tables around the room, hoping to spark curiosity and start conversations.

As people began to trickle in, Anna greeted each participant warmly, her enthusiasm for the project evident in her every interaction. Among the attendees was Mr. Krause, a retired teacher known for his vast knowledge of local history, and Frau Lehmann, whose family had lived in Marzahn for generations.

"Welcome, everyone," Anna began, once all the attendees were seated. "Thank you for joining me today. This workshop is about discovering and sharing the stories that make up the fabric of Marzahn. Each of you carries a piece of this district's history."

Frau Lehmann, a keen participant, was the first to speak. "I've lived here all my life, and I've seen this neighborhood change in so many ways. I think it's important to record these changes, to tell our children and grandchildren what it was like."

"Absolutely," Anna agreed. "Your experiences are a living history of Marzahn. What you've witnessed is valuable not just for historians but for the community itself."

Mr. Krause nodded, adjusting his glasses. "I used to teach history at the local school. There are many stories from the old days, some joyful, some difficult. How do we choose what to share?"

"That's a great question," Anna responded. "I believe every story has its place. The joyful, the difficult, they all contribute to our understanding of the past. During these workshops, I encourage you to share whatever you feel is significant. Our goal is to capture a wide array of experiences."

As the session progressed, participants shared anecdotes, some reaching back to the days of East Berlin, others more recent but no less significant. Anna facilitated the discussion, guiding the participants on how to document their stories, from conducting oral histories to preserving physical artifacts and photographs.

"Think of yourselves as historians," Anna urged the group. "What you're doing by sharing your stories is not just reminiscing—it's an act of preservation. You're ensuring that the history of Marzahn is remembered and understood."

The workshop concluded with participants expressing a renewed appreciation for their own histories and a commitment to continue sharing and documenting their stories. Anna provided them with digital recorders donated by the cultural foundation and instructions on how to use them.

As the participants left, many stayed back to thank Anna and to speak with her about their plans to document their family histories. Mr. Krause approached her, his expression thoughtful.

"Anna, what you're doing here—it's vital," he said earnestly. "Marzahn has many stories that are seldom heard. You're giving them a voice."

"I hope to," Anna replied, feeling both humbled and motivated by his words. "And I hope the project grows, that more voices are heard."

As the last of the attendees departed, Anna packed up her materials, her mind buzzing with ideas and the potential impacts of the workshops. She stepped outside, the late afternoon sun casting long shadows across the community center's facade. The stories shared today had added depth to her understanding of Marzahn, each one a thread in the larger tapestry of Berlin's history.

Walking back through the quiet streets of the district, Anna felt a profound connection to the place and its people. Her project was more than just an academic endeavor; it was a bridge linking past to present, memory to history. Each step was a step forward in this vital journey of discovery and preservation.

The next phase of Anna's workshop series took her deeper into the community of Marzahn, where she planned an interactive session at a local library, designed to teach residents how to research their family histories using both digital and traditional archival resources. The session attracted a diverse group, from teenagers eager to explore their heritage to older residents interested in preserving their legacies.

As Anna prepared the room, setting up laptops for online research and spreading out maps and old city directories, she was approached by a young woman, Elise, who seemed particularly keen to start.

"Ms. Richter, I've heard about your workshops and I'm so excited to be here," Elise said, her eyes bright with curiosity. "I've always wanted to know more about my family's history, especially since my grandparents were part of the original settlers in Marzahn after the war."

"That's wonderful, Elise," Anna replied, pleased with her enthusiasm. "Today, we'll start by looking at some online archives. I'll also show you how to access and use city records that can give you clues about your family's past."

As the participants gathered around, Anna began the session by introducing the basics of genealogical research. "Researching family history can be like detective work. You'll follow clues, sometimes hit dead ends, and then find a detail that opens up a whole new avenue of inquiry," she explained.

A middle-aged man, Mr. Weber, raised his hand. "I've tried looking into my family's history before, but I got stuck. The records just seemed to stop at a certain point. What do you suggest when that happens?"

"That can be frustrating," Anna acknowledged. "When you hit a roadblock, it's helpful to widen your search. Look into the historical context of the time and place. Sometimes, broader social and economic conditions can help explain why records stop or where people might have moved."

The group nodded, absorbing her advice as they turned to their computers and documents. Anna walked among them, offering guidance and answering questions. She stopped beside an elderly woman, Frau Schmidt, who was carefully examining an old map.

"Can you help me understand this map, Ms. Richter?" Frau Schmidt asked, pointing to a faded area. "I believe my family lived somewhere here in the 1940s, but I'm not sure how to correlate this map with the current city layout."

"Let's see," Anna said, leaning closer. "Old maps like this are valuable tools. You can use this as a base and overlay it with a current map. The city's geography office has digital tools for this, which I can show you how to use."

As they worked through the process, Elise, who had been listening, chimed in. "Is it also possible to use old newspapers and directories to find information?"

"Absolutely," Anna responded, turning to include the rest of the group in the conversation. "Newspapers are great resources. They can provide personal notices, business advertisements, and other community news that might mention your family."

The workshop continued with high engagement, participants sharing discoveries and sometimes surprises as they unearthed small but significant details about their ancestors. Anna felt a deep satisfaction in facilitating these personal discoveries, knowing that each piece of information added to a richer understanding of both personal and community history.

As the session drew to a close, Anna gathered the group for a final discussion. "I hope today's workshop has given you the tools to continue your research. Remember, each of you is now a keeper of your family's history."

The participants expressed their gratitude, many lingering to discuss their findings or ask for further advice. Elise approached Anna with a smile. "Thank you, Ms. Richter. This has opened up a new world for me. I feel like I'm connecting with my grandparents in a way I never thought possible."

"I'm glad to hear that, Elise," Anna replied, feeling the emotional weight of her work. "Keep exploring, and keep sharing your stories."

As the library began to quiet down and the participants slowly departed, Anna packed up her materials, her thoughts on the next workshop. Each session reinforced her belief in the power of personal histories to enrich lives and connect generations. Walking out of the library, she felt the gratifying weight of her contributions, each step a continuation of her journey through the living history of Berlin.

Anna's project in Marzahn had begun to bear fruit, and word of its success spread to other districts, stirring interest and generating invitations from community centers eager to host her workshops. Among these was a vibrant community center in Neukölln, a district with its own rich tapestry of histories and cultures. Anna, embracing the opportunity to expand her reach, organized a special workshop focused on integrating immigrant histories into the broader narrative of Berlin's past.

The venue was bustling as Anna set up her materials; the walls of the center were adorned with colorful artwork and photographs depicting various facets of Neukölln's community life. The attendees were a diverse group, representing the multicultural fabric of the district, each with their own unique stories and heritage.

As people settled in, a man named Omar, with roots in Turkey, spoke first, his voice curious and eager. "Ms. Richter, how do we start documenting histories that seem so scattered? Many of us have family stories that span different countries and languages."

"That's a fantastic question, Omar," Anna replied, adjusting her projector. "The key is to start with what you have—family photos, letters, even oral stories told by elders in your family. Document these stories in whatever language they are told. The authenticity of language can add depth to the narratives."

A woman named Aisha, whose family had come from Lebanon, added, "But what if there are gaps? My family lost a lot of their belongings when they moved here, and much of our history seems fragmented."

"That happens often," Anna acknowledged, nodding sympathetically. "In cases like these, public records can be helpful. You can also reach out to extended family members or even the communities where your families lived. Sometimes, other community members might have stories or photographs that include your family."

The group listened intently, many taking notes as Anna displayed examples of public records on her projector. "Here's how you can access city archives and immigration records. These documents can provide context for your family's stories and help fill in some of those gaps."

An older gentleman, Mr. Schneider, who had been quiet, spoke up, "I've written some of my experiences down, but I'm not sure how to preserve these writings. How can I ensure they last for my grandchildren to see?"

Anna smiled, pleased by his foresight. "Physical documents should be stored in acid-free folders and kept in a dry, cool place. Digitally, you can scan them and store them on a computer or cloud service. It's also wise to share these documents with several family members to ensure they aren't lost."

The discussion turned lively as participants shared snippets of their histories, seeking specific advice on how to document and preserve them. Anna facilitated the conversation, her expertise guiding each person through their unique challenges.

As the workshop neared its end, a young girl named Leyla, with a keen interest in history, asked, "How can we, as young people, contribute to this project? I want to help but I'm not sure where to start."

"Start by being curious, Leyla," Anna encouraged, her enthusiasm infectious. "Ask questions, and record the stories your family tells you. You could even create a project at school to document the histories of your classmates' families. Every story matters, and your generation is key to keeping these histories alive."

The participants clapped, energized and motivated by the workshop. They gathered around Anna afterwards, thanking her and discussing plans to begin their own documentation projects.

As the room slowly emptied, Anna packed up her materials, her heart full from the connections made and stories shared. Each workshop not only preserved more of the city's diverse histories but also reinforced the importance of her work.

Leaving the community center, the voices of the workshop participants echoed in her mind, a chorus of the past and present merging into a narrative of shared history and hope. Each conversation, each piece of advice given, and each story told spun a richer, more inclusive tapestry of Berlin's historical narrative.

Chapter 18
A Moment's Respite

Winter was approaching once more, and with it came the conclusion of Anna's series of community workshops across Berlin. Yet, instead of winding down, her efforts seemed only to be gaining momentum. To discuss future directions and new opportunities, Anna arranged a meeting with Henrik at the same small café where they had planned many of her initial workshops.

As they sat down, the café bustling quietly around them, Henrik was the first to speak. "Anna, your workshops have truly exceeded our expectations. The feedback has been phenomenal. It's clear you've touched a nerve in these communities."

Anna smiled, grateful for the support. "Thank you, Henrik. It's been more rewarding than I could have imagined. People are really connecting with their history in a way that feels personal and alive."

"I'm not surprised," Henrik replied, sipping his coffee. "You have a way of making history accessible. So, what's next? How do you see this project evolving?"

Anna took a moment to gather her thoughts. "I've been thinking about that a lot. The interest in these workshops has shown there's a strong desire for this kind of historical engagement. I'd like to formalize this into a more permanent program, perhaps even establish a dedicated center for personal history here in Berlin."

"A center for personal history—that's an ambitious plan," Henrik noted, his interest piqued. "Tell me more about what you envision for such a place."

"Well," Anna began, excitedly outlining her idea, "it would be a place where people can come to learn about researching their own histories, but also a place where they can contribute to a larger narrative. We could host exhibitions, offer classes, provide research resources, and much more. It would be both a resource center and a community hub."

"That sounds incredible, Anna," Henrik responded, clearly impressed. "It aligns perfectly with our foundation's mission of promoting cultural heritage. What kind of support would you need to get something like this off the ground?"

"For starters, funding for the physical space and initial setup," Anna said, listing the essentials. "We'd need a location that's accessible and welcoming. Then, there's staffing, technology for research and archiving, and funding for outreach programs to ensure the community knows about and uses the center."

Henrik nodded thoughtfully. "It sounds like a significant undertaking, but a worthwhile one. I think the foundation would be interested in supporting this, especially given the success of your workshops. We could start by looking for potential locations and maybe drafting a more detailed proposal?"

"That would be fantastic," Anna agreed, her mind already racing with possibilities. "I'll start working on a proposal right away. I can include potential programs, staffing needs, and a budget."

"Great," Henrik said. "And let's think about partners too. Local universities, other cultural institutions—they might be interested in collaborating or even co-funding."

"Absolutely," Anna replied. "The more community involvement we can get, the better. I'll reach out to my contacts and see who might be interested in joining the project."

As their meeting drew to a close, both Anna and Henrik were energized by the potential of creating something lasting and impactful. They agreed to meet again soon to review the initial proposal and start the next steps.

Leaving the café, Anna felt a profound sense of anticipation and responsibility. Her project had started as an effort to preserve individual stories, but it was growing into something much larger—a center that could serve as a guardian of personal and community histories for generations to come. As she walked through the crisp air, her thoughts were on the future, on the stories that were yet to be told, and on the legacy she hoped to build in the heart of Berlin.

The momentum behind Anna's project continued to build as she finalized partnerships and began scouting locations for the new center for personal history. On a crisp morning, she met with Henrik and several members of the foundation at a potential site in a historically rich part of Berlin. The building they considered was once a factory during the early 20th century, now an empty shell waiting for a new purpose.

"This could be the perfect place," Henrik noted as they walked through the spacious, sunlit halls. "It has historical significance, and there's enough space for exhibitions, workshops, and research areas."

Anna nodded, her eyes scanning the structure, envisioning what it could become. "I agree, Henrik. The history of this building could serve as a great inspiration for the center. It ties directly into our mission."

As they discussed the logistics of acquiring and renovating the building, a representative from the city's historical preservation society, Mrs. Weber, who had joined the tour, added her thoughts. "You'll have our full support. This building is a gem, and repurposing it to preserve and explore history is a fitting next chapter."

"I'm thrilled to hear that," Anna responded. "Our goal is to make history accessible and engaging. This location could really help anchor the center in the community."

Henrik pulled out some preliminary renovation plans. "Let's walk through some of these ideas. We need to ensure that whatever modifications we make preserve the integrity of the original structure while making it functional for modern use."

As they moved through the rooms, discussing potential layouts and uses, Anna's phone rang. Excusing herself, she stepped aside to take the call from Dr. Hoffmann, who had news from the university.

"Anna, I've just come from the meeting with the university board," Dr. Hoffmann began, his voice filled with excitement. "They've officially approved the partnership. We're all set to integrate our history programs with your center."

"That's fantastic news, Dr. Hoffmann!" Anna exclaimed, her heart lifting with joy. "Your students will bring so much vitality to the center, and the academic partnership will strengthen the quality of our programs."

"I believe so too," Dr. Hoffmann agreed. "We're looking forward to being part of this innovative approach to history. When can we meet to discuss the next steps?"

"How about next week at the university? We can outline the integration process and start planning some joint initiatives," Anna suggested, her mind already racing with possibilities.

"That sounds good. I'll set up a meeting with the relevant departments and confirm the details with you," Dr. Hoffmann replied.

"Thank you, Dr. Hoffmann. I'll see you next week," Anna said, ending the call with a smile. Returning to the group, she shared the good news.

"That's another piece in place," Henrik said, pleased. "With the university on board, the educational aspect of the center is secured."

The group continued their inspection of the building, each member contributing ideas that blended the historical with the functional. By the time they finished, there was a shared vision of what the center could become—a dynamic space where history was not just stored but actively explored and discussed.

As they left the site, Anna felt a profound sense of accomplishment and anticipation. The dream of the center was slowly becoming a reality, a tangible part of Berlin's cultural landscape. Walking back through the city, the historical narratives she had always cherished now felt more alive and imminent, each waiting to be told in the new space they were creating.

With the partnership firmly in place and the site for the new center selected, Anna dove into the intricate process of design and planning. Recognizing the need for specialized skills, she organized a meeting with a team of architects, interior designers, and historical preservationists. Their goal was to ensure that the renovation of the old factory preserved its historical essence while creating a modern, functional space for the center.

As they gathered around the large table in a conference room overlooking the site, Anna laid out the vision and the challenges. "This building has a rich history, and it's crucial that we maintain that character. We want the architecture itself to tell a story, just as much as the exhibits and workshops inside it will."

The lead architect, Mr. Jansen, nodded, spreading the blueprints across the table. "We've taken the building's history into account. Our design incorporates the original brickwork and the factory's large windows to keep the industrial feel while updating it for energy efficiency and modern use."

Anna peered over the plans, pointing to a section. "I like how you've integrated the old features. What about the interior layout? We need versatile spaces that can be adapted for different types of exhibitions and workshops."

Mr. Jansen highlighted several areas on the blueprint. "Here we have movable walls that can expand or divide rooms as needed. We've also planned for state-of-the-art audio-visual equipment to be integrated seamlessly into the ceilings and walls, maintaining the aesthetic while providing functionality."

"That sounds excellent," Anna responded, clearly pleased. "What about accessibility? It's important that everyone, regardless of ability, can use and enjoy the center."

The interior designer, Ms. Vogel, chimed in. "We've included ramps and elevators, and all displays will be at heights accessible from both standing and seated positions. We're also incorporating tactile and audio descriptions for all exhibits."

"Thank you, Ms. Vogel, that's vital," Anna said, her attention then turning to the preservationist, Dr. Klein. "Dr. Klein, could you speak to how we're preserving the more delicate aspects of the building's history?"

"Of course," Dr. Klein began, adjusting his glasses. "We're using non-invasive restoration techniques to preserve the original masonry and woodwork. Any new materials will be aged to match. Additionally, we're documenting every step of the process, which we'll include as part of an exhibit on the building's transformation."

"Perfect. It's essential that the center not only houses history but also represents it," Anna noted, satisfied with the team's efforts.

As the meeting drew to a close, Anna summarized the steps ahead. "It sounds like we have a solid plan moving forward. I'll coordinate with the foundation and our other partners to ensure funding is aligned with these phases. Let's aim to break ground by early spring."

"Sounds good, Anna," Mr. Jansen said as the group began to pack up. "We'll finalize the technical specifications and start on the necessary permits."

"Thank you, everyone, for your hard work and dedication," Anna expressed warmly. "This center is going to be something truly special, thanks to all of you."

Leaving the meeting, Anna felt a mixture of relief and exhilaration. The project was complex, certainly more so than any she had undertaken before, but seeing it start to come together was immensely gratifying. As she walked away from the conference room, her thoughts already on the next tasks, she felt deeply connected to the city's past and future. Each step she took was part of a larger journey—not just hers, but that of the entire community poised to rediscover and celebrate its history.

As the initial renovations began at the site of the future center, Anna organized a meeting with community leaders and potential sponsors to discuss the center's role and impact on the local community. The meeting took place in a temporary office overlooking the renovation site, the sounds of construction a backdrop to their conversation.

Anna greeted each attendee as they arrived, offering coffee and pastries before they settled around a makeshift conference table. Once everyone was seated, she opened the discussion with a warm smile.

"Thank you all for coming today. This center is not just a project of mine; it's a community asset, and your input is invaluable. I'd like to start by hearing your thoughts on how the center can serve our community most effectively."

Mr. Ali, a community organizer, was the first to speak. "Anna, we appreciate your efforts in making history accessible to everyone. One thing we really need is a program that engages our youth. Many young people in our district feel disconnected from the historical narrative of Berlin."

"That's a great point, Mr. Ali," Anna replied. "We're planning interactive workshops and storytelling sessions aimed specifically at younger audiences. We want to encourage them to explore their own family histories and see themselves as part of the city's larger story."

Ms. Fischer, a representative from a local educational charity, chimed in, "I believe there's potential for partnership with schools. Perhaps the center could offer field trips or specialized educational programs that align with the school curriculum."

"I love that idea," Anna responded enthusiastically. "We aim to work closely with schools to provide resources and programs that complement their curriculums. I think it's crucial that students understand history through a personal lens."

Dr. Baumgartner, a potential sponsor from a technology firm, raised a question. "Anna, how do you plan to integrate technology into the center? Our company might be interested in funding tech-driven exhibits or resources."

"We're very interested in making the center a state-of-the-art facility," Anna explained. "This includes digital archives accessible to visitors, virtual reality experiences that bring historical events to life, and interactive kiosks where visitors can research their own histories."

"That sounds quite innovative," Dr. Baumgartner noted, nodding approvingly. "We would be interested in discussing how our technologies could support your vision."

"I would welcome that, Dr. Baumgartner," Anna said, making a note. "I believe your technology can greatly enhance the interactive aspects of our exhibits."

Mrs. Weber, a local historian, then asked, "How will the center handle the preservation of historical artifacts and documents? It's important that these items are not only displayed but also preserved for future generations."

"Absolutely, Mrs. Weber," Anna assured her. "We are implementing top-tier preservation techniques, and part of our facility will be dedicated to archival storage that meets international conservation standards. We'll also offer workshops on preservation techniques for community members who want to preserve their own artifacts."

As the meeting drew to a close, Henrik from the cultural foundation added his final thoughts. "This center is shaping up to be a cornerstone of cultural preservation and education in Berlin. We are proud to support it and excited to see its impact."

"Thank you, Henrik, and thank you all for your valuable insights and support," Anna concluded. "I'll follow up with each of you to discuss how we can bring these ideas to fruition."

The attendees began to disperse, exchanging handshakes and enthusiastic conversations about the future. Anna felt a surge of gratitude and determination as she watched them leave, each conversation adding layers to the foundation of the center.

Turning back to the window, she watched the workers on the site, each movement a step closer to realizing her vision. The center was more than a building; it was a beacon of community and history, bridging past and future. As the echoes of the meeting mingled with the sounds of construction, Anna was reminded of the tangible impact of her work, her commitment deepening with each passing moment.

Chapter 19
Betrayal Uncovered

As spring returned to Berlin, bringing with it the promise of renewal and growth, the construction of the center for personal history was nearing completion. The structure had begun to take shape, transforming the old factory into a modern hub of historical exploration. In anticipation of the upcoming opening, Anna organized a series of meetings with her team to finalize the launch plans and the initial exhibitions.

Gathered in the nearly completed main hall of the center, which still echoed with the subtle sounds of construction, Anna, Henrik, and the team of curators were deep in discussion about the layout and content of the inaugural exhibits.

"Let's focus on ensuring that the personal touch we've talked about so much is evident right from the opening exhibits," Anna suggested, unrolling a large blueprint across the table. "I want visitors to feel connected to the stories as soon as they walk in."

Henrik, looking over the plans, nodded in agreement. "The entrance hall is the first impression they'll get. What do you have in mind for this space?"

Anna pointed to a section of the blueprint labeled 'Entrance Exhibit'. "Here, I think a multimedia presentation would work well, showcasing short clips of personal stories from different eras. It's like introducing the visitors to the voices of history themselves."

"That sounds engaging," one of the curators, Lisa, chimed in. "We could use projections on the walls and even the floor, making it an immersive experience as they walk through."

"Exactly," Anna replied, pleased with the suggestion. "And for the main exhibit hall?"

Henrik pulled out another set of documents. "We have space here for several interactive installations. Perhaps we can start with the city's post-war recovery period—it's rich with personal narratives and pivotal in shaping modern Berlin."

"That's a critical era," another curator, Tom, added. "We could pair artifacts from that time with digital screens where visitors can access detailed stories and additional photographs. It would allow them to dive deeper into the subjects that interest them."

"I like that approach," Anna responded. "Let's make sure there are plenty of interactive elements. We want to encourage visitors not just to observe but to engage actively with the material."

Lisa brought up a logistical point. "We'll need to coordinate closely with the tech team to ensure all the digital content is ready and tested before we open. The last thing we want is technical issues during the launch."

"Agreed," Anna said, making a note. "Henrik, could you oversee that? We need the installations up and running flawlessly."

"Of course, Anna. I'll schedule a run-through with the tech team next week," Henrik confirmed, jotting down the action item.

As the meeting progressed, the team discussed marketing strategies, educational programs, and community outreach efforts to ensure a successful launch and sustained interest in the center.

"We should partner with local schools and universities," Tom suggested. "Offering tailored tours and workshops could really draw in the educational sector and get students excited about their city's history."

"And let's not forget about community groups," Lisa added. "Hosting special community days might help bring in families and local historians who could be invaluable in spreading the word."

"That's a great point, Lisa," Anna said. "Engaging with the community is key. We want this center to be a living part of Berlin, not just a place to visit."

As the meeting drew to a close, the team felt a collective sense of anticipation and readiness. They agreed to meet again the following week to finalize details and begin the countdown to the opening.

Stepping out of the main hall, Anna paused to look back at the space that would soon be filled with the voices and stories of Berlin's past. The journey from concept to creation had been long and challenging, but as she looked around at the nearly completed center, she felt a profound connection to every story it would soon tell. The last rays of the afternoon sun filtered through the large windows, casting a warm glow that seemed to affirm the promise of the center: to illuminate the past, enlighten the present, and inspire the future.

As the opening day of the center for personal history approached, the final touches on the exhibitions and installations were being meticulously applied. Anna spent her days bustling between coordinating with technicians, curators, and the marketing team to ensure everything would be perfect for the visitors. The air was thick with anticipation and a touch of nervous excitement as they all worked towards a common goal.

One afternoon, Anna met with Claudia, the lead graphic designer, in one of the newly finished exhibit halls, surrounded by interactive displays that were in the final stages of testing.

"Claudia, how are the interactive timelines coming along?" Anna asked, eyeing a screen that flickered momentarily before displaying a detailed timeline of Berlin's post-war recovery.

"They're almost ready," Claudia assured her, tapping on her tablet to bring up the status report. "We're just ironing out some minor bugs in the software to ensure the touch responsiveness is fluid. It should be done by tomorrow."

"That's great to hear," Anna responded, visibly relieved. "The timelines are a cornerstone of our educational approach. It's crucial they work flawlessly."

"Absolutely," Claudia agreed. "I'll be here late tonight to oversee the final updates. We want everything to be seamless for the opening."

Anna nodded appreciatively, then glanced around at the other installations. "And the audio stations? I remember you mentioned some issues with the audio clarity last week."

"We've upgraded the speakers, and the sound checks we ran this morning were successful. The narratives are clear, and the volume adjusts automatically to the ambient noise levels, which should enhance the visitor experience," Claudia explained.

"Perfect. Sound quality is essential, especially when it's personal stories being shared," Anna noted, her attention then shifting to the visual displays. "The visual storytelling elements look stunning, Claudia. Your team has done an incredible job."

"Thank you, Anna. We wanted to ensure that the visuals were compelling and that they complemented the stories rather than overshadowing them," Claudia replied, her pride in her team's work evident.

As they continued their inspection, Henrik joined them, his expression one of cautious optimism. "Everything seems to be coming together nicely. How are you feeling about the opening, Anna?"

"Optimistic," Anna said with a smile, though the hint of anxiety was not lost on Henrik. "And a bit anxious, of course. We've all put so much into this project."

"It's going to be a significant addition to Berlin's cultural landscape," Henrik reassured her. "The community feedback has already been overwhelmingly positive. The pre-opening tours for school groups were a hit."

"That's reassuring to hear," Anna admitted, her smile becoming more confident. "Engaging the younger generation in our city's history was one of our main goals."

"Yes, and it seems we're on track to achieving that," Henrik observed, looking around. "Once we open the doors, I believe we'll see even greater interest."

"I hope so," Anna said, her gaze lingering on a nearby display that detailed a personal story from the Berlin Wall era. "These stories deserve to be heard. They're what make this city so unique."

With the conversation winding down, Claudia and Henrik excused themselves to attend to other tasks, leaving Anna alone in the hall for a moment. She walked slowly between the displays, each step resonating with the gravity and excitement of bringing the past alive in such a dynamic way.

As the sun began to set, casting long shadows through the large windows of the center, Anna stood reflecting on the journey that had brought her to this point. The center was more than just a museum or an educational facility; it was a testament to the power of personal history in shaping public consciousness. Now, on the eve of its opening, she felt a profound connection to every story it held, a deep sense of responsibility, and an eager anticipation to share it with the world. Each narrative, carefully curated and presented, was a thread in the vibrant tapestry of Berlin's history, soon to be explored by visitors who would add their own perspectives to the ever-evolving story of the city.

The grand opening of the Center for Personal History was set under a clear Berlin sky, the early morning sunlight casting a warm glow over the freshly painted facade of the building. Inside, the final preparations buzzed with energy as Anna and her team made their last rounds to ensure everything was in place.

Anna, walking briskly alongside Henrik, checked in with each department. "Henrik, how's the setup for the opening ceremony looking?"

"Everything's on track," Henrik replied, checking off items on his digital tablet. "The seating is arranged, the sound system has been tested twice, and the catering team is setting up in the reception area as we speak."

"Great to hear," Anna said, her voice a mix of relief and anticipation. "And the guest speakers? Has everyone confirmed?"

"Yes, all confirmed. The mayor will be here at ten to give the opening address, followed by Dr. Hoffmann from the university, and then you'll take the stage. Everyone's excited, Anna. This is a big day."

"I can hardly believe it's finally here," Anna admitted, her gaze sweeping over the bustling activity. "Let's make sure the volunteers at the information desk are ready to handle inquiries and guide the visitors."

As they approached the information desk, Anna greeted the volunteers, a group of university students who had been involved in the project from early on. "Morning, everyone! Are you all set for the day?"

"We are, Ms. Richter," one of the students, a bright-eyed young woman named Sophie, responded enthusiastically. "We've got the maps and schedules ready, and we've familiarized ourselves with the layout so we can answer questions and give directions."

"Excellent, Sophie. Thank you all for being here and for your help," Anna said, her gratitude genuine.

Moving on to the exhibition halls, Anna met with Claudia, who was overseeing the final touches to the interactive displays. "Claudia, how are things looking here?"

"We're all set, Anna," Claudia confirmed, a touch of pride in her voice. "All interactive elements are fully operational, and the last-minute graphics updates look fantastic."

"Perfect. I'm especially looking forward to seeing the visitors interact with the timelines and personal story stations," Anna said, her excitement barely contained.

"They're going to love it," Claudia assured her. "It's been amazing to see this project come to life."

Anna's next stop was the special exhibits hall, where Tom was coordinating the placement of last-minute signage. "Tom, are the exhibit descriptions all in place?"

"Just finishing up now," Tom replied, securing a sign next to a display. "Each description has been double-checked for accuracy and clarity. We want to make sure the visitors get the most out of these stories."

"That's what today is all about," Anna smiled, her eyes briefly meeting Tom's as they shared a moment of mutual understanding of the project's importance.

Finally, as guests began to arrive, filling the lobby with a murmur of voices and the clicking of cameras, Anna took a deep breath, standing beside Henrik as they prepared to greet the first wave of visitors.

"This is it, Henrik. It feels like everything we've worked for is coming together today," Anna said, watching as people started exploring the center with interest and awe.

"It's more than just coming together, Anna. It's the beginning of something that will continue to grow and influence," Henrik responded, his tone supportive. "You've made history today, not just preserved it."

As the opening ceremony began, Anna felt a profound sense of accomplishment and anticipation. The center was alive, thrumming with the energy of visitors engaging with the exhibits, their expressions of curiosity and wonder a clear sign that the Center for Personal History was set to become a cherished institution in Berlin.

Throughout the day, Anna mingled with guests, answering questions, sharing insights, and soaking in the feedback. Every comment, every smile from a visitor added to the deep satisfaction of seeing her dream realized. This was not just an opening; it was a celebration of history, of community, and of the countless personal stories that, together, wove the rich, complex tapestry of Berlin's past and present.

The grand opening of the Center for Personal History was not just a single day's celebration but the kickoff of an ongoing series of events designed to embed the center deeply into the cultural life of Berlin. In the weeks that followed, Anna organized various follow-up activities, including expert-led history talks, family genealogy workshops, and school partnership programs.

One late afternoon, as another successful event wrapped up at the center, Anna sat down with Henrik and Claudia in a quiet corner of the café that had become their unofficial meeting spot. They reviewed feedback from the opening series and discussed strategies for maintaining momentum.

"It's been an incredible start," Anna began, her voice tinged with both fatigue and satisfaction. "The feedback has been overwhelmingly positive, but we need to think about how we keep people coming back and ensure the center remains a vibrant part of the community."

Henrik, sipping his coffee, nodded in agreement. "We've started strong, but sustaining that interest will be key. Perhaps we could introduce a monthly theme that explores different aspects of Berlin's history through various interactive and multimedia displays."

"That's a great idea," Claudia added, her mind already turning over the possibilities. "Each month could culminate in a special event or workshop that ties back to the theme. It would keep the content fresh and engaging."

Anna considered this, her strategic mind mapping out how such a program could work. "I like that. It keeps our exhibits dynamic and gives people a reason to visit regularly. We could partner with local historians and cultural figures to bring each theme to life."

"Exactly," Henrik said. "And let's not forget about the educational programs. The school visits have been a hit, but we can expand on that. Maybe create tailored educational packages that schools can use throughout the year."

Claudia was quick to pick up on the suggestion. "That would tie nicely into the monthly themes. Schools could participate in projects related to each theme, which we could then display at the center."

Anna wrote down these ideas, her enthusiasm growing. "These are fantastic suggestions. Let's put together a proposal for the next six months, outlining potential themes and activities. We can include a section on educational outreach to really solidify that aspect of the center."

As they wrapped up their meeting, the sun began to set, casting long shadows across the café. They stood, gathering their materials, each feeling a renewed sense of purpose.

"I'll start reaching out to potential collaborators for the themes and get their input," Henrik offered, his role as a liaison proving invaluable.

"And I'll draft some initial designs for the exhibits and promotional materials," Claudia said, always ready to bring their ideas to visual life.

"Thank you both," Anna said, feeling immensely grateful for her team. "Let's meet again next week to finalize the plan. I'm excited to see where we can take this."

As they left the café, the crisp evening air felt invigorating. Anna walked slowly towards the center, reflecting on the journey it had taken to get here and the future she was helping to shape. The center was more than a repository of history; it was a living, breathing space that encouraged exploration and understanding of the personal narratives that made up the city's rich tapestry.

Each step she took was a reminder of the impact of her work. The center was not just preserving history; it was actively participating in the creation of new historical understandings. This was her vision come to life, a vision that continued to evolve with each new story uncovered and shared within its walls.

Chapter 20
Desperate Measures

Several months after the opening of the Center for Personal History, Anna sat down with Henrik and a new team member, Julia, a cultural anthropologist recently hired to manage the center's community outreach and educational programs. The trio met in a small conference room within the center, surrounded by walls adorned with historical maps and photographs, to discuss the integration of an exciting new project focusing on the diverse cultural heritage of Berlin's immigrant populations.

"Julia, we're thrilled to have you on board," Anna began, her eyes reflecting genuine enthusiasm. "Your expertise in cultural anthropology is exactly what we need to expand our outreach. I'd like to hear your initial thoughts on integrating the immigrant history project into our current offerings."

"Thank you, Anna. I've been reviewing our resources and the community feedback," Julia responded, her voice calm and confident. "There's a rich tapestry of immigrant stories that are integral to Berlin's history. I propose we start by launching a series of workshops that not only tell these stories but also involve the immigrant communities in creating these narratives."

"That sounds wonderful," Henrik interjected. "Involvement from the community could really help make the project authentic and vibrant. How do you envision structuring these workshops?"

"My idea is to host bi-weekly sessions where community members can come in and share their stories, artifacts, and even family recipes that highlight their cultural heritage," Julia explained. "We can document these narratives and create a living archive that grows with each contribution."

Anna nodded thoughtfully. "I like that. It gives the project a grassroots feel while ensuring it remains structured. How will we ensure that the communities feel welcomed and valued through this process?"

"That's crucial," Julia agreed. "We'll need to do extensive outreach, working closely with community leaders and local organizations that are already engaged with these populations. Building trust and showing genuine interest in their history is key."

Henrik, who had been taking notes, looked up. "I can help coordinate the initial outreach. We should also consider multilingual support to ensure no one is excluded because of language barriers."

"Absolutely," Anna said. "Let's make sure all our materials and communications are available in at least the three most spoken languages in each community we're engaging with."

Julia added, "I also think it would be beneficial to involve local artists from these communities. They could help illustrate the stories or create installations that represent their cultures' contributions to the city."

"That's an excellent idea," Anna responded, her enthusiasm growing. "Art can be a powerful medium for storytelling. Plus, involving local artists not only enriches the project but also strengthens community ties."

"The visual impact of art combined with personal narratives could truly make this project unique," Henrik noted. "It could become a model for how cities can integrate immigrant histories in a respectful and engaging way."

"Let's formalize this plan," Anna suggested. "Julia, can you draft a detailed proposal based on today's discussion? Include potential costs, resources needed, and a timeline. Henrik, start identifying potential community leaders and organizations we can partner with."

"Will do," both Julia and Henrik affirmed, ready to move forward with the tasks assigned.

As the meeting concluded, the three stood, energized by the potential of the project. They stepped out of the conference room into the main hall of the center, where visitors were engaged with exhibits, their expressions a mix of curiosity and reflection.

"This project," Anna said, watching the visitors, "is going to add another layer to our understanding of Berlin. Each story we uncover and share will help paint a fuller picture of our city."

"Exactly," Julia agreed, her eyes bright with anticipation. "And it's about time these stories found their rightful place in the city's historical narrative."

As they parted ways to start their respective tasks, the center buzzed around them, a hub of activity and history in the making. Anna paused for a moment, feeling a deep connection to the work unfolding within these walls, work that would help bridge histories and cultures in one of the world's most dynamic cities.

As the immigrant history project began to take shape, Anna and Julia dedicated their efforts to creating a framework that would not only gather stories but also weave them into the rich historical tapestry of Berlin. They organized a pilot workshop aimed at testing their approach with a small group of participants from various immigrant communities.

The workshop was scheduled to take place in one of the newly renovated rooms at the center, a space designed with versatility in mind, able to transform into a cozy setting for discussions or a lecture hall. On the morning of the workshop, Anna reviewed the setup, ensuring that every detail was in place—from the seating arrangements to the audio-visual equipment used to record the sessions, which they planned to archive.

As the participants began to arrive, Anna greeted each one at the door. Her welcoming demeanor helped ease the initial awkwardness that often accompanied such gatherings. Once everyone was settled, Julia took the lead, her background in cultural anthropology giving her a unique insight into facilitating discussions that were both sensitive and enlightening.

"Thank you all for joining us today," Julia started, standing at the front of the room with a calm and inviting smile. "This workshop is part of a larger project aimed at celebrating and understanding the diverse cultures that contribute to our city's identity. We are here not just to talk about history, but to share it, to recognize it, and to preserve it."

The group, though initially quiet, gradually began to open up, sharing snippets of their personal and familial journeys to Berlin. Each story, distinct yet interconnected, painted a picture of struggle, resilience, and hope. A woman from Turkey shared a poignant tale of her grandfather, a master tailor, who brought his craft to Berlin in the 1960s, contributing to the city's fashion industry. A young man from Vietnam talked about his mother's small grocery shop that became a gathering place for the Vietnamese community.

Julia facilitated the discussion, encouraging participants to delve deeper into what these stories meant to them and how they shaped their identities. "These narratives are more than just personal memories," she explained. "They are threads of a larger historical fabric. By weaving these threads together, we create a more complete picture of our city's past and present."

As the session continued, Anna took notes, her mind already on how these stories could be integrated into permanent exhibits at the center. The richness of the dialogue reinforced the importance of their project, highlighting the need for such platforms where histories that are often overlooked can be brought to the forefront.

After the workshop concluded, participants lingered, some exchanging contact information, others discussing further the stories they had shared. The atmosphere was one of camaraderie and mutual respect, indicative of the project's potential to foster community ties.

Anna and Julia debriefed after everyone had left. "This was incredibly fruitful," Anna remarked, her voice filled with a mix of exhaustion and satisfaction. "Seeing people connect over shared histories and experiences reaffirms the value of what we're trying to achieve here."

Julia nodded in agreement. "There's a powerful sense of validation that comes from having your story heard and acknowledged. We need to keep this momentum going, perhaps with more frequent workshops and a dedicated space for these stories within the center."

As they discussed next steps, planning further outreach and considering new methods to capture and display these histories, the center around them buzzed with the quiet activity of visitors and staff. Each person there, whether they knew it or not, was a part of a larger story being told within those walls—a story of diversity, unity, and the shared human experience.

Anna walked through the exhibit halls before locking up for the evening, each display, each artifact whispering echoes of the stories shared earlier. The center was more than just a building; it was a living, breathing space where history was not only preserved but also created, day by day, story by story.

The immigrant history project had quickly become one of the most popular initiatives at the Center for Personal History, driven by the enthusiastic response from the community. To build on this momentum, Anna and Julia planned an extensive series of themed storytelling nights. Each event would focus on different cultural groups within Berlin, showcasing their unique contributions to the city's tapestry through personal stories, music, and art.

One evening, as they prepared for a storytelling night dedicated to Berlin's African communities, Anna and Julia reviewed the final details in the center's cozy seminar room, transformed into an inviting space with vibrant fabrics and traditional decorations.

"Julia, how are the preparations for tonight?" Anna asked, checking the sound setup for the guest speakers and musicians.

"Everything looks good, Anna. The speakers are all confirmed, and the musician doing the closing performance just arrived for a sound check," Julia replied, scrolling through her digital planner. "We also have a local artist displaying their work, inspired by African heritage, in the lobby."

"That's wonderful. I think these events really highlight how interconnected our histories are, and how each community has shaped Berlin," Anna said, her voice reflecting a deep appreciation for the project's impact.

"Absolutely," Julia agreed. "It's about creating a dialogue and understanding that everyone's history matters. Tonight is a perfect example of how we can celebrate those contributions."

As the first guests began to arrive, Anna greeted each with a warm smile, guiding them towards the refreshments before the presentations began. The atmosphere was lively, the air filled with the rich aromas of African cuisines prepared by local caterers.

Once everyone had settled, Julia took the stage to introduce the evening. "Thank you all for joining us tonight. This event is a celebration of the stories and cultures that make up our city. We are honored to have members of Berlin's African communities share their personal histories with us."

The first speaker, Mr. Adebowale, stepped up, his presence commanding. "Good evening, everyone. I am delighted to share a bit about my journey from Nigeria to Berlin, a journey filled with challenges and triumphs. Our stories are not just about where we come from but how we've woven our lives into the fabric of this city."

His story was a poignant narrative of migration, adaptation, and integration, resonating deeply with many in the room. After him, a young poet, Kemi, recited a piece about her dual identity, blending languages and cultural references, which drew enthusiastic applause.

"Thank you, Kemi, for that beautiful poem," Julia said, returning to the stage. "It's incredible how art and storytelling can express so much about our identities and experiences."

The event continued with a few more speakers, each sharing stories of heritage, struggle, and contribution, which not only enriched the understanding of the audience but also created a sense of shared community experience.

As the final speaker concluded, a Senegalese musician began setting up his kora, a traditional harp-like instrument, preparing for the last performance of the evening. His music, intricate and soulful, provided a perfect end to the night, weaving the narratives together through melody.

After the applause had faded and the guests began mingling again, Anna and Julia came together, observing the interactions.

"Julia, see how stories can turn strangers into neighbors? This is exactly what the center was meant to do," Anna remarked, watching a lively group discussing the night's stories.

"It's really heartwarming," Julia responded. "Every event like this builds more bridges, deepens our understanding, and enriches our community."

The evening wound down with guests reluctant to leave, lingering to talk more with the speakers, exchange contacts, and even share bits of their own stories.

As the last guests departed and the staff began to clean up, Anna and Julia reviewed the night's success. Each feedback, each smile, each thank you from the attendees reinforced their commitment to the project. Walking through the now quiet halls of the center, Anna felt a profound connection to every story shared, every life touched by the history they were preserving and celebrating.

As the Center for Personal History entered its first year of operation, it had already become a cornerstone of cultural preservation and education within Berlin. The success of the immigrant history project prompted Anna and Julia to consider how they could expand the center's outreach to include even more of Berlin's diverse communities. Today, they were meeting with representatives from various cultural associations to discuss new collaborations.

In a bright, airy meeting room within the center, decorated with artifacts and photos from recent events, Anna began the discussion with an enthusiastic welcome. "Thank you all for joining us today. The center has seen incredible engagement from the community, and we're excited to explore new partnerships that can help us continue this work."

A representative from the Middle Eastern community, Mr. Hamid, was the first to speak. "We've been thrilled to see the inclusion of diverse histories in your programs. Our community is eager to participate more actively. We have many stories that we believe could contribute to a deeper understanding of Berlin's multicultural identity."

"That's exactly what we hope to achieve," Anna replied. "We believe that every community has unique stories that are essential to the complete historical narrative of our city. Julia, could you share some of the ideas we've been considering?"

Julia nodded, opening her notebook to reveal a list of potential projects. "We're considering several new series, including oral history projects, cultural festivals, and even a digital archive where people can contribute their personal stories directly."

"I like the idea of a digital archive," remarked Ms. Schneider from the Polish community association. "Many of our members are tech-savvy and would appreciate the ability to interact with history in a digital format. How can we help make this a reality?"

"We'd love to have community members contribute both content and expertise," Julia responded. "Perhaps we could set up workshops to train people on how to record and upload their stories. We could use some technical support to ensure the platform is user-friendly and accessible."

"That sounds feasible," Mr. Hamid added. "We could also organize a series of events where community members can come together to share their stories in person, which could then be recorded and added to the digital archive."

"An excellent suggestion," Anna agreed. "These stories are not just for us to tell—they belong to everyone, and this kind of active participation could really enrich the archive."

The discussion then turned to the logistics of these collaborations, with each representative expressing eagerness to contribute. "We could also look into co-hosting some cultural festivals here at the center," suggested Ms. Lee from the Korean community. "It would be a fantastic way to celebrate our traditions while educating others about our history and culture."

"We would be honored to host such events," Anna said with a smile. "Cultural festivals could bring our communities together and show the vibrancy of our city's cultural fabric."

As the meeting drew to a close, Henrik, who had been listening intently, chimed in. "It's inspiring to see such enthusiasm and collaboration. The foundation is fully supportive of these initiatives and is prepared to assist with funding and resources."

"Thank you, Henrik," Anna said, feeling grateful for the support. "And thank you all for your valuable input today. We'll follow up with each of you to discuss the next steps and start putting these plans into action."

As the representatives left, exchanging handshakes and words of anticipation for future projects, Anna and Julia remained behind, reflecting on the meeting's outcomes.

"These collaborations are going to bring so much more to the center," Julia remarked, packing up her notes.

"Yes, they will," Anna agreed, looking around the room filled with the echoes of the day's productive conversations. "It's more than just preserving history. It's about creating a space where history is lived and breathed."

As they stepped out of the meeting room, the center buzzed with the usual visitors and staff, each person contributing to the dynamic environment that the Center for Personal History had become. Anna felt a deep satisfaction, knowing that the center was not just a repository of the past but a vibrant part of Berlin's present and future.

Chapter 21
Along the Riviera

The streets of Berlin buzzed with a strange energy, a mixture of tension and hope. As Anna walked through the city, she felt the weight of the past months pressing on her shoulders. The familiar sights now seemed tinged with a sense of foreboding. The mission was nearing its climax, and every step felt like it carried the fate of countless lives.

She entered a small café, a known meeting point for those working in the resistance. The air was thick with the aroma of coffee and the quiet murmur of conversations. At a corner table, James sat, his eyes scanning the room as if perpetually on alert. Anna approached him, her presence drawing his gaze.

"Any news?" she asked, sliding into the seat across from him.

James nodded, leaning in to speak quietly. "Our contact confirmed the location of the final rendezvous. It's an old warehouse by the river, heavily guarded but with a few exploitable weaknesses."

Anna sighed, relief and anxiety mingling in her chest. "Good. We need to be ready for anything. The intel suggests they might be moving sooner than expected."

James glanced around before pulling out a folded map from his jacket. He spread it on the table, pointing to the marked location. "We enter from here, through the service tunnels. It's risky, but it's our best shot at avoiding the main guards."

Anna studied the map, her mind racing with the details. "What about the escape route? We need a clear plan for getting everyone out safely."

James traced a path on the map with his finger. "There's an old sewer line that leads to a safe house on the outskirts. It's a tight squeeze, but it should be manageable."

Their conversation was interrupted by the arrival of Sophie, their trusted ally. She slid into the seat beside Anna, her expression serious. "I've got the equipment you asked for," she said, passing a small, inconspicuous bag under the table.

Anna peeked inside, confirming the presence of communication devices and other necessary tools. "Thanks, Sophie. You've been a lifesaver."

Sophie smiled, though it didn't reach her eyes. "Just doing my part. We all know what's at stake."

James leaned back, his eyes scanning the room again. "We need to finalize our team. Who do we have?"

"Besides us," Anna began, "there's Ingrid, who knows the layout of the warehouse, and Karl, our tech expert. That should cover most of our bases."

James nodded, his mind already calculating the roles and responsibilities. "Alright, let's meet tonight at the safe house to go over the plan one last time. We can't afford any mistakes."

Sophie looked at Anna, her expression softening. "Are you ready for this? It's going to be dangerous."

Anna met her gaze, her resolve clear. "We don't have a choice. If we succeed, we can change everything. If we fail…"

"Failure isn't an option," James interjected, his voice firm. "We've come too far to turn back now."

They finished their drinks, the gravity of their mission hanging heavy in the air. As they exited the café, the sun had begun to set, casting long shadows across the city. Anna felt a sense of unity with her team, a shared determination that would carry them through the coming challenges.

Back at the safe house, the team gathered in a dimly lit room, the map spread out on the table. Ingrid and Karl listened intently as James and Anna briefed them on the plan.

"Ingrid," James began, "you'll lead us through the service tunnels. Karl, you handle the security systems. Anna and I will secure the hostages and lead them to the escape route."

Ingrid nodded, her expression confident. "I've studied the layout. We can bypass most of the guards if we're quick and quiet."

Karl adjusted his glasses, his focus intense. "I'll disable the cameras and alarms. We should have a few minutes of undetected movement, but we need to be fast."

Anna looked around at her team, her heart swelling with a mixture of pride and fear. "This is it. We move tomorrow at dawn. Get some rest, and be ready."

The room fell silent as they dispersed to prepare. Anna lingered, her mind replaying the plan, searching for any potential flaws. James approached, his presence comforting.

"We've got this," he said softly, placing a reassuring hand on her shoulder.

Anna nodded, steeling herself for what lay ahead. "We have to. For everyone depending on us."

The dawn broke gently over Berlin, casting a pale light on the quiet streets. Anna and her team were already in position, gathered near the entrance to the service tunnels that would lead them to the warehouse. The air was thick with anticipation, each breath they took laced with the weight of what lay ahead.

James adjusted his equipment, glancing at the others. "Everyone ready?"

Ingrid gave a curt nod, her face set with determination. "I've memorized the route. We'll move quickly and stay out of sight."

Karl, fiddling with a small device, added, "I've synchronized our comms. We'll be in constant contact. If anything goes wrong, we regroup at the secondary exit."

Anna tightened her grip on her flashlight, her heart pounding in her chest. "Let's do this."

They descended into the tunnels, the dim light from their flashlights casting eerie shadows on the walls. The silence was broken only by the sound of their footsteps and the occasional drip of water echoing through the narrow passageways. Anna felt the tension in the air, every step bringing them closer to the critical moment.

"We're nearing the entrance to the warehouse," Ingrid whispered, her voice barely audible. "Stay close and keep quiet."

The team moved as one, a well-coordinated unit driven by a shared purpose. They reached the end of the tunnel, where Ingrid pointed to a rusted metal door. "This leads to the lower level of the warehouse. From there, we split into our assigned tasks."

Karl approached the door, working quickly to disable the alarm system. "Give me a minute. I need to bypass the security."

Anna watched, her nerves on edge as Karl deftly manipulated the wires. Moments later, the door clicked open. Karl gave a thumbs-up, his face breaking into a relieved grin. "We're in."

They entered the warehouse, their movements careful and precise. The interior was a maze of storage rooms and corridors, dimly lit by the occasional flickering light. Anna and James headed towards the main storage area where the hostages were being held, while Ingrid and Karl moved to their designated positions.

"Remember," James whispered, "we only have a few minutes before the alarm resets. We need to move fast."

Anna nodded, her focus sharp. They approached the door to the storage area, listening for any signs of guards. Hearing nothing, they slipped inside, finding a group of frightened faces staring back at them.

"We're here to help," Anna whispered urgently. "Stay quiet and follow us."

The hostages, their relief palpable, quickly gathered their few belongings and prepared to move. Anna led them back towards the tunnels, every step filled with tension. They were halfway there when the sound of footsteps echoed down the corridor.

"Guards!" James hissed, pulling Anna and the hostages into a side room. "Stay hidden."

The guards passed by, their conversation casual, unaware of the group hiding just a few feet away. Once they were out of earshot, James signaled for the group to continue.

"We're almost there," Anna encouraged, her voice steady despite the fear gnawing at her. "Just a little further."

They reached the tunnel entrance without further incident, slipping back into the darkness below. Anna's heart hammered in her chest as they moved quickly through the passageways, every second feeling like an eternity.

Back at the secondary exit, Ingrid and Karl were waiting, their expressions tense but hopeful. "Did you get them all?" Ingrid asked, her eyes scanning the group.

"Yes," Anna confirmed, relief flooding her. "Let's get out of here."

They emerged from the tunnels into the early morning light, the city just beginning to stir. The safe house was only a short distance away, but the danger was far from over. They moved swiftly through the streets, avoiding main roads and keeping to the shadows.

As they approached the safe house, Anna felt a surge of hope. They had made it this far; freedom was within their grasp. She looked at James, who gave her a reassuring smile. "We did it," he said quietly, his voice filled with determination.

Anna nodded, feeling a sense of triumph and relief. "Yes, we did. But we're not done yet. We need to keep moving, keep fighting."

The safe house door opened, and a familiar face greeted them. Sophie, her eyes bright with relief and determination, ushered them inside. "You made it," she said, her voice filled with emotion. "Welcome back."

Anna stepped inside, feeling the weight of their journey lift slightly. There was still much to do, but for now, they were safe. She looked at her team, each of them battle-worn but resolute, and knew they would face whatever came next together.

Inside the safe house, the atmosphere was a mix of relief and urgency. The small group of hostages, now free, huddled together in the main room, their faces etched with exhaustion but glimmers of hope in their eyes. Anna and James took a moment to catch their breath, but they knew their work was far from over.

Sophie moved quickly, distributing blankets and water to the new arrivals. "We need to keep a low profile until it's safe to move again," she said, her voice calm and reassuring. "Everyone should rest while we figure out our next steps."

James approached Anna, his expression serious. "We need to debrief with Karl and Ingrid. Make sure we haven't missed anything."

Anna nodded, glancing at the hostages. "I'll join you in a minute. I want to make sure everyone here is settled."

She turned to the group, offering a reassuring smile. "You're safe now. Take this time to rest and regain your strength. We'll be moving again soon, but for now, you're among friends."

A young woman, her eyes wide with gratitude, spoke up. "Thank you… we didn't think anyone would come for us."

Anna knelt beside her, her tone gentle. "We don't leave anyone behind. You're safe now, and we'll get you to a better place."

James called from the other room, and Anna joined him, Karl, and Ingrid around a small table covered in maps and notes. The safe house, dimly lit by a single lamp, offered a sense of security, but the urgency in their mission was clear.

"Alright, let's review," James began, his voice low. "Karl, any issues with the security systems?"

Karl shook his head, adjusting his glasses. "No, everything went as planned. We disabled the alarms and cameras, and it should be a while before anyone realizes what happened."

Ingrid added, "The tunnels were clear, and we avoided the main patrols. But we need to be ready for increased security at the borders. They'll tighten the net once they realize we've extracted the hostages."

Sophie entered the room, joining the discussion. "We have a window of a few hours before they ramp up their search efforts. We need to move quickly."

Anna leaned over the map, tracing a route with her finger. "Our best bet is to split into smaller groups and head to the secondary safe houses. It's safer than traveling in one large group."

James nodded in agreement. "Anna and I will lead one group. Ingrid, you take the second. Karl, you'll stay behind and handle communications. Sophie, you coordinate with our contacts to ensure the safe houses are ready."

Sophie looked at Anna, concern in her eyes. "Are you sure you're ready for this? It's a lot to manage."

Anna met her gaze, her determination unwavering. "We have to be. These people are depending on us."

James squeezed Anna's shoulder. "We'll make it through. We always do."

The group dispersed to prepare for the next leg of their journey. Anna took a moment to gather her thoughts, feeling the weight of their mission but also the strength of their resolve.

As she moved to gather supplies, James joined her. "We should leave within the hour. The sooner we're on the move, the better."

Anna nodded, packing a bag with essentials. "I know. I just hope we're not pushing them too hard. They've been through so much already."

James's eyes softened. "You're doing everything you can, Anna. They're stronger than they look, and they have us to lead them."

Ingrid approached, her face set with resolve. "My group is ready. We'll take the northern route and meet at the designated point."

Anna embraced her briefly. "Stay safe, Ingrid. We'll see you at the rendezvous."

With everything in place, the groups prepared to depart. The hostages, though weary, were bolstered by the courage and organization of their rescuers. As they stepped out into the night, the safe house faded behind them, replaced by the vast unknown of their journey ahead.

Anna led her group through the quiet streets, every sense heightened, every shadow a potential threat. James stayed close, his presence a steady anchor. They moved with purpose, driven by the hope of freedom and the knowledge that they were not alone in their fight.

As they navigated the city, Anna couldn't help but think of the countless others still waiting for their chance at liberation. Each step they took was a step toward a brighter future, a testament to their resilience and the unbreakable bond they shared.

The road was long and fraught with danger, but together, they were unstoppable. Their journey was far from over, but with every step, they drew closer to their goal, their hearts united in the pursuit of freedom.

The streets of Berlin were eerily quiet as Anna and James led their group through the labyrinthine alleyways, every footstep echoing in the night. The weight of their mission pressed heavily upon them, yet each step forward felt like a small victory. They were determined to reach the next safe house, a crucial waypoint on their path to freedom.

Anna glanced back at the group of hostages, their faces a mix of exhaustion and hope. "We're almost there," she whispered, her voice carrying a promise of safety. "Just a little further."

James moved to her side, his eyes scanning the darkness for any sign of danger. "How are you holding up?" he asked softly.

"I'm fine," Anna replied, though the tension in her voice was palpable. "We need to keep moving."

They continued in silence, their senses on high alert. Suddenly, a shadow moved in the distance, causing the group to freeze. James held up a hand, signaling for everyone to stay quiet.

"Did you see that?" Anna whispered, her heart pounding.

James nodded, his eyes narrowing. "Could be a patrol. We need to find cover."

Quickly, they ducked into a narrow alleyway, pressing against the cold, damp walls. The sound of footsteps grew louder, accompanied by the muffled voices of guards on patrol. Anna held her breath, her hand gripping James's arm.

"Stay calm," James murmured, his voice barely audible. "They'll pass."

The footsteps grew closer, the guards' conversation now discernible. "I heard there was a breakout at the warehouse," one guard said. "We need to be on high alert."

Another guard replied, "Don't worry. They won't get far. We've tightened security across the city."

Anna's heart raced as the guards' voices faded into the distance. She exhaled slowly, relief flooding through her. "That was too close," she whispered.

James nodded, his expression grim. "We need to keep moving. It's not safe here."

They emerged from the alley and continued their journey, the tension palpable. As they neared the edge of the city, the streets became narrower and less patrolled. The safe house was just a few blocks away, a beacon of hope in the darkness.

Sophie's voice crackled through the small comm device in Anna's ear. "Anna, do you copy?"

Anna pressed the device closer. "I'm here. We're almost at the safe house."

"Good," Sophie replied, relief evident in her voice. "Ingrid's group made it safely. We're ready for you."

James heard the exchange and gave Anna a nod. "Let's pick up the pace. We're almost there."

They moved swiftly, the safe house coming into view. It was a modest building, inconspicuous among the surrounding structures. As they approached, the door opened, revealing Sophie's familiar face.

"Welcome," Sophie said, her eyes filled with relief. "Come in, quickly."

Anna and James ushered the hostages inside, the weight of their journey lifting slightly. The interior of the safe house was warm and inviting, a stark contrast to the cold streets outside.

Sophie addressed the group, her voice calm and reassuring. "You're safe here. Take a moment to rest. We have food and blankets."

James approached Anna, his expression softening. "We did it."

Anna nodded, a smile breaking through her exhaustion. "Yes, we did. But we still have a long way to go."

Sophie joined them, her eyes reflecting the same determination. "We have contacts ready to help with the next leg of the journey. We'll get everyone to safety."

One of the hostages, an elderly man with kind eyes, approached them. "Thank you," he said, his voice trembling with emotion. "You've given us hope when we had none."

Anna's eyes met his, her heart swelling with empathy. "We're in this together. We won't stop until everyone is free."

James placed a hand on Anna's shoulder. "Rest for a moment. You've earned it."

She nodded, sinking into a chair, her body finally succumbing to the exhaustion she had been holding at bay. James sat beside her, their shoulders touching in a silent show of solidarity.

"Do you ever wonder if we'll truly be free?" Anna asked quietly, her voice barely above a whisper.

James looked at her, his gaze steady. "I believe we will. We have to. For them," he gestured to the hostages, "and for us."

Sophie joined them, her presence a comforting reminder of their shared mission. "We're stronger together," she said. "And as long as we stand together, we have a chance."

Anna smiled, feeling a renewed sense of hope. "Then we keep fighting. For all of us."

The room buzzed with quiet conversations, the air filled with a sense of cautious optimism. They had made it this far, and with each other's support, they would continue their journey toward freedom. The road ahead was uncertain, but their resolve was unshakeable. Together, they were unstoppable.

Chapter 22
The Safe House

In the wake of the cultural festival's success, Anna sought to expand the educational programs offered by the Center for Personal History. Recognizing the potential for a more formalized relationship with local schools, she arranged a meeting with several school administrators and teachers to discuss collaborative opportunities. The meeting took place in a conference room at the center, arranged to foster an atmosphere conducive to open discussion and creative ideas.

As the attendees gathered around the large oak table, Anna began with an enthusiastic welcome. "Thank you all for coming today. The center has developed a range of interactive and educational programs that we believe can significantly enhance your history curricula. I'm eager to explore how we can collaborate to bring these resources directly into your classrooms."

Mr. Fischer, a high school principal, responded warmly. "We've heard great things about your recent festival and the workshops you've been running. I'm interested in how these can be adapted for our students."

"Absolutely," Anna replied. "One of our main goals is to make history tangible and relevant. We can offer workshops here at the center, where students can engage directly with historical documents and artifacts, and even meet and interview people who have firsthand experiences of historical events."

Ms. Browning, a middle school history teacher, leaned in, intrigued. "That sounds fantastic. Many of my students are visual and experiential learners. Do you have programs that cater specifically to younger age groups?"

"We do," Anna confirmed. "For younger students, we focus on storytelling and hands-on activities. For example, they can participate in a 'day in the life' workshop, where they experience historical living conditions and tasks. It's very engaging and informative."

Dr. Hennings, an administrator, asked, "What about integration with our existing curriculum? Can these programs be tailored to complement specific historical periods or topics we're covering in class?"

"That's a great question," Anna replied. "We can absolutely tailor programs to fit specific curriculum needs. We already have modules that cover major periods in Berlin's history, and we can adapt these to focus on particular aspects as needed. Additionally, we can develop new content together based on your requirements."

Mr. Fischer looked thoughtful. "And beyond one-off visits, is there scope for ongoing projects or partnerships?"

"Yes, there is," Anna answered. "We're very interested in establishing long-term partnerships. For instance, we could set up a semester-long project where students create a documentary or digital archive based on their research and interviews conducted here."

Ms. Browning seemed particularly interested. "That would be an invaluable experience for them. How do we handle the logistics of scheduling and transportation?"

"We can work together to schedule sessions well in advance, and we can also help coordinate transportation if needed," Anna explained. "We want to remove as many barriers as possible to student participation."

Dr. Hennings nodded, jotting down some notes. "What about metrics or feedback mechanisms? How do we measure the success of our collaboration?"

"We gather feedback from all participants after each session, and we can provide you with detailed reports on student engagement and learning outcomes," Anna detailed. "We can also adjust the programs based on this feedback, ensuring that they meet the students' needs and learning goals effectively."

The meeting continued with a lively exchange of ideas and possibilities. Each administrator and teacher brought different perspectives and needs, enriching the discussion and helping Anna and her team shape a versatile educational outreach program.

As the meeting concluded, the group agreed to start with a pilot program involving schools from each educational level. They scheduled a follow-up meeting to finalize the details and begin the implementation phase.

Anna felt energized by the productive discussion and the potential impact of these partnerships. Walking back to her office, she reflected on how the center was becoming a vital part of the educational landscape in Berlin, not just preserving history, but actively participating in the educational development of the city's youth.

After the successful meeting with local educators, Anna was motivated to ensure that the pilot educational programs launched without a hitch. Over the next few weeks, she and her team worked tirelessly, preparing customized educational materials and training the center's staff to handle the influx of students expected from the collaboration.

The first of these sessions was designed for a group of high school students studying World War II and its impact on Berlin. The center had curated a special exhibition that included personal letters, photographs, and artifacts from the era, which were interspersed with interactive digital displays allowing students to explore historical events through personal stories.

On the morning the students arrived, the air at the center was charged with a sense of purpose. As the young visitors filed in, their expressions ranged from curiosity to awe as they gazed around at the high ceilings and the historical treasures on display. Anna welcomed them with a brief introduction about the center and its mission, emphasizing the importance of understanding history through personal narratives.

"Today, you will get a chance to see history from a personal perspective, which can often be quite different from what you read in textbooks," she explained to the group, her voice echoing slightly in the large open space.

The students were then divided into smaller groups and assigned a guide who led them through the exhibition. They were encouraged to interact with the displays, listening to audio recordings of personal accounts, and using tablets provided by the center to dig deeper into the historical context of each artifact.

One display, in particular, captured their attention—a series of letters exchanged between a soldier on the Eastern Front and his family in Berlin. The raw emotion and everyday concerns expressed in these letters provided a stark contrast to the grand narratives of war strategies and political alliances that dominated their textbooks.

Throughout the visit, the students took notes and asked thoughtful questions, engaging with the material in a way that was both respectful and keenly inquisitive. Anna observed from a distance, pleased with the level of engagement and the insightful discussions sparked by the exhibits.

As the session came to an end, the students gathered for a closing discussion led by one of the center's historians. They shared their reflections on what they had learned and how the personal stories had affected their understanding of the historical events.

"It's one thing to learn about history. It's another to feel it," one student remarked, summarizing the sentiment of many in the room.

The feedback from the teachers accompanying the students was overwhelmingly positive. They appreciated the depth of the material and the unique approach the center took towards historical education. Many expressed interest in arranging more visits and even suggested topics for future sessions.

After the students left, Anna and her team debriefed, discussing what had gone well and what could be improved for future sessions. The success of the day was evident not only in the positive feedback but also in the animated discussions it had inspired among the students.

The pilot program's initial success gave Anna and her team the confidence to expand their offerings, and they began to plan additional sessions for other schools and age groups, each tailored to different aspects of Berlin's complex history.

As the day wound down, Anna walked through the now-quiet exhibition space, reflecting on the profound impact that these personal stories had on young minds. She felt a deep satisfaction knowing that the center was fulfilling its mission, making history accessible and engaging for a new generation. This was just the beginning, she thought, as she turned off the lights and closed the doors for the night. The center would continue to grow, evolve, and serve as a bridge between the past and the present, helping to shape a more informed and thoughtful future.

Buoyed by the success of the pilot educational program, Anna was eager to explore further opportunities to enrich the Center for Personal History's offerings. To gather ideas and input, she organized a brainstorming session with her team and several invited experts in history education and multimedia technology. The session was held in a collaborative space at the center, walls lined with inspiring quotes and images from Berlin's past, fostering a creative and reflective environment.

As the team gathered around a large, round table cluttered with notes and laptops, Anna initiated the discussion. "Thank you all for joining today. We've seen fantastic results from our initial school collaborations, and I'd like to explore how we can use technology to enhance our programs further. Any thoughts on how we might integrate new tech to make history even more tangible for our visitors?"

Miles, a tech consultant specializing in educational tools, was quick to respond. "One idea could be to use augmented reality (AR) to bring historical photos and scenes to life. Imagine students being able to point a device at a photo and see the scene unfold in front of them as if they were there."

"That sounds fascinating," Julia interjected, her eyes alight with excitement. "It would be a compelling way to connect visitors with history, making it feel immediate and immersive. Could we also incorporate interactive timelines or maps that evolve as you walk through the exhibit?"

"Yes, that's entirely feasible," Miles confirmed. "We can create interactive, augmented displays that respond to the user's movements, providing information and visuals that change depending on where they stand or what they point their device at."

Anna, pleased with the direction of the conversation, turned to a history educator, Dr. Larson. "Dr. Larson, from an educational perspective, how can we ensure that these technologies enhance learning without overwhelming the historical content?"

Dr. Larson nodded thoughtfully. "It's important to maintain a balance. The technology should serve as a bridge to deeper understanding, not a distraction. Each interactive element should be carefully designed to expand on the narrative or provide context that deepens the visitor's connection to the material."

"Absolutely," Anna agreed. "We need to integrate technology in a way that complements and enhances the storytelling, not competes with it. Could we pilot a small project to test these ideas?"

"I think a pilot would be an excellent way to gauge effectiveness and gather feedback," Miles suggested. "Perhaps start with a single exhibit or event to see how visitors respond and what impact it has on their understanding and engagement."

"I like that approach," Anna said. "Let's identify a forthcoming exhibit that could benefit from this technology. We could design the AR components to supplement the existing materials and see how it enhances the visitor experience."

As the meeting drew to a close, the team outlined a plan to develop the AR pilot, assigning tasks and setting deadlines. Anna thanked everyone for their contributions. "This has been an incredibly productive session. I'm excited to see how these ideas will come to life and enhance our mission here at the center."

After the team dispersed, Anna stayed behind, looking over the notes and sketches that covered the table. The potential to further bridge past and present through technology was thrilling. As she collected the papers, her thoughts were on how each new tool and approach could help demystify history, making it more accessible and engaging.

Leaving the meeting room, Anna felt energized by the creative possibilities ahead. The center was quickly becoming not just a repository of history, but a dynamic space where the past met the future, engaging new audiences in ways that once seemed the realm of fiction. This, she reflected, was just the beginning of a new chapter in how history could be experienced and learned.

The selected exhibit to pilot the augmented reality (AR) project was one focusing on the Berlin Wall, a topic rich with personal stories and historical significance. As the project team gathered to discuss the integration of AR elements into the exhibit, the excitement was palpable. The meeting took place in a small, informal setup within the center, surrounded by artifacts and images from the era.

Anna initiated the discussion, her tone infused with enthusiasm. "This AR project has the potential to transform how our visitors connect with the history of the Berlin Wall. I think it's crucial we get every detail right. Let's start with the content. What specific stories or elements do we want to bring to life using AR?"

Miles, ready with his tablet, showcased a mock-up of the AR interface. "We can start by animating several key events, like the construction of the wall, major escapes, and its eventual fall. Users can point their devices at different sections of the exhibit to see these events unfold."

"That's fantastic," Julia chimed in. "We should also include personal stories. I can gather narratives from individuals affected by the Wall—those who lived in its shadow, those who were separated from family, and even guards who were stationed there."

"Absolutely," Anna agreed. "These personal narratives are what set our center apart. How will these stories be presented in the AR experience?"

"We can use audio clips, triggered by the AR app," Miles suggested. "As visitors point their device at specific photos or objects, they can hear people narrate their experiences in their own words. It would be a powerful way to make history feel immediate and personal."

Dr. Larson, who had been listening intently, added, "It's important that we contextualize these stories. Each AR experience should be accompanied by historical facts that help visitors understand the broader implications of these personal experiences."

"Good point," Anna nodded. "We need to ensure that while the AR makes the exhibit more engaging, it also educates. We'll include pop-up texts or a narrated guide that provides this context."

Julia, taking notes, looked up. "What about the technical side, Miles? What do we need to ensure the AR is seamless and user-friendly?"

"We'll need high-quality visuals and stable software to make sure the AR is responsive and doesn't detract from the experience with technical issues," Miles explained. "I'll work closely with the software developers to make sure the app is intuitive and informative. We should also have several testing phases to collect feedback and make adjustments."

"That sounds like a solid plan," Anna confirmed. "Let's also think about accessibility. We want everyone, regardless of their tech-savvy, to benefit from this AR experience."

"We can have volunteers on hand to assist visitors with the AR technology," Julia suggested. "And maybe also offer simpler, non-AR versions of the same narratives for those who prefer it."

"Great idea," Anna smiled. "Ensuring accessibility is key. Alright, team, let's proceed with these ideas. Miles, you'll oversee the technical development with the developers. Julia, you gather the narratives and work on the content with Dr. Larson. I'll coordinate with the rest of the center's staff and start planning for the exhibit's launch."

As the meeting wrapped up, the team felt a collective anticipation about the project. They were not just creating an exhibit; they were setting a new standard for historical engagement. As they left the meeting room, their conversation continued, buzzing with ideas and possibilities.

Anna stayed behind for a moment, looking over the plans laid out across the table. The potential to bring history to life in such a dynamic way was both exhilarating and daunting. But she knew that with her team's passion and expertise, they were on the brink of something truly special.

Stepping out of the room, Anna was ready to guide this ambitious project to fruition, envisioning the day when visitors would not only learn about history but would feel as if they had stepped right into it, thanks to the wonders of augmented reality.

Chapter 23
Closing In

As the augmented reality (AR) project neared completion, the atmosphere at the Center for Personal History was one of focused intensity. The exhibit on the Berlin Wall was set to be a groundbreaking blend of technology and storytelling, designed to transport visitors directly into the heart of Berlin's past. With just a few weeks until launch, Anna oversaw the integration of the AR elements into the physical setup, ensuring that the digital enhancements seamlessly complemented the physical artifacts and displays.

The final element of the project involved a detailed review of the historical content and the technological functionality. Anna worked closely with Miles and a team of software developers who were busy debugging the final version of the AR application. The application was designed to be intuitive, allowing users to simply point their smartphones or tablets at different markers throughout the exhibit to activate various AR experiences.

Each station within the exhibit focused on a key aspect of the Berlin Wall's history—from its sudden construction in 1961, which cleaved the city in two, to the poignant stories of separation and the jubilant scenes of its fall in 1989. One station, in particular, featured a poignant audio recording of a family divided overnight, complemented by ghostly AR images of family members on either side of the wall, reaching out toward one another.

Meanwhile, Julia curated the content with a meticulous hand, ensuring every story was respectfully and accurately presented. She had spent weeks interviewing contemporary witnesses and digging through archives to gather personal stories that were both impactful and representative. These narratives were now embedded within the AR experience, giving voices to those who had lived through the historical events.

Dr. Larson contributed by ensuring all supplemental historical information was factually accurate and provided the necessary context for the AR visuals. His expertise helped balance the vivid personal stories with a broader historical perspective, enriching the visitors' learning experience.

As the project came together, Anna often walked through the exhibit after hours, testing the AR features. With each marker she scanned, the history of the Berlin Wall came alive around her. She watched as a virtual crowd gathered at Brandenburg Gate, listened to the whispers of a secret tunnel excavation, and felt the tension of a checkpoint crossing—all rendered in stunning visual detail through the AR interface.

The integration of AR technology into historical exhibits was a bold move, and Anna felt the weight of expectation to deliver a meaningful, engaging experience. She knew that the success of this exhibit could set a precedent for future displays, not just within her center but in museums and educational settings everywhere.

In the final days before the exhibit's launch, the center buzzed with activity. Technicians adjusted lights and audio levels, while historians and educators reviewed every piece of content for accuracy and impact. Anna coordinated these efforts with a calm yet commanding presence, driven by a vision of making history accessible and immersive through modern technology.

As the launch day approached, the team held a final meeting to discuss logistics and visitor flow. Anna encouraged her team, emphasizing the importance of this project not just as an exhibit but as an educational tool that could redefine how history was experienced and understood.

The day before the launch, Anna walked through the exhibit one last time, watching as the final adjustments were made. Each step through the exhibit reassured her that they had achieved what they set out to do—create a space where history was not just displayed but experienced, where past events were not just remembered but felt.

With everything in place, the center closed for the evening, and Anna stepped out into the cooling air of Berlin, the city's own history reflecting back at her from every stone and corner. Tomorrow, she would see her vision become a reality, and she was ready to share this new way of experiencing history with the world.

Launch day for the augmented reality (AR) exhibit at the Center for Personal History arrived with an air of electric anticipation. Early in the morning, Anna, alongside her team, gathered in the main exhibit hall to go over the day's schedule and address any last-minute details.

"Team, this is a big day for us," Anna began, looking around at the assembled group, each member attentive and ready. "We've all worked incredibly hard to bring this project to life. Let's ensure we provide our visitors with an unforgettable experience today. Any final thoughts or concerns before we open the doors?"

Miles, who had been double-checking the AR equipment, looked up. "All the AR stations have been tested and are fully operational. I'll be on hand to troubleshoot any issues, but we shouldn't expect any major problems."

"That's great to hear, Miles," Anna responded, her tone conveying both relief and confidence. "Julia, how are we handling the guided tours today?"

Julia, clutching a clipboard with the day's schedule, nodded. "We have guided tours starting every half hour. I've briefed all our guides this morning, and they're ready to assist visitors and enhance their experience with additional insights about the Wall and the personal stories integrated into the AR experience."

"Perfect, Julia. And the reception area?" Anna asked, turning to Henrik who was overseeing the front of house operations.

"We're all set up," Henrik confirmed. "The reception team is ready. We've also set up additional signage to help guide visitors through the exhibit, ensuring a smooth flow."

"Excellent," Anna said, her gaze sweeping the room. "Let's remember, today is not just about showcasing our technological advancements but about making a deep, meaningful impact on how people understand history through personal narratives. Let's make it a day to remember."

As the doors opened to the public, the first group of visitors entered, their expressions a mix of curiosity and excitement. Anna watched from a distance as families, students, and history enthusiasts began interacting with the AR features. She approached a family that was using their device to unlock an AR scene depicting a dramatic escape attempt from East to West Berlin.

"How are you finding the experience?" Anna asked the group, a smile playing on her lips.

"It's incredible," replied the father, holding up his tablet that displayed the vivid AR scene. "We've read about the Wall, but seeing it like this, hearing the stories—it's very powerful."

"I'm glad to hear you think so," Anna said. "We hope it makes the history more relatable."

Nearby, a group of students clustered around another AR station, where a virtual scene of a famous speech at the Wall was playing. Julia, who was guiding the group, asked, "What do you all think about the way the speech has been presented?"

"It's like stepping back in time," one student exclaimed, her eyes wide with amazement. "It's one thing to hear about these events, but it's another to see and feel them as if you're there."

Julia nodded, pleased with the feedback. "That's exactly what we aimed for. We want you to not only learn history but to experience it."

Throughout the day, Anna and her team interacted with visitors, gathering feedback and observing the engagement. The response was overwhelmingly positive, with many expressing a deeper connection to the historical events through the personal stories brought to life by the AR technology.

As the day drew to a close, Anna convened a brief meeting with her team to debrief. "Today was a testament to what we can achieve when we combine technology with storytelling. The reactions from our visitors were incredibly affirming," she reflected, the fatigue of the day overshadowed by her enthusiasm.

"Yes, they were," Miles agreed. "It's rewarding to see how the technology can enhance understanding and empathy for historical events."

"Let's build on this," Anna concluded, her mind already racing with ideas for future projects. "The potential for expanding our use of AR is vast. Today was just the beginning."

With the successful launch behind them, the team felt a renewed sense of purpose. As they left the exhibit hall, turning off lights and closing doors, the echoes of the day's success lingered in the air, a promise of more innovative historical storytelling yet to come.

The success of the augmented reality (AR) exhibit on the Berlin Wall set a new precedent at the Center for Personal History, sparking ideas for additional technologically-enhanced exhibits. Riding the wave of this success, Anna planned a strategy meeting to explore these new ideas further. She invited her core team along with several external experts in history, technology, and educational theory to brainstorm the potential expansions.

The meeting room buzzed with anticipation as participants gathered around a large conference table, each equipped with notes and devices. Anna opened the discussion with a nod to their recent success.

"First, I want to say thank you to everyone for the roles you've played in making the Berlin Wall exhibit a landmark project for the center," Anna began, her voice filled with genuine gratitude and excitement. "Today, I'd like us to think about how we can apply what we've learned to other areas of our historical narrative. What other periods or events in history could benefit from an AR approach?"

Miles, ever eager to push the envelope on technological integration, was quick to respond. "I think the post-war reconstruction of Berlin could be an incredible story to tell through AR. Imagine visitors being able to see the city rebuild around them, perhaps even participate in decision-making processes about the city's layout and architecture through interactive scenarios."

"That's an excellent idea," Julia chimed in. "It ties in well with our educational goals. Students could really benefit from a hands-on understanding of urban development and historical consequences."

Dr. Larson, the resident historian, added, "We could also consider expanding the scope to include the Cold War era. There's a wealth of untapped personal stories and unseen footage that could be brought to life, providing a vivid contrast between East and West Berlin during that tense period."

Anna nodded thoughtfully, jotting down notes. "Those are both compelling suggestions. How do we ensure that these experiences are not only technologically engaging but also historically accurate and respectful of the narratives?"

"We should continue to collaborate closely with historians and eyewitnesses," Dr. Larson suggested. "Perhaps even more rigorously than before. For every technological feature we want to implement, we need a solid historical foundation."

"That's a crucial point," Anna agreed. "Julia, could you elaborate on how we might enhance the educational impact of these new exhibits?"

Julia leaned forward, her enthusiasm evident. "Certainly. Alongside the AR experiences, we could develop a series of workshops and seminars that delve deeper into the themes presented. For instance, following an AR experience of the Cold War, we could have a seminar on the political ideologies at play, facilitated by experts in the field."

"That would be a valuable addition," Anna responded. "It would provide depth and encourage more profound reflection and discussion among our visitors."

Miles, tapping on his tablet, brought up another point. "We should also consider the technology aspect—ensuring our infrastructure can handle more complex AR applications and increased visitor interactions. This might mean upgrading our hardware or even designing a dedicated app to manage content delivery."

"That's a good point, Miles. Let's make sure we have the IT infrastructure to support these ideas," Anna noted. "Now, thinking about logistics, how do we phase these projects? Should we focus on one exhibit at a time, or parallel develop several?"

"I think a phased approach might work best," suggested Henrik, who had been listening intently. "It allows us to build on the momentum of each successful launch and continuously refine our process based on visitor feedback."

"Agreed," Anna concluded, feeling a surge of excitement for the future. "Let's start detailed planning on the post-war reconstruction exhibit first, then use that as a springboard for the Cold War exhibit."

As the meeting drew to a close, the team was animated, discussing various ideas and potential partnerships that could help bring these projects to life. Anna felt a profound sense of pride and responsibility as she facilitated these discussions. The center was not just preserving history but was actively engaging a broad audience in its living narrative.

Leaving the conference room, the echoes of the day's energetic planning filled the corridor, resonating with the promise of new projects that would further bridge the gap between past and present.

As the Center for Personal History moved forward with its ambitious plans for expanding AR exhibits, Anna convened a project kickoff meeting with the newly formed development teams. The focus was on the upcoming post-war reconstruction exhibit. The room was set with multiple displays, each ready to show visualizations of potential AR experiences, as team members from various disciplines—history, technology, design, and education—gathered to align their visions and responsibilities.

"Good morning, everyone," Anna began, standing at the front of the room with an air of calm authority. "Today marks the beginning of a significant project for our center—one that will not only expand our use of augmented reality but also deepen our audience's understanding of Berlin's post-war reconstruction. Each of you plays a crucial role in this. Let's start by defining the main historical themes and technological innovations we want to incorporate. Miles, can you kick us off with the tech overview?"

Miles nodded, clicking his presentation to life. "Certainly, Anna. For the post-war reconstruction exhibit, we're planning to implement a layered

AR approach. This means visitors can select different levels of information—architectural, personal stories, or political context—depending on their interest. Each layer will be accessible via user-controlled settings in the AR app, which we'll develop to be intuitive and user-friendly."

"That sounds excellent," Julia interjected. "For the content layers, I suggest we start with personal stories that highlight how individuals contributed to the rebuilding efforts, how daily life changed, and the challenges they faced. These stories can be powerful draws that engage visitors emotionally."

Dr. Larson, the team's historian, added, "I agree with Julia. Additionally, we should include an architectural layer that shows before-and-after visuals of key Berlin landmarks. It would be fascinating to provide historical context and then allow visitors to 'rebuild' these sites through interactive AR simulations."

"That's a great idea," Anna responded, visibly pleased. "It aligns perfectly with our educational goals. How do we ensure the historical accuracy of these simulations?"

Dr. Larson nodded thoughtfully. "We'll need to conduct thorough research, perhaps collaborate with local archives and universities. We can also consult with historians who specialize in this era. Accuracy is paramount, as these reconstructions will heavily influence visitor perceptions."

Henrik, overseeing the logistical aspects, then spoke up. "On the practical side, we'll need to scale up our hardware installations in the exhibit space to handle these interactive elements. I'll coordinate with tech suppliers to ensure we have the necessary equipment installed and tested well before launch."

"Thank you, Henrik," Anna said. "Now, turning to the educational programs tied to the exhibit—Julia, what's your vision there?"

Julia was quick to outline her plans. "I'm thinking of setting up a series of workshops for students and adults alike. These could include hands-on sessions where participants learn about the materials and techniques used in post-war construction, or discussions led by contemporary witnesses or experts in the field."

"That would certainly enrich the exhibit," Anna agreed. "Let's ensure those programs are as interactive and engaging as the AR components. Also, let's think about accessibility. We want everyone, regardless of their familiarity with AR technology, to benefit from this exhibit."

Miles reassured her, "We'll design the app with various accessibility features, including voice narration for those who might find AR interfaces challenging."

As the meeting drew to a close, the team felt energized and aligned with a clear sense of direction. "This project is a step forward in how we engage with history," Anna concluded. "Let's keep communication open and regular. We're breaking new ground here, and I'm confident we'll create something truly impactful."

With that, the team dispersed, ready to tackle their individual tasks. Anna remained behind, reviewing the notes from the meeting. Each line spoke of potential and promise, each task a piece of the puzzle that was bringing a forgotten chapter of Berlin's history back to vivid life.

Chapter 24
The Ambush

As the development of the post-war reconstruction exhibit progressed, Anna organized a review meeting with the project team to assess the progress and integrate any necessary adjustments based on the initial feedback from a closed beta testing group. The group had been selected to experience the exhibit's AR features and provide insight into both its educational impact and user experience.

Gathered in the conference room, the team listened intently as Anna initiated the discussion. "Thank you all for coming. Today, we need to evaluate the feedback from our beta testers and decide how it might influence our final adjustments. Let's start with the general reactions. Miles, could you summarize the feedback on the AR technology?"

Miles nodded, pulling up data on his laptop. "Overall, the reactions to the AR technology were quite positive. Testers were impressed with the ability to interactively 'rebuild' historical sites. However, there were comments about the interface being a bit complex for first-time users. We might need to simplify the navigation and ensure the instructions are clearer."

"That's a good point," Anna replied. "It's crucial that our exhibit is accessible to everyone, regardless of their tech experience. Julia, what feedback do we have on the content, particularly the personal stories and historical information?"

Julia flipped through her notes. "The personal stories were very well-received. They added a human element to the historical events that really resonated with our testers. But there was a suggestion to increase the number of stories from diverse perspectives to provide a broader understanding of the period. Also, some testers wanted more in-depth historical context to fully appreciate the significance of what they were seeing."

"I see," Anna said thoughtfully. "Dr. Larson, could you work with Julia to incorporate more diverse narratives and ensure we have robust historical details accompanying each AR scene?"

"Absolutely," Dr. Larson agreed. "I'll consult additional sources and maybe reach out to some more contemporary witnesses. We need to ensure the historical accuracy and comprehensiveness of the narratives."

Henrik, who had been managing the logistical aspects, then brought up another point. "Regarding the physical layout of the exhibit, some testers felt that the flow between sections was a bit disjointed. We might need to rethink the spatial arrangement to ensure a more intuitive visitor journey."

"That's important feedback," Anna acknowledged. "Let's make sure the physical journey through the exhibit mirrors the chronological and thematic progression of the history we're presenting. Henrik, can you coordinate with the design team on that?"

"Will do," Henrik confirmed. "I'll work with them on rearranging the sections for a smoother flow."

Anna then addressed the group with a note of encouragement. "This feedback is invaluable. It's exactly why we conduct these tests—to make our exhibit as impactful and user-friendly as possible. Any other thoughts or concerns before we proceed with the adjustments?"

Miles mentioned, "We should also consider enhancing the support for the AR app. Maybe add a quick help feature or even staff-assisted stations for those who need assistance."

"That's an excellent idea," Julia supported. "Engagement shouldn't be hindered by technological hurdles."

Anna concluded the meeting with a reaffirmation of the project's goals. "Our mission with this exhibit is not only to educate but to immerse and move our visitors. Each adjustment we make should aim to enrich their experience. Let's take this feedback and use it to refine our exhibit into an educational tool that truly resonates."

The team dispersed, each member clear on their responsibilities and motivated by the constructive feedback. Anna stayed back to review the notes once more, ensuring no detail was overlooked. As she organized her papers, her commitment to bringing history to life in a meaningful, accessible way was stronger than ever. This project was more than just an exhibit; it was a bridge connecting past to present, inviting everyone to explore and understand the complexities of Berlin's history.

In preparation for the public launch of the post-war reconstruction exhibit, Anna scheduled a final team meeting to go over the adjustments made following the beta feedback. The meeting was held in the center's main hall, where sections of the exhibit had been updated and refined. As team members gathered around the designated area, the sense of anticipation was palpable.

Anna started the meeting with a warm greeting, "Thank you, everyone, for joining today. We've made significant changes based on the feedback, and I believe we've greatly improved our exhibit. Let's go through these adjustments and ensure everything is aligned for the launch."

Miles, who had been instrumental in refining the AR technology, was eager to share the updates. "We've simplified the user interface of the AR app, making navigation more intuitive. We've also added quick-help icons that are easily accessible from every screen, ensuring users can get assistance without needing to leave their current session."

"That sounds great, Miles. How about the responsiveness issues that were raised?" Anna asked, focusing on ensuring the technical aspects were flawless.

"The app is now faster, with less lag between user actions and AR responses," Miles confirmed. "We've optimized the software and even upgraded some of the hardware on our end to handle the processing more efficiently."

Julia chimed in, discussing the content enhancements, "We've enriched the personal narratives within the exhibit. I've added stories from a wider range of perspectives, including women and children, who were particularly affected by the post-war reconstruction. Each story is now accompanied by archival images and documents, where available, to deepen the visitor's engagement."

Dr. Larson, always concerned with historical accuracy, added, "I've reviewed all the historical content again, ensuring everything is up to academic standards. We've also expanded the informational pop-ups to include more context about the socio-political climate of post-war Berlin, giving visitors a better understanding of the magnitude of the city's transformation."

Anna nodded appreciatively, then turned to Henrik, who was overseeing the exhibit layout. "Henrik, how have we addressed the flow issues within the exhibit space?"

"We've rearranged the exhibit sections to create a more logical chronological flow. Now, visitors will move through the exhibit in a way that mirrors the historical timeline of events, making the entire experience more coherent," Henrik explained. "We've also increased signage and added directional floor markings to guide visitors through the space more effectively."

"That's excellent," Anna said, satisfied with the progress. "What about the integration of the new sections into the existing layout?"

"We've managed to integrate seamlessly," Henrik assured her. "The new sections don't just fit in terms of space, but they also complement and enhance the stories told in the older parts of the exhibit. It feels like a complete narrative now, rather than disjointed pieces."

Anna looked around at her team, feeling a surge of pride. "This has been a massive effort, and I want to thank each of you for your dedication and expertise. We are not just launching an exhibit; we are setting a new standard for how history can be experienced and understood. Let's make sure we maintain this level of excellence through to the launch and beyond."

As the meeting concluded, the team dispersed to handle their respective tasks, each person motivated by the project's potential. Anna lingered in the exhibit space, reviewing every detail of the installation. The stories of the past were about to come alive in a way they never had before, and she felt both the weight of responsibility and the excitement of innovation. This was not just another exhibit; it was a portal to the past, crafted with the technology of the future.

On the eve of the exhibit's public launch, Anna convened a final walkthrough with her team to ensure that every element of the post-war reconstruction exhibit was perfected. As they gathered in the main hall of the Center for Personal History, the sense of collective accomplishment was palpable, yet underscored by a keen awareness of the details that needed last-minute attention.

Anna addressed her team with a mix of command and encouragement. "This is our final check before we open our doors tomorrow. I want us to go through the exhibit one last time, focusing on the functionality of the AR features, the clarity of the informational content, and the overall visitor experience. Let's start with the AR functionality. Miles, have all the updates been fully integrated?"

"Yes, Anna," Miles replied, holding up his tablet with the AR application running. "All updates are integrated and functioning smoothly. The interface is cleaner, and the response time has improved significantly. We've also added a feature that allows users to leave feedback on each AR experience directly through the app."

"That's excellent," Anna responded, visibly pleased. "Let's make sure that feedback feature is easily noticeable to users. Julia, how about the content? Are all the new narratives integrated and clearly displayed?"

Julia nodded, her eyes scanning her clipboard filled with notes. "Yes, all narratives are in place, and we've included QR codes next to each exhibit that visitors can scan to access further detailed stories and historical documents. We've made sure that these are both visible and accessible."

"Good work, Julia. Dr. Larson, have all historical dates and facts been double-checked against our latest research to ensure accuracy?"

Dr. Larson, always meticulous, confirmed, "I've personally reviewed all the historical content this morning. Everything is accurate and reflects the latest academic research. We've also included additional context for some of the more complex events to ensure that all visitors, regardless of their prior knowledge, can fully appreciate the significance of what they're experiencing."

"Thank you, Dr. Larson. Henrik, talk to us about visitor flow and signage," Anna directed her attention next to the logistical aspects, critical for a smooth opening day.

Henrik spread out a map of the exhibit on a nearby table. "We've set up directional signage throughout the exhibit, and I've coordinated with the staff to manage visitor flow, especially in the AR interactive zones, to prevent any bottlenecks. Additionally, we've scheduled group tours at staggered times to evenly distribute visitors throughout the day."

"Excellent foresight, Henrik. It's crucial that our first visitors have a positive experience. They will be our advocates moving forward," Anna said, turning to address the entire group. "Everyone, this exhibit is more than just a collection of dates and facts. It's a narrative tapestry that we've woven together, each thread enriched by our dedication and expertise. Tomorrow, we share that story with the world."

As they moved through the exhibit during the walkthrough, testing each interactive station and reviewing every panel, the team felt a growing sense of pride. They paused occasionally to discuss minor tweaks—adjusting the lighting here, repositioning an informational placard there—but the overall sense was one of readiness.

"Thank you, everyone, for your hard work and dedication," Anna concluded as they finished their tour. "Let's meet here early tomorrow to prepare for the opening. We're ready to make history come alive like never before."

The team dispersed, leaving Anna alone in the quiet hall. She took a moment to reflect on the journey that had brought them to this point. Each decision, each discovery, had been a step towards this day. Now, on the cusp of unveiling their work to the public, Anna felt a profound connection to the past they were about to bring to life, and a hopeful gaze towards the future it would inspire.

The morning of the exhibit's launch dawned clear and bright, casting a hopeful light over the Center for Personal History. The team gathered early, buzzing with last-minute preparations and the excitement of showcasing their hard work to the public. Anna, calm yet visibly eager, checked in with each member of her team to ensure everything was in order for the grand opening.

"Good morning, everyone. Let's start with a quick round to confirm that all systems are go," Anna began, addressing her team assembled in the main lobby, which was already beginning to fill with early visitors.

Miles, checking his tablet, reported first. "All AR systems have been booted up and are running smoothly. I've done a final sweep, and all interactive points are responsive. The feedback feature is live and prominently displayed within the app."

"That's great to hear, Miles. Thank you," Anna nodded with satisfaction. "Julia, are the docents ready with their material, and is the educational content all set?"

Julia, who had been coordinating with the educational team, confirmed, "Yes, all docents are briefed and ready. They're excited to engage with the visitors and share the rich stories we've prepared. The educational materials for schools have been distributed to our first visiting groups."

"Perfect. Dr. Larson, any last-minute concerns about the historical content or the informational accuracy within the exhibit?" Anna turned to Dr. Larson, who had taken a final walk through the exhibit earlier.

"No concerns, Anna. Everything is accurate, and I've placed supplementary reading material at key points for visitors who want deeper dives into specific topics," Dr. Larson responded, adjusting his glasses with a satisfied look.

"And Henrik, how are we looking on logistics? Is the exhibit flow as smooth as we hoped?" Anna's final check was on the visitor experience, crucial for the day's success.

Henrik, looking over the layout map, replied, "All is set. Signage is clear, and the flow guides visitors naturally through the exhibit. We've also prepared for high traffic, with additional staff on hand to guide our guests."

"Excellent," Anna said, her voice carrying a blend of relief and anticipation. "Thank you, everyone, for your incredible efforts. Let's open the doors and welcome our guests."

As the doors officially opened, visitors began streaming in, their faces filled with curiosity. Anna and her team watched as people of all ages engaged with the AR features, listened intently to the docents, and interacted with the exhibit. The real-time feedback started coming in through the app, and Miles monitored it closely, ready to make any necessary adjustments.

Throughout the day, Anna spoke with many visitors, gathering their impressions and experiences. "What did you think of the AR features?" she would ask, or "Did the stories resonate with you?"

One visitor, a local history teacher, was particularly impressed. "The way you've brought these personal stories into the broader historical narrative is fantastic. It's engaging for students and really brings the history to life."

"Thank you," Anna replied, genuinely pleased. "We hope it makes the history more accessible and impactful."

As the day progressed, the feedback was overwhelmingly positive. Visitors appreciated the depth of the narratives and the innovative use of technology. The educational aspects were also well-received, with several teachers expressing interest in arranging school trips.

By late afternoon, as the visitor flow began to slow, Anna gathered her team for a brief recap of the day. "This has been a remarkable launch. The feedback we've received today is invaluable, and it seems we've truly touched our visitors with the history we've presented."

The team shared their observations and discussed minor tweaks to improve the experience further, but the overall sentiment was one of accomplishment and pride.

As the sun began to set, casting long shadows across the exhibit halls, Anna took one last walk through the exhibit. Watching the history of Berlin come alive around her, she felt a deep connection to every story told and every visitor who walked the halls. The project was more than just an exhibit; it was a new way to experience history, a bridge connecting the past to the present, and she was already looking forward to the future possibilities.

Chapter 25
The Final Run

Several months after the successful launch of the post-war reconstruction exhibit, the Center for Personal History had seen a significant increase in visitor numbers and educational engagement. Riding on this wave of success, Anna decided it was time to plan further expansions and improvements. She organized a strategic planning meeting with her team and key stakeholders to discuss the future direction of the center.

As they assembled in the conference room, equipped with notes and laptops, Anna began the session with an overview of the center's achievements and the opportunities ahead. "Thanks to everyone's hard work, we've had a phenomenal response to our recent exhibits. Today, I want us to think about what comes next. How can we build on our current success to further our mission?"

Henrik, who had been instrumental in improving the visitor experience, was the first to respond. "One area we could expand is our interactive technology. The AR has been a hit, but I think there's potential to integrate virtual reality (VR) for more immersive experiences. This could especially enhance exhibits that are heavy on narrative, like historical events or personal stories."

"That's an intriguing idea," Anna replied, nodding thoughtfully. "VR could indeed take our immersive experiences to the next level. Julia, from an educational perspective, how do you see us integrating this into our programs?"

Julia leaned forward, her enthusiasm evident. "VR could be revolutionary for our educational workshops. We could create simulations that allow students to 'live' through historical events, making complex concepts more accessible and engaging. It would also be an excellent tool for special needs education, providing alternative learning modalities."

Dr. Larson, always concerned with the integrity of the historical content, added, "While I see the potential benefits of VR, we must ensure that our use of such technology remains grounded in accurate historical representation. It's crucial that these experiences are not only engaging but also educationally sound and historically precise."

"Absolutely," Anna agreed. "We'll need to work closely with historians and technologists to develop content that is both compelling and correct. Miles, could you look into the technical feasibility and cost implications of integrating VR?"

Miles nodded, already jotting down notes. "I'll start researching the latest VR technology and reach out to potential tech partners. We'll need to consider not just the installation and maintenance costs, but also ongoing content development and updates."

"Good," Anna said, turning her attention back to the group. "Another area for expansion is our community outreach. We've made great strides in involving local communities in our projects, but I think there's room to grow, especially in reaching underrepresented groups."

"I agree," Julia chimed in. "Perhaps we could develop targeted outreach programs that specifically address the needs and interests of these groups. This could include multilingual tours, workshops designed with community input, and even traveling exhibits that go into community centers and schools."

"That's an excellent approach," Anna responded. "It ensures that our educational impact extends beyond the walls of the center. Henrik, could you work with Julia on a proposal for this?"

"Will do," Henrik confirmed, making a note. "I think these programs could significantly boost our community engagement and help in securing additional funding from sources interested in educational and cultural outreach."

As the meeting continued, the team discussed various logistical and strategic aspects of these initiatives. They set preliminary goals, assigned responsibilities, and agreed on timelines for researching and implementing the new ideas.

With a clear plan in place, the meeting concluded on a high note, with the team feeling motivated and optimistic about the future. As they left the conference room, Anna lingered for a moment, reflecting on the journey so far and the exciting path ahead. The center was evolving, not just as a repository of history but as a vibrant, interactive hub that brought history to life for all ages and backgrounds. This new chapter was just beginning, and Anna was ready to lead her team into the future, where history was not only told but experienced.

With the strategic initiatives outlined and the team charged with new responsibilities, the following weeks at the Center for Personal History were bustling with activity. Anna was focused on tracking the progress of the new projects, particularly the integration of virtual reality (VR) into the existing exhibits, which had the potential to redefine the visitor experience significantly.

One afternoon, Anna convened a progress meeting in her office, where Miles was ready to report on the technical aspects of incorporating VR into the center's offerings. The sunlight filtered softly through the blinds, casting a warm glow over the room as they prepared to delve into the specifics of the project.

"How is the VR integration coming along, Miles?" Anna asked, her tone a mix of curiosity and urgency.

Miles, enthusiastic as ever, began detailing the technical side. "We've made good headway. I've been in discussions with several VR platform developers and have identified a couple of potential partners who are excited about our project. The technology has advanced significantly, allowing us to create truly immersive historical environments."

"That sounds promising," Anna replied. "But what are the cost implications? We need to ensure that this investment is justifiable and sustainable."

"Absolutely," Miles agreed. "The initial setup isn't cheap, but the vendors are willing to work on a phased implementation, which spreads out the cost. Plus, they're interested in co-developing content, which could reduce our expenses on the creative side."

Anna nodded, satisfied with the pragmatic approach. "What about the content development for these VR experiences? Julia, how are we doing on that front?"

Julia, who had been collaborating closely with historians and educators, chimed in. "We're progressing well. Dr. Larson and I have outlined several key historical events that we believe will benefit most from VR—like the fall of the Berlin Wall and the 1948 Berlin Airlift. We're focusing on creating narratives that are engaging yet educational, ensuring they adhere to historical accuracy."

"Good," Anna responded, her mind already considering the educational potential. "It's vital that these experiences don't just wow our visitors but also deepen their understanding of history."

Dr. Larson, joining the conversation via video call, added, "I've been overseeing the historical accuracy of these scripts. It's a fascinating challenge to adapt our usual exhibit formats to something as dynamic as VR. We're making sure that the 'wow' factor of the technology doesn't overshadow the educational content."

"That balance is crucial," Anna acknowledged. "And speaking of balance, Henrik, how are we preparing to manage visitor flow once these VR experiences are integrated into the exhibits? We anticipate higher interest and potentially longer dwell times at each station."

Henrik had been carefully considering this aspect. "I've been working on a visitor management plan. We're considering timed entry slots for the VR sections to prevent bottlenecks. Additionally, we might need temporary staff or volunteers to assist during peak times and ensure that all visitors have a smooth experience."

"That's well thought out," Anna approved. "It sounds like we're on the right track. Let's continue pushing forward with these initiatives, and keep me updated with weekly reports. Our goal is not just to implement new technology but to set a new standard in historical education."

As the meeting wrapped up, the team felt a renewed sense of purpose. They were not only part of an innovative project but were also at the forefront of transforming how history could be experienced by future generations.

With the meeting concluded, Anna stayed back to review the detailed plans once more. Each step taken was a step towards redefining the educational impact of the Center for Personal History, blending the richness of the past with the possibilities of the future.

As the virtual reality (VR) project moved from the conceptual phase toward implementation, Anna focused on ensuring the seamless integration of this new technology into the existing fabric of the Center for Personal History. She arranged a specialized session to train the staff and volunteers who would be directly interacting with visitors using the VR setups. Held in one of the center's larger education rooms, the session was designed to familiarize the team with the VR equipment and prepare them for common visitor inquiries and technical troubleshooting.

Before the session began, Anna gathered her team for a quick briefing. "Today's training is crucial," she explained. "It's not just about learning to operate the VR equipment; it's about understanding how this technology can enhance our storytelling and help visitors connect more deeply with history. We need to be prepared to guide them through this new experience and answer any questions they might have."

Miles took the lead in the technical training, demonstrating the setup and use of the VR headsets. "When you fit the headset to a visitor, make sure it's snug but comfortable. Like this," he demonstrated, adjusting the straps on a headset. "You'll need to familiarize yourselves with the start-up and shutdown procedures, how to navigate the menus, and what to do in case something doesn't work as expected."

As the staff and volunteers took turns trying the equipment, Julia reviewed the content that visitors would experience. "Each VR session is designed to be immersive and informative. For example, in the 1948 Berlin Airlift experience, visitors will feel as though they are witnessing the events firsthand from the Tempelhof Airport. It's powerful, and it's important we help them process that experience."

Dr. Larson added, "Be ready to provide historical context before and after each session. The impact of these experiences can be profound, and having additional historical information can help visitors understand and appreciate what they've just seen."

Henrik, overseeing the operational logistics, discussed visitor flow management. "With the addition of VR, we expect increased interest and longer visit durations. We'll be implementing a timed ticket system to manage the flow and ensure that all visitors have a chance to engage with the VR without overcrowding. It's important that you all understand the scheduling and can assist visitors with any confusion over timing."

Anna concluded the session with some final thoughts. "This new technology is a tool, but the real magic happens with the interactions you foster and the stories you help to unfold. Our visitors come here to learn and to feel connected to history. Your role in facilitating that connection is absolutely key."

As the training wrapped up, the staff and volunteers expressed their excitement and a few nerves about the new responsibilities. They lingered in the room, discussing the potential impacts and sharing their thoughts on how best to integrate this technology into their daily interactions with visitors.

After everyone had left, Anna remained behind, reviewing her notes and planning the next steps. She was determined to ensure that the introduction of VR technology would not only meet but exceed the expectations of all who came to the center. This project was more than just an upgrade in technology; it was an enhancement of the center's mission to make history accessible and engaging through innovative storytelling. The days ahead would be busy, but Anna was ready to lead her team through this exciting evolution.

With the VR systems fully integrated and the staff trained, the Center for Personal History prepared for the public unveiling of the new virtual reality experiences. Anna decided to host a special preview day for educators, historians, and members of the press to foster initial interest and gather external feedback before opening the experience to the broader public.

On the morning of the preview, Anna walked through the exhibit halls, ensuring that each VR station was perfectly set up. The air was charged with a palpable sense of anticipation. As the guests began to arrive, Anna greeted each one personally, her enthusiasm for the project evident in her warm welcomes.

"Thank you for joining us today," Anna addressed the gathered guests in the central hall, her voice echoing slightly off the high ceilings. "We're excited to show you how we're using virtual reality to bring history to life. Each of you plays a role in educating and informing the public, and we hope this technology will become a valuable tool in your efforts."

As the guests dispersed to explore the VR stations, Anna joined a group led by Miles, who was eager to demonstrate the capabilities of the new system. "Right here, we have the Berlin Airlift experience," Miles explained, handing a VR headset to a guest. "You'll be able to see Berlin in 1948, experience the effort of the airlift, and hear from the people who lived through it."

A historian in the group, after trying the experience, shared his thoughts with Anna. "It's incredibly immersive. I've read and taught about the airlift countless times, but seeing it like this adds a whole new dimension to my understanding."

"I'm glad to hear that," Anna responded, pleased with the reaction. "We believe these experiences can help deepen understanding and empathy for historical events."

As the guests moved from one station to another, Julia facilitated discussions, emphasizing the educational aspects of the VR content. "In addition to the immersive experiences, we've developed accompanying lesson plans and discussion guides. We aim to make these tools as useful as possible for educators."

One teacher, intrigued, asked Julia, "How can we integrate these experiences into our current curriculums?"

"We've designed the content to be modular," Julia explained. "This means you can use it as a standalone experience or integrate it into broader teaching units. We're also here to support you in customizing the content to fit your needs."

Throughout the day, Anna and her team received valuable feedback, which ranged from technical tweaks to content suggestions. Henrik took notes on operational feedback, particularly focusing on visitor flow and the management of wait times, which could be critical once the exhibit opened to the general public.

As the preview day drew to a close, Anna gathered her team for a quick debrief. "Today was a great success, but our work isn't done. We need to review all the feedback and make any necessary adjustments. Our goal is not only to impress but to create a meaningful and educational experience that resonates with all our visitors."

Miles, energized by the day's successes and the challenges ahead, added, "I'll look into fine-tuning the interface based on today's observations. We want to make sure it's as user-friendly as possible."

"And I'll organize the feedback into a report," Henrik offered. "We can use it to improve not just the VR experiences but also how we manage our visitors."

With the preview day concluded, the team felt a mixture of exhaustion and exhilaration. As they left the center that evening, the halls quieted down, and the lights dimmed, leaving Anna looking back over the spaces that had buzzed with life and historical exploration just hours before. She knew they were on the cusp of something special, ready to bring history into the future.

Chapter 26
Aboard the Vessel

The successful preview of the virtual reality (VR) experiences at the Center for Personal History fueled a sense of momentum among Anna's team. With the official public launch just around the corner, Anna convened a strategic meeting with her core team to ensure that every aspect of the visitor experience was polished and ready.

Gathered in the main conference room early in the morning, the team was eager to finalize the details. Anna opened the meeting with a focus on operational readiness.

"Good morning, everyone. We're on the brink of launching our VR experiences to the public, and I want to ensure we have everything in place. Henrik, let's start with you. How are we looking on visitor management and staff readiness?"

Henrik responded promptly, "We've adjusted our staffing schedules to ensure we have ample support during peak times. All team members have undergone additional training to handle the increased foot traffic and to assist visitors with the VR equipment. We've also set up designated areas for VR use to manage flow and prevent overcrowding."

"That sounds well-prepared. Miles, can you update us on the final tech checks and the integration of the feedback system into the VR experiences?"

Miles nodded, his expression serious but confident. "All systems are go. We've conducted extensive tests on the VR setups to ensure there are no technical issues. The feedback system is integrated seamlessly, allowing visitors to leave their thoughts on each experience right as they finish. This should give us real-time data to continuously improve the experiences."

Anna turned her attention to Julia, who was coordinating the educational content. "Julia, how are we incorporating the educational aspects into the VR experiences?"

Julia, enthusiastic about the educational potential, replied, "We've developed comprehensive educational packets that align with the VR content. These are available for schools and groups to download from our website and include pre-visit materials, in-depth guides to the experiences, and post-visit discussion questions. We're also ready to host webinars and Q&A sessions for educators interested in integrating this technology into their curricula."

"That's excellent, Julia. It's important that our offerings are not only technologically advanced but also educationally enriching," Anna said, clearly pleased with the progress. "Dr. Larson, how are we ensuring the historical accuracy and integrity of the narratives within the VR experiences?"

Dr. Larson, always meticulous about details, reassured her, "I've personally reviewed all the historical scripts and visuals again after our last adjustments. We've made sure that every piece of content is not only accurate but also contextually rich, providing a deep dive into the periods we're showcasing. The integration of real historical artifacts and documents within the VR narratives also enhances the authenticity."

"Thank you, Dr. Larson. That's crucial for maintaining our credibility," Anna acknowledged. "Now, regarding the marketing and public relations aspect, Henrik, what's the status of our outreach?"

"Henrik, prepared with the latest updates, shared, "Our marketing team has been very active. We've launched a multi-platform advertising campaign that includes social media teasers, email newsletters, and local media partnerships. We're also hosting a media day right before the public launch to generate buzz and provide press with a firsthand look at the VR experiences."

Anna, satisfied with the updates, concluded, "This is a pivotal moment for our center. These VR experiences are not just exhibits; they represent a new way for people to engage with history. Let's make sure that from the moment our visitors step in, they feel transported and enlightened. We have a chance to set a new standard for historical education."

As the meeting adjourned, the team dispersed with a clear sense of purpose and immediate tasks at hand. Anna stayed behind for a moment, reviewing her notes and contemplating the journey ahead. The center was about to embark on a groundbreaking path, and she was ready to lead it into this new chapter of historical engagement.

As the day of the public launch approached, the entire team at the Center for Personal History worked tirelessly to ensure that everything was in perfect order. The new virtual reality (VR) exhibits were poised to revolutionize how visitors interacted with history, offering immersive experiences of significant historical events that were previously confined to text and static displays.

Anna spent the morning touring the facility, double-checking each VR station. She observed the staff as they performed final checks on the equipment, ensuring that every headset was functioning correctly and that each interactive display was perfectly calibrated. The air was filled with a mix of anticipation and quiet confidence as the staff moved with purpose, each member fully aware of their role in the day's events.

In the background, technicians ran through the software one last time, verifying that the recent updates—incorporating feedback from the preview day—had been successfully integrated. These updates had enhanced user interfaces and increased the accessibility of the content, making the narratives not only more engaging but also easier for all visitors to enjoy and understand.

Miles, overseeing the technical setup, briefly caught up with Anna. "All systems are green," he assured her, his tone reflecting both readiness and a hint of excitement. "We've also set up additional charging stations and spare units, just in case."

"That's great to hear, Miles. Let's keep an eye on those first interactions to ensure everything runs smoothly," Anna responded, her attention already shifting to the next detail.

Meanwhile, Julia and her educational team were setting up information booths that offered supplementary materials. These booths were strategically placed at the exits of each VR experience, where visitors could pick up educational packets or speak with historians and educators about what they had just experienced. The packets included detailed discussions of the events, additional resources for further study, and suggestions for related historical sites in Berlin that could extend the learning experience.

Outside, Henrik coordinated with the visitor services team to manage the expected influx of guests. Signs were posted clearly marking the entrance, exit, and various paths through the exhibit, designed to facilitate an intuitive flow and prevent any congestion. He also briefed the volunteers, who were tasked with guiding visitors and answering any questions they might have about the technology or the content.

As the doors finally opened to the public, Anna watched from a discreet distance. She saw families, students, and history enthusiasts stream in, their faces alight with curiosity. As they approached the VR stations, their initial hesitation quickly gave way to awe and deep engagement. Children and adults alike were captivated by the lifelike historical scenes unfolding before their eyes, and the air buzzed with excitement and the murmur of impressed visitors.

Throughout the day, Anna circulated among the visitors, occasionally stopping to observe or to ask for feedback. The responses were overwhelmingly positive, with many expressing amazement at the depth and realism of the experiences. The historical narratives, enriched by the immersive technology, allowed them to feel as though they were stepping directly into the past, an encounter that many described as moving and profound.

As the sun began to set, casting long shadows through the high windows of the center, the crowd began to thin. Anna took a moment to stand amidst the now-quiet VR stations, reflecting on the day's successes. The launch had not only met but exceeded her expectations, affirming her belief in the power of technology to make history accessible and visceral.

With the closing of the day, the staff gathered to debrief, sharing observations and noting any areas for improvement. But for Anna, the enduring image was that of a young boy, headset lifted, eyes wide with wonder, asking his mother if they could go through the experience again. It was a clear sign that the Center for Personal History had opened a new chapter, not just in how history was presented, but in how it was experienced and remembered.

Several weeks after the successful launch of the virtual reality exhibits, Anna convened a follow-up meeting with her team to assess the initial public response and discuss any necessary adjustments. The meeting room was filled with a sense of achievement, but also with a readiness to tackle any challenges that had emerged since the launch.

Anna started the meeting with a direct approach, "I've seen a lot of positive feedback about the VR exhibits, but I want to hear from all of you. What are the visitors saying, and what can we do to enhance their experience even further?"

Miles responded first, detailing the technical feedback. "The overall response to the VR tech has been fantastic. However, we've noticed a few instances where the headsets required resetting due to software glitches. I'm already working on a patch to fix these issues. Also, the feedback feature within the app has provided us with a lot of constructive suggestions which we can use to improve the interface."

"That's good to hear, Miles. It's important that we stay on top of these technical aspects to maintain a smooth visitor experience," Anna acknowledged. She then turned to Julia, "How about the educational content? Are the teachers and students finding the materials helpful?"

Julia, enthusiastic, shared her insights, "The educational packets have been very well received, especially by school groups. Teachers appreciate the depth of information and the engaging way it's presented. Some have asked for even more detailed follow-up materials they can use back in the classroom. I think we could develop additional resources to complement the VR experiences."

"That's a great idea, Julia. Expanding our educational resources could really solidify our role as an educational hub," Anna noted, pleased with the proactive suggestion. She then looked towards Henrik, "What's the situation with visitor flow and management?"

Henrik, ready with his report, stated, "Visitor flow has been manageable, but the popularity of the VR stations sometimes creates bottlenecks. One solution could be to introduce a reservation system for peak times to ensure that all visitors have a chance to enjoy the experiences without long waits."

Anna considered this, nodding thoughtfully, "A reservation system might indeed improve the visitor experience during peak times. Let's prototype that. And, Dr. Larson, any thoughts on historical accuracy or the content's reception?"

Dr. Larson, who had been closely monitoring visitor reactions and feedback, replied, "The historical accuracy has not been called into question, which is excellent. However, visitors are expressing a desire for more diverse perspectives within the narratives. I suggest we could consider adding additional stories and viewpoints to the existing setups to broaden the narrative scope."

"That's an insightful observation, and aligning with our mission to provide comprehensive historical perspectives," Anna agreed. "Let's look into integrating those additional narratives. Everyone, this feedback is invaluable. It shows that while our launch was successful, there's always room for improvement. Let's keep pushing to not only meet but exceed our visitors' expectations."

As the meeting drew to a close, the team was motivated by the constructive feedback and the clear direction set by Anna. Each member understood their role in the continuous improvement of the VR experiences and was ready to tackle the necessary adjustments.

Leaving the meeting, Anna felt reassured that the center was on the right path. The integration of new technologies like VR into historical storytelling was proving to be a powerful tool in education and engagement. As she walked back to her office, her mind buzzed with possibilities for future expansions and the potential impacts these could have on visitors' understanding of history.

As the Center for Personal History continued to refine its virtual reality (VR) exhibits based on visitor feedback and technological updates, Anna planned a series of community engagement sessions. These sessions were designed to involve the local community more deeply in the ongoing development of the exhibits, ensuring that the center remained a dynamic and responsive part of the city's cultural landscape.

One brisk morning, as Anna prepared the main hall for the first of these sessions, she discussed with her team the agenda and the expected outcomes. "Today, we'll be engaging with various community members, from local historians to students and regular visitors, to gather their direct input on our VR experiences," Anna explained, arranging the chairs into a semi-circle to facilitate an open discussion.

Miles, checking the functionality of a portable VR unit, nodded in agreement. "It's crucial we understand how different groups interact with the technology. Any specific issues they encounter can direct our technical adjustments."

Julia, who had been coordinating the invitations and managing RSVPs, added, "We have a good mix of participants today. Their insights will be invaluable for enhancing the educational aspects of the experiences."

As the participants began to arrive, Anna greeted each one personally, welcoming them to the session. Once everyone was seated, she opened the discussion with a brief overview of the center's objectives. "We're here to listen to your experiences and suggestions. Your feedback is essential for us to continue improving and ensuring our exhibits not only educate but also resonate with our visitors."

A local high school teacher was the first to speak. "The VR experiences are incredibly immersive and a hit with my students. However, they would benefit from a glossary or a reference guide they can access quickly while using the VR, to help them understand some of the historical terms and context in real-time."

"That's a fantastic suggestion," Julia responded, taking notes. "We could integrate pop-up definitions or a companion app that students can refer to on their devices."

A history enthusiast, an older gentleman who frequented the center, shared his perspective. "I appreciate the depth of the narratives, but sometimes the technology can be a bit intimidating. Perhaps simpler, more intuitive controls would help make the VR more accessible for all ages."

Miles acknowledged this point. "That's something we can certainly improve. Making the technology user-friendly is as important as the content it delivers. We'll look into more intuitive interfaces."

A student from a local university suggested, "Maybe you could add more interactive elements within the VR scenarios that allow users to explore different outcomes or perspectives. It could make the learning experience even more engaging."

Anna found the idea intriguing. "That's an excellent point. Interactive scenarios could indeed deepen the engagement and provide richer educational experiences. We'll explore how we can incorporate those elements without compromising historical accuracy."

As the session continued, more ideas were shared, ranging from logistical improvements to enhance visitor flow to content suggestions that would diversify the narratives presented. Anna and her team listened attentively, engaging with the participants and discussing potential implementations of their ideas.

After the session concluded, Anna thanked everyone for their valuable contributions. "Your input today has been incredibly insightful. We are committed to using this feedback to make our exhibits even more informative and engaging."

As the participants left, chatting amongst themselves and with members of Anna's team, there was a palpable sense of community involvement and shared ownership of the center's future.

Gathering her team for a quick debrief, Anna expressed her satisfaction. "Today was a success. Let's start working on integrating this feedback. We have a lot to do, but it's exciting to see how much our community cares and wants to contribute."

With the community's voice now a part of the center's evolution, Anna felt even more confident in the path they were taking. Each piece of feedback was a step toward making history not just something to be observed but something to be truly experienced and understood. As the team discussed the next steps, the hall slowly emptied, leaving behind the echoes of a community becoming ever more connected with its history.

Chapter 27
Reflections at Sea

With the feedback from the community engagement sessions still fresh, Anna initiated a series of targeted upgrades to the virtual reality (VR) exhibits at the Center for Personal History. These updates were designed not only to enhance the visitor experience based on the suggestions received but also to integrate cutting-edge technology that would set the center apart as a leader in historical education.

One of the primary focus areas was the development of a user-friendly interface for the VR systems, aimed at making the technology accessible to all age groups. The technical team, led by Miles, worked diligently, consulting with usability experts to ensure that the interfaces were intuitive and required minimal prior knowledge of VR technology. This involved simplifying navigation and incorporating voice-activated controls that allowed users to interact with the exhibit without being hindered by complicated menus or unfamiliar tech jargon.

Simultaneously, Julia spearheaded the expansion of content within the VR experiences. Taking into account the feedback for more interactive and diverse historical narratives, she collaborated with historians and scriptwriters to craft additional scenarios that visitors could explore. These scenarios included "decision points" where users could make choices that would alter the course of the narrative, thereby providing a more immersive and personal encounter with history.

To complement these interactive scenarios, the educational team developed supplementary materials that provided deeper insights into the consequences of these historical decisions, enhancing the learning experience. These materials were made available both on-site through interactive kiosks and online, allowing teachers to integrate them into their classroom discussions before and after visits to the center.

In the exhibit spaces, Henrik managed a reconfiguration of the layout to improve visitor flow around the new VR stations. This was crucial to avoid congestion, especially during peak hours, and to ensure that each visitor had a fulfilling experience without feeling rushed. New signage was also designed, offering clear directions and information about the exhibits, which helped in maintaining a smooth movement of crowds.

As the updates neared completion, Anna oversaw the installation of the new equipment and the integration of the revised content. She walked through the exhibit halls, observing the new setups and watching as the final pieces were put in place. Her team conducted thorough testing sessions, simulating visitor interactions and making adjustments where necessary to ensure everything operated flawlessly.

Throughout this period, Anna maintained an open line of communication with the center's stakeholders, updating them on progress and the expected outcomes of these enhancements. Her leadership kept the team motivated and focused, ensuring that every task was executed with precision.

As the project reached its final stages, the center began to buzz with anticipation of the re-launch of the VR exhibits. The staff, fully trained on the new systems and content, were eager to see how visitors would respond to the improved experiences.

The day before the re-launch, the center closed early to give the team time to make any last-minute adjustments and to walk through the entire exhibit once more. Anna led this final walkthrough, checking every detail, from the functionality of the VR headsets to the clarity of the informational signage.

As the walkthrough concluded and the team gathered to discuss the next day's plan, there was a shared sense of accomplishment and excitement. They had not only responded to the community's feedback but had pushed the boundaries of what was possible in the realm of historical education.

With everything in place, Anna felt a profound satisfaction in the knowledge that they were about to offer their visitors a richer, more engaging way to connect with history. The center was quiet now, the calm before the storm of visitors who would come the next day, eager to experience the past in a way they never had before.

The re-launch day of the updated virtual reality (VR) exhibits arrived, and the Center for Personal History opened its doors to an eager public. Anna was present at the entrance, greeting visitors as they arrived, her enthusiasm infectious. As groups began to explore the exhibits, Anna joined Miles and Julia at the central VR station, observing the initial reactions and ready to address any questions or concerns.

"How do you think they're responding to the new interfaces?" Anna asked Miles, watching a family adjust their headsets and start the experience.

"It looks like the simplifications we made are working well," Miles replied, carefully monitoring the interactions. "See how easily the children are navigating the menu? The voice commands are definitely a hit. We've reduced the need for manual controls, which seems to make the experience more intuitive for all age groups."

Julia, who had been speaking with a group of teachers, joined the conversation. "The feedback on the educational content has been very positive so far. The teachers especially appreciate the decision points we've added. They say it makes the scenarios more engaging for the students, provoking more discussion and critical thinking."

"That's exactly what we were aiming for," Anna responded with a nod. "Engagement and education. It's crucial that we keep this balance right. Henrik, have the changes to the layout improved the flow like we hoped?"

Henrik, overseeing the floor from a distance, walked over to join them. "Absolutely, Anna. The new layout is managing the crowd much better than before. The spacing between stations helps in maintaining a smooth flow, even with increased numbers. We haven't seen any bottlenecks so far."

"That's great to hear," Anna said, visibly relieved. "It's important that our visitors have a comfortable experience without feeling crowded or rushed."

As they spoke, a visitor approached Anna with a smile. "Excuse me, are you in charge here? I just wanted to say, this VR experience is incredible. I've learned so much about the Berlin Airlift that I never knew before, even though I've read about it in books."

"Thank you very much," Anna replied warmly. "We strive to bring history to life in a way that books sometimes can't. Is there anything you think we could improve?"

"Well, everything has been fantastic, but I was wondering if there could be more personal stories in some of the other scenarios as well. The personal touch really makes the history come alive," the visitor suggested.

"That's valuable feedback, thank you. We're always looking to improve and expand our narratives," Anna assured the visitor, pleased with the constructive suggestion.

Turning back to her team, she said, "Let's keep an eye on that kind of feedback. Personal stories are our strongest tool for engagement. Maybe we can think about incorporating more narratives in future updates."

As the day progressed, more visitors shared similar sentiments, praising the immersive quality of the VR experiences and the depth of the educational content. Anna and her team continued to mingle with the crowd, gathering direct feedback and answering questions.

Towards the end of the day, Anna gathered her team for a brief meeting to discuss the initial feedback. "Today has been a huge success," she began. "The positive responses to the VR updates and the smooth flow of visitors throughout the center have shown that our efforts have paid off. But let's not rest on our laurels. We need to keep listening and keep improving."

"Absolutely, Anna," Miles agreed. "I'll compile the technical feedback we gathered today and see if there are any immediate tweaks we can make."

"And I'll organize the educational feedback," Julia added. "There's a lot we can learn from today about how visitors engage with the content."

As the meeting ended, the team felt a renewed sense of purpose. They had achieved a great deal, but the journey of improvement was ongoing. As the last of the visitors left, Anna stayed behind, looking over the now-quiet exhibits. The day had been a reaffirmation of the center's mission and her own commitment to bringing history to life through innovative, engaging experiences.

As the weeks progressed after the successful re-launch of the virtual reality exhibits, Anna focused on leveraging the momentum to further enhance the Center for Personal History's reputation and outreach. She decided to host a series of public lectures and workshops that tied into the themes explored in the VR experiences, aiming to draw even deeper connections between visitors and Berlin's rich history.

One sunny afternoon, Anna met with Julia and Henrik to plan these events. They gathered in Anna's office, surrounded by books and artifacts that spoke to the depth of the center's collections. The table was strewn with calendars, event flyers, and notes.

"Julia, how are the preparations for the upcoming lecture series?" Anna began, looking over the schedule.

Julia, flipping through her planner, responded enthusiastically, "They're going very well. We've secured several prominent historians who specialize in the periods we cover in our VR experiences. They're excited to participate and share their insights, which will not only enhance the understanding of our exhibits but also attract more academic visitors to the center."

"That sounds promising," Anna nodded approvingly. "And what topics are we covering in these lectures?"

"We have a range of topics," Julia explained. "From the impact of the Berlin Airlift on the city's culture and politics to personal narratives from the Berlin Wall era. Each lecture is designed to complement the VR scenarios, offering a broader context and encouraging deeper engagement."

"Excellent work, Julia. Henrik, what's our strategy for marketing these events to ensure a strong turnout?" Anna shifted her focus to outreach, knowing that the success of these events hinged on effective promotion.

Henrik, who had been coordinating with the marketing team, laid out his plan. "We're targeting local universities and history clubs first, as they're likely to be most interested in the lectures. We're also using social media to highlight unique aspects of each talk, especially snippets that tie directly back to the VR experiences."

"Are we prepared to handle larger groups if the turnout is higher than expected?" Anna asked, always mindful of logistics.

"Yes, we've planned for overflow spaces where the lectures can be streamed live," Henrik assured her. "This way, no one misses out, and it allows us to manage the crowd comfortably."

As they discussed the finer details, Anna's phone buzzed with a reminder about a meeting with the center's educational partners. She looked up, her mind shifting gears. "I have to meet with the school district representatives in a few minutes. They're interested in making regular field trips here part of their history curriculum."

"That's great news," Julia responded, smiling at the prospect. "More regular visits mean more exposure to our exhibits and potentially more feedback to help us improve."

"Exactly," Anna agreed as she stood, gathering her papers. "Let's keep pushing forward. These lectures and partnerships could significantly enhance our educational impact. Keep me updated on the progress, and let's regroup next week to finalize the details."

As Anna left her office to meet with the school representatives, her steps were brisk, her mind already weaving through the possibilities these new initiatives presented. Each lecture, each partnership, was a thread in the larger tapestry of the center's mission to educate and engage the public in meaningful history.

With the sun setting outside her window, the center began to quiet down as visitors and staff departed. Anna watched from her office, considering the day's accomplishments and the work ahead. Each decision, each effort, was building towards a richer understanding of history, not just for the casual visitor but for the community and future generations.

The lecture series at the Center for Personal History had commenced, drawing crowds eager to delve deeper into the historical contexts that shaped Berlin. On one such evening, as guests gathered in the lecture hall, Anna prepared to introduce the speaker, an expert on Cold War Berlin. The room buzzed with anticipation, the attendees ranging from students to seasoned historians.

Anna approached the podium, her presence commanding attention. "Good evening, everyone. Thank you for joining us tonight. Our lecture series is designed to complement our virtual reality exhibits by providing deeper insights into the historical events they depict. Tonight, we are fortunate to have with us Dr. Emily Richter, a renowned historian specializing in Cold War Berlin."

Dr. Richter took the stage with a warm smile. "Thank you, Anna, and thank you all for being here. Tonight, I want to explore the complex dynamics of Berlin during the Cold War, focusing on how this city became the focal point of geopolitical tensions and the everyday lives of its residents."

As Dr. Richter delved into her talk, illustrating her points with vivid photographs and eyewitness accounts, the audience was visibly engaged, some nodding in agreement, others furrowing their brows in thought. After her detailed presentation, the floor was opened for questions.

A young student raised his hand, asking, "Dr. Richter, in your opinion, how did the personal experiences of Berlin's residents influence their perception of the political conflict?"

Dr. Richter responded thoughtfully, "That's an excellent question. Personal experiences during the Cold War were profoundly shaped by the divided city. For many, daily life was directly impacted by the political climate—family separations, travel restrictions, and constant surveillance. These personal narratives provide us with a unique lens to understand the broader political and social upheavals."

Another attendee, a local teacher, inquired, "How can we use the information from tonight's lecture to help our students better connect with this period in history?"

Anna chimed in before Dr. Richter could answer. "That's precisely why we host these lectures. We aim to provide educators with deeper historical contexts that can be integrated into classroom discussions. Additionally, our VR experiences allow students to 'experience' history, making it more relatable and impactful."

Dr. Richter added, "Using interactive technologies like VR in conjunction with traditional educational methods can profoundly enhance students' understanding. It allows them to visualize and 'live' through scenarios that were once just pages in a textbook."

As the Q&A session continued, the dialogue ranged from specific historical details to broader discussions about the implications of the Cold War on modern geopolitical landscapes. The engagement was deep, the questions reflective of a genuine desire to understand the complexities of history.

As the evening drew to a close, Anna thanked Dr. Richter and the audience for their participation. "Thank you, Dr. Richter, for your insightful presentation, and thank you all for your thoughtful questions and engagement."

Guests slowly began to disperse, some staying back to discuss further with Dr. Richter or to thank Anna for organizing the lecture. Anna lingered in the hall, satisfied with the success of the evening. Each lecture served not only to educate but also to build a community of informed individuals passionate about history.

As the last of the guests left and the staff began to tidy up the room, Anna stayed behind, reviewing the evening in her mind. The discussions had sparked ideas for future lectures and potential enhancements to the VR experiences, demonstrating the vibrant, ongoing dialogue between past and present that she had always envisioned for the center.

Leaving the lecture hall, Anna felt a renewed sense of purpose. These events were crucial in furthering the center's mission, bridging historical scholarship with public interest, and she was eager to continue this journey, bringing history to life for all who walked through the doors of the Center for Personal History.

Chapter 28
New Beginnings

Several months after the successful launch of the lecture series and the enhancement of the VR experiences, the Center for Personal History had not only solidified its place as a cultural cornerstone in Berlin but also expanded its influence through partnerships with educational institutions and historical societies. As autumn ushered in cooler weather and the leaves began to turn, Anna planned an ambitious new project: an outdoor exhibit that would bring history into the public spaces of Berlin, making it accessible to a broader audience.

The project, titled "Echoes of Berlin," was to feature a series of installations across various key historical sites in the city. Each installation would use augmented reality (AR) to allow visitors to see and interact with historical events as if they were happening in real time. This initiative aimed to connect the physical geography of Berlin with its rich historical narratives, providing a contextual and immersive learning experience.

Anna spent weeks coordinating with city officials to secure the necessary permissions and with technology developers to ensure the AR could be seamlessly integrated into the urban landscape. She also worked closely with historians to select the events and sites that were not only historically significant but would also resonate with both locals and tourists.

One crisp morning, Anna met with her team to discuss the project's progress. The meeting took place in her office, which was filled with maps of Berlin and diagrams of the proposed installations. "How are we doing with the permissions from the city?" she inquired, looking over at Henrik, who was handling the logistical aspects of the project.

"We've secured most of the permissions needed," Henrik replied, shuffling through his papers. "There are a couple of locations still under review, but we're on track. The city is quite supportive of the project, seeing its potential to boost local engagement and tourism."

"That's excellent," Anna said, her tone reflecting both relief and determination. "And the technology? Miles, are we ready to implement AR in these environments?"

Miles, always enthusiastic about the technological challenges, nodded confidently. "We've done preliminary tests, and the AR integration is looking good. The next step is to conduct site-specific tests to adjust the visuals and interactions based on the actual locations. We need to ensure that the historical content is accurately aligned with the physical landmarks."

"Good, let's prioritize those tests. We need to be sure of the accuracy before we go live," Anna emphasized, aware of the importance of historical integrity in their presentations.

As the project moved forward, Julia focused on developing educational programs around the outdoor exhibits. She envisioned guided tours, school group activities, and even interactive workshops that could be conducted at the sites. "The educational potential here is vast," she mused aloud during one of her planning sessions. "We can connect with schools across the city, inviting students to explore their history right where it happened."

Anna often visited the proposed sites herself, walking the grounds and envisioning how visitors would interact with the past through their mobile devices. She imagined families and school groups gathered around an invisible Berlin Wall, watching historical events unfold through their screens, or tourists standing by the Brandenburg Gate, witnessing the joyous scenes of its liberation.

As preparations for the outdoor exhibit continued, Anna's leadership and vision drove the project forward. She was deeply involved in every detail, from the placement of AR markers to the narratives that would be told at each site. Her commitment to making history accessible and engaging was evident in her tireless efforts and the collaborative energy she fostered among her team.

With the launch date approaching, the center buzzed with activity, and the excitement was palpable. "Echoes of Berlin" promised to be more than just an exhibit; it was poised to become a new way for Berliners and visitors to connect with the city's history, to walk through time as they walked through the city, discovering the echoes of the past that shaped the vibrant metropolis they knew today.

With the preparations for "Echoes of Berlin" in full swing, Anna convened a key meeting to address the final elements needed for a successful launch. Gathered in the conference room, the team was surrounded by blueprints and digital mock-ups of the augmented reality (AR) installations. Anna was keen to ensure that every detail was accounted for, and the atmosphere was one of focused anticipation.

"Let's go through the checklist for each site installation," Anna began, her voice steady and commanding. "Henrik, what's the status on the last of the city permissions?"

Henrik, looking up from his notes, responded, "We received the final approvals this morning. All sites are cleared for installation. The city has been very cooperative, especially after seeing the potential benefits of the project."

"That's excellent news," Anna replied with a nod of approval. "Miles, tell me about the technical preparations. Are we ready to roll out the AR components smoothly?"

Miles adjusted his glasses, his face lit by the glow of his laptop screen. "Yes, we've completed all site-specific calibrations. The AR software is fully integrated and responsive. We've also set up remote monitoring systems to manage any issues that might arise in real-time."

"Good work. Now, Julia, how are the educational programs shaping up? I want to make sure we're ready to engage with schools and the general public from day one," Anna said, turning her attention to the educational outreach component.

Julia, ever enthusiastic about the project's educational impact, was quick to share her updates. "We've developed a series of guided tours and interactive workshops that will be offered at each site. These are designed to enhance the AR experience and provide deeper historical insights. We're also coordinating with local schools to schedule field trips throughout the opening month."

"That sounds promising. It's important that our educational content complements the technology and makes history tangible for our visitors," Anna commented thoughtfully. "Henrik, have we addressed the logistics for the opening day? With the expected crowd, we need to ensure a smooth experience for everyone."

Henrik, who had been meticulously planning the logistics, detailed his strategy. "We have arranged for additional staff and volunteers to be on-site at each installation. They will assist visitors with the AR technology and help manage crowd flow. We've also coordinated with local transportation services to handle increased traffic to the sites."

"Excellent," Anna said, visibly pleased with the team's thoroughness. "Now, let's talk about the launch event itself. I want to make sure we have a strong media presence to maximize our exposure. Miles, have we confirmed the tech demos for the press?"

Miles nodded. "Yes, we have set up exclusive previews for the media on the morning of the launch. This includes hands-on demos and interviews with our team. It's a great opportunity to showcase the technology and the historical narratives we've developed."

"Great. This project is a significant step forward for us in integrating technology and history in a public setting," Anna reflected, looking around at her team. "We are not just launching an exhibit; we are transforming how people interact with our city's past. Let's ensure that 'Echoes of Berlin' sets a new standard in historical engagement."

As the meeting concluded, the team dispersed, each member clear on their responsibilities. Anna remained behind, reviewing the project timelines and promotional materials. The anticipation for the launch was building, not just within the walls of the center but across the city. "Echoes of Berlin" was poised to become a landmark project, one that would bring history to life in the streets of Berlin, allowing people to explore the past where it happened. As she left the conference room, Anna felt a profound connection to the project, knowing it would soon offer everyone a new lens through which to view their city.

As the launch date for "Echoes of Berlin" approached, the city buzzed with anticipation. Posters and digital billboards advertised the upcoming augmented reality (AR) installations, beckoning residents and tourists alike to experience Berlin's history where it unfolded. Under Anna's guidance, the Center for Personal History was transforming from a place of learning within four walls into an expansive, interactive historical journey across the city.

The morning of the launch was brisk and sunny, perfect for an outdoor event. Anna arrived early at the first installation site, located in a historically significant park where remnants of the Berlin Wall still stood. As her team conducted final checks on the AR equipment, she surveyed the area, ensuring everything was perfectly set for the guests and media who would soon arrive.

Technicians discreetly placed AR markers around the park, each one a gateway to a different era of Berlin's tumultuous past. Nearby, a small podium had been set up for the opening ceremony, with rows of chairs for special guests, including local dignitaries, historians, and school groups.

Anna's team moved efficiently, their familiarity with the project's details evident in their precision and calmness under pressure. They tested each AR headset, confirming that the historical simulations were accurately aligned with the physical environment, allowing for a seamless blending of past and present.

As guests began to arrive, Anna greeted them with a warm smile and shared enthusiasm. She handed out leaflets that explained how to use the AR headsets and what they could expect to experience. The leaflets also included QR codes linking to further reading and resources, enriching the learning experience beyond the visual spectacle.

The official opening was brief but poignant. Anna addressed the gathering with a few words about the importance of remembering and engaging with history, not just in books and museums but in the very places where it happened. "Today," she said, "we bridge the gap between past and present, using technology to peel back the layers of time. We invite you to walk through history, to see, hear, and feel the moments that have shaped our city."

As the ribbon was cut, the crowd dispersed to explore the installations. Children and adults alike donned the AR headsets, gasping in delight as historical scenes came to life around them. A group of tourists found themselves standing by the Berlin Wall as it was first erected; their expressions turned solemn as the reality of the division sank in through the narratives and images that surrounded them.

At another site, schoolchildren followed a map to various points around a plaza, each stop revealing different aspects of the city during the Cold War. They listened to stories of espionage, watched scenes of daily life under surveillance, and learned about the global politics that played out in their hometown.

Throughout the day, Anna moved between the various sites, observing and occasionally assisting guests with the technology. The feedback was overwhelmingly positive, with many expressing a new appreciation for the city's history and the innovative way it was presented.

As the sun began to set, casting long shadows over the historical sites, the crowds thinned. Anna stood for a moment at the park, watching a family as they discussed what they had learned. The children were animated, retelling the stories they had heard, clearly moved by the experience.

Content, Anna finally started to make her way back to the center. Today had been more than just a successful launch; it had been a demonstration of how history could be made vivid and accessible to all ages. The project was not just about looking back but about moving forward with a deeper understanding of the past.

Her steps were unhurried as she left the site, the echoes of the day's successes still resonant in the cool evening air. The journey of bringing history into the public space had just begun, and Anna was already envisioning the next chapters that would unfold under her stewardship at the center.

In the weeks following the launch of "Echoes of Berlin," the augmented reality (AR) installations continued to draw crowds, becoming a talked-about attraction in the city. Anna observed with pride how the project connected people of all ages with the city's history in a deeply personal way. Now, to build on this success, she planned to introduce a series of evening events at various AR sites, combining historical lectures with live reenactments—a further step to deepen the immersive experience.

Under a clear evening sky, the team gathered at one of the most popular sites near the remains of the Berlin Wall. As they set up temporary seating and lighting, Anna coordinated with the performers and speakers who would bring the evening to life. The site was bathed in soft light, creating a poignant backdrop for the night's event.

"Everything looks great," Anna remarked to Henrik, who was overseeing the setup. "These evening events could really enhance the way visitors engage with the installations."

Henrik nodded, checking his clipboard. "We've got everything on schedule. The first group should be arriving soon. We're expecting a good turnout based on the registrations."

As the guests began to arrive, Anna greeted them warmly, her enthusiasm for the project evident. "Welcome, everyone! Tonight, we're going to experience history not just through technology but through storytelling and performance. I hope you find it as enlightening as it is entertaining."

The event began with a short introduction by a local historian, who set the scene by describing Berlin in the late 1980s, just before the Wall fell. As the historian spoke, actors dressed in period-appropriate clothing mingled with the crowd, their interactions designed to mimic the tensions and hopes of the time.

Following the introduction, guests were invited to put on AR headsets. The historical lecture continued, with the narrator guiding the audience through the events leading up to the fall of the Wall. As the narrative unfolded, the AR technology overlaid scenes of historical marches, speeches, and the jubilant crowds that gathered as the Wall was breached.

Anna watched as guests looked around in awe, their faces illuminated by the glow of the AR displays. They were not just spectators but participants in the unfolding drama, experiencing the collective emotion of a pivotal moment in history.

As the reenactment reached its climax with the symbolic 'fall' of the Wall, the audience erupted in applause, moved by the powerful combination of live action and augmented reality. After the applause died down, the floor was opened for a Q&A session, where guests could ask questions about the historical events and the technology used to recreate them.

One guest, a local schoolteacher, expressed her appreciation during the Q&A. "This is an incredible way to teach history. Seeing it, living it like this, makes it so much more real and memorable than reading about it in a textbook."

Anna responded, "Thank you. That's exactly what we strive for. We want to make history accessible and engaging for everyone, using every tool at our disposal."

As the evening wound down, guests lingered, discussing what they had learned and experienced. Anna and her team circulated among them, gathering feedback and answering lingering questions.

The success of the evening was a reaffirmation of the project's value. As the last guests departed and the team began to pack up, Anna took a moment to savor the success. The city's past had been brought to life in a new and innovative way, fostering a deeper connection and understanding among its residents and visitors.

Walking away from the site, Anna felt a profound sense of accomplishment. The "Echoes of Berlin" project was more than just an exhibition; it was becoming a vital part of the city's cultural and educational landscape, bridging generations and histories in the heart of Berlin. As she looked back at the dimming lights and the historic backdrop, she was already thinking ahead to the next steps, eager to expand and deepen the project's impact.

Chapter 29
Building a Home

Several months had passed since the launch of the "Echoes of Berlin" AR project, and its success had continued to grow, drawing attention not just from locals and tourists but also from academic institutions and cultural organizations worldwide. In light of this attention, Anna was approached by an international consortium of historical museums interested in adapting the AR project for their own cities. This opportunity led her to organize a conference at the Center for Personal History, where she could share insights, strategies, and potential collaborations with her peers from around the globe.

On the day of the conference, the center was abuzz with excitement. Delegates from museums in Europe, Asia, and the Americas gathered in the main hall, which had been set up with round tables to facilitate discussion and exchange. Anna, ever the gracious host, opened the conference with a warm welcome.

"Good morning, everyone. I'm thrilled to see so many faces from around the world gathered here today," Anna began, standing confidently at the podium. "The success of our 'Echoes of Berlin' project has not only deepened our connection with our city's history but has also sparked a global conversation about how we use technology to engage with our past."

Miles, who was scheduled to speak about the technical aspects of the project, joined Anna on stage. "The AR technology we used was designed to be adaptive and interactive, making historical events accessible and engaging. By overlaying historical images and narratives onto the modern landscape, we've managed to create a dynamic way of experiencing history."

A delegate from a museum in London raised a question. "Could you elaborate on how you ensured the accuracy of the historical content within the AR environment?"

Anna nodded to Dr. Larson, who was prepared to address such inquiries. "We worked closely with historians and used primary sources to script the narratives. Each piece of content underwent rigorous peer review to ensure its accuracy and to respectfully present our city's history."

Another delegate, this time from Tokyo, was curious about the public's response. "How did you gauge and handle the feedback from visitors, especially in terms of educational impact?"

Julia took the opportunity to respond. "We set up feedback kiosks at each installation site and also used mobile apps to collect responses. This data helped us tweak the content and user experience continuously. We also partnered with local schools to integrate these experiences into their history curricula, enhancing the educational impact."

The morning progressed with discussions on potential challenges when implementing similar projects in different cultural and urban contexts. A delegate from Buenos Aires asked, "What major obstacles should we anticipate in deploying this technology in a city with a significantly different historical infrastructure?"

Miles answered, "One of the key challenges is the integration of AR with existing urban landscapes, which might not always be as conducive to such technology as Berlin. It requires custom solutions for mapping and content delivery to adapt to different architectural and geographical conditions."

As lunch approached, Anna facilitated a brainstorming session on collaboration. "Given the diverse urban and historical landscapes we represent, I believe there's tremendous potential for cross-cultural exchange and learning. Perhaps we could form a working group to explore these ideas further and support each other in developing our respective projects."

The idea was met with enthusiastic approval, leading to the formation of preliminary committees to explore various aspects of collaboration, including technology sharing, historical research, and educational programming.

As the delegates mingled and exchanged contact information, the conference continued to buzz with the lively exchange of ideas and mutual enthusiasm for the potential of augmented reality to bring history to life.

By the time the afternoon sessions began, Anna felt a renewed sense of purpose and excitement about the possibilities ahead. The conference was not only a platform for sharing but also a catalyst for new projects and partnerships that could reshape historical education across the globe. As the discussions delved deeper into the specifics of potential projects, Anna observed the interactions with a keen eye, already envisioning the future collaborations that would emerge from today's dialogue.

In the wake of the productive morning sessions at the conference, the atmosphere in the afternoon was charged with enthusiasm as delegates prepared for a series of workshops. These workshops were designed to dive deeper into the practical aspects of implementing augmented reality (AR) projects in various cultural and historical settings. Anna had arranged for breakout groups to focus on specific topics, facilitating a more hands-on approach to problem-solving and project planning.

As the delegates split into their respective groups, Anna joined the workshop focused on "Adapting AR to Diverse Historical Contexts," where participants from museums in regions with complex histories like the Middle East and Southeast Asia gathered. She initiated the session with an open question to the group, setting the tone for a collaborative discussion.

"How can we ensure that our AR projects respect and accurately represent the diverse narratives within our histories, especially in regions where historical interpretation can be contentious?" Anna asked, encouraging input from all participants.

A delegate from Jerusalem was the first to respond. "In our city, history is a living part of our identity, but it's also a source of conflict. Our approach has been to involve multiple stakeholders in the creation of any historical narrative, ensuring that all voices are heard. This not only enriches the content but also promotes a sense of shared ownership and respect among the communities."

"That's a valuable strategy," Anna acknowledged. "Involving community stakeholders not only in the planning but also in the ongoing review of content can indeed help mitigate conflicts and misrepresentations. Does anyone have experience with integrating such stakeholder feedback into the technological development process?"

A participant from Vietnam chimed in, "We've used community forums and digital platforms to gather ongoing feedback, which is then directly fed back to our tech teams. This continuous loop helps us adjust content quickly and keep our narratives up-to-date and balanced."

The conversation then shifted to the technical aspects, particularly the challenge of developing AR content that could adapt to various physical environments. A delegate from Singapore raised a concern, "Our challenge has been adapting AR to highly urbanized settings where historical sites are often overshadowed by modern infrastructure. How can we enhance visibility and engagement in such environments?"

Miles, who had joined the workshop to provide technical insight, replied, "One approach is to use geo-tagging combined with visual cues that can trigger AR experiences even in crowded, modern spaces. By creating visually compelling entry points, we can draw attention to the less noticeable historical sites."

The discussion then turned towards educational integration, a topic of great interest to Anna and her team. "How can we better integrate these AR experiences into formal education systems to ensure that they're not just seen as novelties but as valuable educational tools?" Anna posed to the group.

A representative from Australia provided their insight. "We've partnered directly with educational authorities to embed AR projects into the curriculum. By aligning the content with national education standards and providing teachers with detailed guides and lesson plans, we've seen AR become a more accepted and effective educational tool."

As the workshop drew to a close, Anna summarized the key points discussed. "It's clear that while we face diverse challenges, the strategies we've shared today—from stakeholder involvement to educational integration—offer a roadmap for making AR a valuable tool in historical education and community engagement."

The participants exchanged contact information, eager to keep the conversation going beyond the conference. As they left the room, there was a consensus that the insights gained from these discussions would greatly enhance their respective projects.

Anna remained behind for a few moments, reflecting on the discussions. The collaborative spirit of the workshop had not only reinforced her commitment to the "Echoes of Berlin" project but had also inspired new ideas for future expansions. Energized by the day's exchanges, she was more convinced than ever of the transformative potential of technology in bringing history to life.

As the international conference drew to a close, Anna organized a final panel discussion with key experts from the AR and historical research fields. The panel was designed to address future trends in technology and historical presentation, providing insights into how these could be harmoniously integrated. With the room filled to capacity, the atmosphere was ripe with curiosity and the eager anticipation of knowledge.

Anna introduced the panelists, each a respected leader in their field. "Today, we are fortunate to have with us experts who have pioneered the use of technology in historical interpretation. Our discussion will focus on what the future holds for integrating technology like AR in our museums and historical sites."

The first question was directed at a panelist specializing in technological innovations. "Could you share your thoughts on emerging technologies that could further enhance our historical narratives?" Anna asked, facilitating the start of a dynamic exchange.

"Certainly," the expert responded. "Beyond AR, we're looking at the integration of AI to create more personalized visitor experiences. Imagine AI that can interact with visitors, answering their questions in real-time and adapting the narrative to suit their interests. This could revolutionize the way we engage with history."

Anna nodded thoughtfully and turned to a historian on the panel. "How do you see these technological advancements impacting our historical accuracy and the authenticity of the narratives we present?"

The historian adjusted his glasses before replying, "It's a double-edged sword. While technology like AI can provide dynamic interactions, there's a challenge in ensuring that the adaptive narratives remain true to historical facts. We must be diligent in our oversight, ensuring that our sources are impeccable and our interpretations are sound."

The conversation sparked interest among the attendees, prompting a question from the audience. "How do we balance the excitement of technology with the need to maintain scholarly rigor in our historical presentations?"

Another panelist, an expert in museum education, took this question. "It's about integration rather than replacement. We use technology to enhance, not overshadow, the factual content. By involving historians in the development process of these technologies, we ensure that our educational goals are not compromised by the allure of new tech."

Anna interjected, "That's a crucial point. Our role as educators and preservers of history should guide the development and application of these technologies. It's about enhancing the learning experience while staying true to the historical narrative."

The discussion then shifted towards practical applications, with a delegate asking, "What are some of the practical challenges you've faced in integrating advanced technologies into historical sites and museums?"

A panelist who had recently overseen the installation of AR in a historical museum shared her experience. "One major challenge is the physical infrastructure of historical sites which often aren't designed to support modern technology. We've had to be creative in embedding technology without disturbing the integrity of these sites."

As the panel discussion drew to a close, the participants clapped enthusiastically, appreciative of the insights shared. The exchange of ideas didn't end with the panel; many continued to discuss these topics as they congregated after the session.

Anna, feeling satisfied with the success of the conference, thanked the panelists and attendees for their active participation. "Thank you all for your valuable contributions. These discussions are just the beginning.

Let's take what we've learned and continue to explore these exciting possibilities."

As the delegates began to disperse, Anna stayed back to chat with a few attendees who lingered, seeking advice or sharing their experiences. The energy in the room was a testament to the passion and commitment shared among those present, all dedicated to the task of bringing history to life through the lens of technology.

Reflecting on the day's discussions, Anna felt energized by the potential collaborations and projects that might arise from this gathering. The future of historical education was bright, with new technologies opening up unprecedented ways to engage and educate. As the center quieted down after the day's events, Anna's thoughts lingered on the possibilities, her mind busy with plans for harnessing these innovations for the Center for Personal History.

In the weeks following the conference, the impact of the discussions and the insights shared became evident. Anna found herself at the center of a growing network of international collaborators eager to implement augmented reality (AR) technologies in their historical presentations. The conference had not only sparked interest but had also set the stage for global partnerships.

Back at the Center for Personal History, Anna was busy planning the next steps. She was determined to capitalize on the momentum from the conference by launching a pilot program that would test new AR features based on collaborative input from her international peers. This program would serve as a model for other institutions, demonstrating how technology could enhance historical education.

With her team gathered around in the main meeting room, Anna mapped out the structure of the pilot program. "We'll start with the 'Berlin Blitz' experience," she explained. "It's one of our most popular segments, and I believe it's ripe for enhancement with the new AI-driven narrative tools we discussed at the conference."

Miles, who had been instrumental in the technical setup of the AR installations, added his thoughts. "The AI component can adapt the narrative based on the visitor's reactions and interactions. For instance, if a visitor spends more time at a particular station, the AI can provide additional detailed content about that event."

Julia, responsible for educational outreach, was keen on integrating the feedback mechanisms. "We can use this pilot to gather real-time data on visitor engagement and understanding. This data can help us refine not just the narratives but also the educational materials we provide."

As the preparations for the pilot program advanced, Anna took a hands-on approach, overseeing every detail from the software development to the training of guides who would assist visitors in using the new features. She often walked through the exhibit spaces, imagining how the new technologies would transform the visitor experience.

One morning, while reviewing the progress with Henrik, Anna discussed the logistical aspects of rolling out the pilot. "We need to ensure that our staff are well-prepared to handle questions about the new features. Also, let's set up dedicated feedback stations where visitors can leave their impressions immediately after experiencing the enhanced AR."

Henrik nodded, making notes. "I'll arrange for additional training sessions for our staff. The feedback stations are a great idea; they'll provide us with invaluable insights from day one."

The pilot program was met with enthusiasm from visitors, who marveled at the seamless integration of AI-driven narratives that seemed to anticipate their interests and questions. The feedback collected was overwhelmingly positive, with many expressing amazement at the depth and personalization of the experience.

As Anna reviewed the visitor feedback reports, she felt a sense of accomplishment. The pilot was not only a testament to her team's hard work but also a confirmation that the path they were on was the right one. The possibilities for expanding the program and introducing these technologies to other parts of the exhibit—or even to other institutions—seemed endless.

One late afternoon, after most of the staff had left, Anna stood in the exhibit hall, watching as the last few visitors of the day interacted with the

"Berlin Blitz" experience. The expressions of curiosity, surprise, and engagement on their faces were a clear indicator of the project's success.

With the success of the pilot program, Anna was already planning the next phase of expansion. The integration of technology into historical education had proven not only viable but vital. As she left the exhibit hall, her mind buzzed with future possibilities, each more promising than the last, as she continued to push the boundaries of how we interact with and understand our past.

Chapter 30
Return to Lisbon

As the pilot program for the augmented reality (AR) enhancements proved successful, Anna decided it was time to expand the project to include additional periods of Berlin's history. She believed that by broadening the scope, they could attract even more visitors and provide a richer educational experience. To plan this expansion, she organized a strategy meeting with her team to discuss potential new historical periods and themes to cover.

Gathered in the conference room, with the morning light streaming through the windows, the team was abuzz with ideas and possibilities. Anna opened the meeting with a focused agenda. "The success of our AR pilot has given us a tremendous opportunity to expand. I want us to consider which historical periods or events we could include next. Let's brainstorm ideas based on historical significance and visitor interest."

Miles was the first to suggest, "Given the current interest in the Cold War era, particularly the espionage stories, why not develop an experience centered around spy tales in Berlin during the 1960s? It's rich with intrigue and could attract a diverse audience."

"That's a compelling idea," Julia chimed in. "The spy narratives are not only fascinating but also provide a window into the geopolitical dynamics of the time. We could incorporate real-life stories of spies and the tools they used, making it interactive and educational."

Henrik added, "We should also consider incorporating the rise of Berlin as a cultural hub in the early 20th century. The Weimar Republic, for example, was a time of incredible artistic and cultural blossoming in Berlin. It could offer a contrast to the more political narratives and appeal to those interested in art and culture."

Anna nodded thoughtfully. "Both are excellent suggestions. The Cold War spy tales can indeed captivate an audience with their suspense and intrigue, while the Weimar Republic could attract those interested in culture and arts. How feasible is it to integrate these into our existing AR setups?"

Miles responded, "Technically, we can leverage the same platforms we've developed for the pilot. The modular nature of our AR software makes it relatively straightforward to introduce new content. We'll need to develop new scripts and perhaps some additional visual assets, but it's certainly doable."

Julia, thinking about the educational aspect, proposed, "For the Weimar Republic, we could collaborate with local art schools and cultural institutions to create content that's not only historically accurate but also richly detailed in terms of art and music of the era. It would make the experience multidimensional."

"That's an excellent approach," Anna agreed. "Collaborations could also extend our reach and bring in new audiences. What about visitor engagement strategies? How do we ensure these new experiences resonate with our visitors?"

Henrik, ever focused on logistics and visitor experience, suggested, "We could start with temporary installations as part of special event nights, allowing us to gather feedback and make adjustments before fully integrating them into the regular visitor route. Additionally, hosting special events could generate buzz and attract media attention."

"Perfect," Anna concluded. "Let's develop a detailed plan for each proposed theme, starting with temporary installations as Henrik suggested. Miles, coordinate with the tech team on the requirements for new scripts and visuals. Julia, begin reaching out to potential collaborators for the Weimar Republic content. I want us all to reconvene next week with progress updates and a more detailed implementation timeline."

As the meeting adjourned, the team felt energized by the clear direction and the creative possibilities ahead. They dispersed to their respective tasks, each person contributing to the expansion of a project that was rapidly becoming a cornerstone of cultural education in Berlin.

Anna stayed back for a moment, reviewing her notes and reflecting on the discussion. The potential to deepen and diversify the historical narratives presented through AR was immense, and she was committed to ensuring its success. As she left the conference room, her thoughts were already turning to how these new stories would be woven into the fabric of the city's rich history, eagerly anticipating the continued evolution of the project.

Following the strategy meeting, the team at the Center for Personal History embarked on the development phase for the new AR experiences focusing on the Cold War espionage and the cultural vibrancy of the Weimar Republic. Anna was particularly keen on ensuring these narratives were not only engaging but also historically meticulous and educationally sound. She scheduled a series of follow-up meetings with each subgroup responsible for different aspects of the project.

In her office, surrounded by stacks of historical texts and digital tablets displaying AR mockups, Anna met with Miles and the technical team to discuss the integration of the new content. "Miles, how are we progressing with the technical aspects of the new modules?" she inquired, looking over the interactive blueprints laid out before them.

"We've made good headway," Miles replied, pointing to the screen showing an interactive map of 1960s Berlin. "The espionage experience is particularly complex, given the need for a more narrative-driven approach. We're incorporating GPS-triggered content that activates at specific locations, simulating the spy routes and dead drops used during the Cold War."

"That sounds fascinating," Anna remarked, genuinely impressed. "What challenges are we facing?"

"The main challenge is ensuring the GPS accuracy and the seamless integration of visual and audio content without disrupting the urban environment," Miles explained. "We're also working on making the interface as user-friendly as possible, especially for those who might not be familiar with AR technology."

Anna nodded, understanding the delicate balance required. "Let's keep testing with various user groups to refine the usability. I want everyone, regardless of their tech proficiency, to enjoy and learn from this experience."

The conversation then shifted to Julia's update on the collaborations for the Weimar Republic project. She had been in discussions with several local cultural institutions. "We've secured a partnership with the Berlin Art School," Julia announced, her face bright with enthusiasm. "They're excited to help us create authentic reproductions of Weimar-era art and music, which will be integrated into the AR experience."

"That's excellent news," Anna responded warmly. "Incorporating authentic art and music will certainly enrich the experience and provide a deeper understanding of the era's cultural context. How are we planning to present these elements in the AR environment?"

"We're thinking of using virtual galleries and concert halls where visitors can explore art pieces or listen to contemporary music of the Weimar Republic," Julia detailed. "These spaces will be virtually reconstructed within the AR platform, allowing visitors to immerse themselves in the artistic ambiance of the period."

"That sounds like a truly immersive approach," Anna complimented, pleased with the innovative ideas. "Keep me updated on the development, and let's make sure we have detailed educational materials to accompany these artistic displays."

As the meeting drew to a close, Anna felt confident in the team's progress and the direction of the new projects. She appreciated the complexities involved in bringing such rich historical content to life through technology. After the team left, Anna stayed behind, reviewing the notes and planning the next steps.

She reflected on the importance of these expansions not only for the center but for the community at large. By bringing history to life through AR, they were providing a bridge between the past and the present, making history accessible and engaging for everyone.

With a thoughtful gaze out of her office window, Anna contemplated the upcoming testing phase. She was eager to see how the public would react to these new narratives and how they could further refine the experiences based on real-world interactions. The journey of expanding the "Echoes of Berlin" project was well underway, filled with challenges but also with immense opportunities to make a lasting impact on historical education and public engagement.

As the new augmented reality (AR) experiences neared completion, Anna organized a series of internal previews to fine-tune the content and technical aspects before the public launch. These previews were crucial for gathering initial reactions and feedback from the center's staff and selected guests, including historians and technology experts.

On a cool, overcast morning, the team assembled at one of the primary AR sites dedicated to the Cold War espionage theme. Anna, Miles, and Julia were joined by a small group of testers equipped with the latest AR headsets, ready to walk through the experience.

"Alright, let's start with the espionage route," Anna instructed as she handed out the devices. "Pay close attention to how the narrative unfolds and how intuitive the interactions are. I want to know how seamlessly the story integrates with the physical environment."

Miles, overseeing the technical execution, added, "Keep an eye on the responsiveness of the app. We need to ensure that the triggers activate correctly based on your location and that there are no delays in content delivery."

The group embarked on their journey through the streets of Berlin, following the AR prompts that led them to various 'dead drop' locations and secret meeting points used by spies during the Cold War. The AR provided immersive narrative segments, reconstructing tense exchanges and crucial moments of espionage with detailed historical accuracy.

After completing the route, the group gathered to discuss their experiences. A visiting historian specializing in Cold War history was the first to offer feedback. "The storyline is compelling and well-researched. However, at several points, the audio narration seemed slightly out of sync with the visual cues. It might confuse visitors who are not familiar with the history."

Miles took note immediately. "That's good to know. We can adjust the timing of the audio to ensure it matches the visual elements more precisely."

Julia, focusing on the educational impact, asked, "How did you find the interactive elements, like the virtual document folders and the coded messages you had to decipher?"

"They were engaging and really drew me into the role of a spy. It felt like I was part of the history," one of the testers, a local school teacher, replied. "But maybe you could add more context about the significance of the documents we're interacting with. It would help those less familiar with the history to understand the bigger picture."

"That's a fantastic suggestion," Anna said, pleased with the constructive criticism. "Julia, let's work on integrating pop-up contextual information that users can access if they want deeper insights into the historical significance of their actions."

As the discussion continued, more feedback highlighted areas for improvement, such as enhancing user navigation and providing clearer instructions on how to use the AR interface. Anna listened attentively, ensuring every point was documented for further review.

"We'll take all these observations and refine the experience," Anna concluded. "Our goal is to make these historical events as accessible and engaging as possible while maintaining rigorous educational standards."

With the espionage route feedback session wrapping up, the team prepared to move on to the next site, focused on the Weimar Republic's cultural vibrancy. This part of the day was devoted to testing the AR experiences that showcased Weimar-era art and music through virtual galleries and concert halls.

As the previews continued, the input from the testers proved invaluable. Each comment and suggestion was a stepping stone towards perfecting the experiences. Anna was heartened by the team's dedication and the testers' enthusiasm, knowing that these efforts would culminate in a launch that would significantly enhance the public's connection to Berlin's history.

With the day coming to a close and the notes from the sessions compiled, the team felt a mix of exhaustion and excitement. There was much work to do, but the path forward was clear, and the potential to transform how people learned about and interacted with history was immense. As the testers departed, Anna and her team remained, discussing the next steps deep into the evening, driven by a shared commitment to bringing history to life through technology.

The final phase before the public launch of the new augmented reality (AR) experiences was dedicated to incorporating all the feedback gathered during the internal previews. Anna and her team had a series of intensive work sessions planned, aimed at refining and perfecting the experiences to ensure they met both educational and engagement standards.

In a well-lit conference room, Anna, Miles, and Julia sat surrounded by laptops, tablets, and piles of feedback forms and notes. The atmosphere was focused, with a sense of urgency palpable in the air.

Anna initiated the meeting with a clear directive. "Let's go through the feedback systematically. We start with the technical issues Miles identified during the espionage route preview. What's the status there?"

Miles responded, adjusting his glasses, his screen filled with lines of code. "I've adjusted the timing of the audio to better sync with the visual cues. This should resolve the dissonance some testers experienced. Additionally, I've enhanced the GPS accuracy to make the location-based triggers more reliable."

"That's great to hear," Anna acknowledged. "How about the user interface improvements? We need that to be as intuitive as possible."

"We've simplified the navigation commands and added more on-screen instructions," Miles continued. "I believe this will make the experience more user-friendly, especially for those who are less familiar with AR technology."

Turning to Julia, Anna asked, "And the educational enhancements for the Weimar Republic experience?"

Julia, whose laptop was open to a colorful display of Weimar-era art and music, was eager to share her updates. "Based on the suggestion to add more context to the interactive elements, we've embedded brief historical descriptions for each artwork and musical piece featured in the virtual galleries. This should enrich the visitor's understanding and appreciation of the cultural context."

"That sounds perfect, Julia. Have we addressed the school teacher's request for more in-depth educational materials?" Anna asked, mindful of the project's significant educational goals.

"Yes, I've developed a supplementary educational packet that includes detailed descriptions of the key events and figures of the Weimar Republic, along with discussion questions that teachers can use in their classrooms," Julia explained. "These materials will be available for download on our website and handed out at the sites."

Anna nodded in approval, satisfied with the progress. "Excellent work, Julia. Now, let's talk about the final preparations for the launch. Henrik isn't here, but he sent in his report on the logistics and staffing for the event. We are well-prepared on that front, with extra guides and staff scheduled for the first week to assist our visitors and manage the expected crowds."

Miles added, "I'll also be on-site for the first few days to monitor the systems in real-time. We can't afford any technical hiccups during the launch."

"That's a good plan, Miles. I want us all on deck to ensure everything goes smoothly," Anna affirmed. "Let's also prepare a brief for all staff members on how to gather feedback from our visitors. This feedback will be crucial for any immediate tweaks and for future enhancements."

As the meeting drew to a close, the team felt a mixture of nerves and excitement. They had worked tirelessly to bring these new historical narratives to life through cutting-edge technology, and the launch was just around the corner.

"Thank you, everyone, for your hard work and dedication," Anna said as they began to pack up their materials. "Let's make sure that these next few days go as planned. We are about to make history more engaging and accessible than ever before."

With a final review of their timelines and responsibilities, the team dispersed, each member clear on their tasks. As Anna left the conference room, she felt the weight and thrill of their endeavor. This launch was not just a culmination of months of work; it was the beginning of a new chapter in how people experienced and interacted with history.

Conclusion

As Anna and James continue their skillful dance of cryptic exchanges across enemy lines, their intellectual connection blossoms into a profound bond, woven through the fabric of war yet rooted in a shared longing for peace and understanding. Through their coded dialogues, they have discovered a sanctuary within each other—a rare space of shared dreams, hopes, and subtle admissions of affection that challenge the very foundations of their wartime roles.

In the final moments of our story, as the war's relentless tide begins to ebb, Anna finds herself at a crossroads, her heart heavy with the weight of her contributions to the war yet buoyed by the promise of a new beginning with James. They decide to meet in person, in a neutral place far removed from the echoes of war, where their conversations can finally transcend the barriers of coded language and secrecy.

As they stand together under the vast expanse of a peaceful sky, their eyes meet for the first time without the veil of war. Here, in this quiet enclave untouched by conflict, Anna and James find the courage to lay down the cryptographic tools of their trade and speak openly of their aspirations, fears, and dreams for a future where their bond can flourish free from the shadows of war. They make a pact, not just as cryptographers or soldiers, but as individuals whose friendship has endured the harshest of conditions—a testament to the enduring power of human connection against the backdrop of turmoil.

This meeting marks the beginning of a new chapter for Anna and James, one filled with possibilities. Together, they step into a future where their conversations, once a lifeline amid chaos, now pave the way for a deeper exploration of life's ordinary yet profound joys. Their story, a tapestry of intellect, resilience, and quiet rebellion against the roles imposed by war, serves as a beacon of hope and a reminder of the indomitable spirit of connection.

Made in United States
North Haven, CT
01 September 2024

56802773R10159